GREED, CR

Carole Hayman was born in Kent. She is a BA Honours graduate from Leeds University and a graduate from the Bristol Old Vic Theatre School. She devised and co-wrote *The Refuge* for Channel 4. She also created and wrote the BBC television drama series *Rides*. Her first novel, *All the Best, Kim*, was serialized on *Woman's Hour*. *Ladies of Letters*, a co-written comic novel, has also been heard on *Woman's Hour*. *Greed, Crime, Sudden Death* is the second of the Warfleet novels. The first, *Missing*, is also available in Vista. Carole Hayman lives in London.

Also by Carole Hayman

ALL THE BEST, KIM

LADIES OF LETTERS
co-written with Lou Wakefield

MISSING
Book One of the Warfleet Chronicles

CAROLE HAYMAN

Greed, Crime, Sudden Death

Book Two of the Warfleet Chronicles

VISTA

First published in Great Britain 1998
as a Vista paperback original

Vista is an imprint of the Cassell Group
Wellington House, 125 Strand, London WC2R OBB

Copyright © Carole Hayman 1998

The right of Carole Hayman to be identified as author
of this work has been asserted by her in accordance with
the Copyright, Designs and Patents Act, 1988.

A catalogue record for this book is
available from the British Library.

ISBN 0 575 60383 6

Printed and bound in Great Britain by
Cox & Wyman Ltd, Reading, Berkshire

All rights reserved. No part of this publication may be
reproduced or transmitted in any form or by any means,
electronic or mechanical including photocopying,
recording or any information storage or retrieval system,
without prior permission in writing from the publishers.

This book is sold subject to the condition that it shall not,
by way of trade or otherwise, be lent, resold, hired out, or
otherwise circulated without the publisher's prior consent in
any other form of binding or cover other than that in which
it is published and without a similar condition including this
condition being imposed on the subsequent publisher.

98 99   10 9 8 7 6 5 4 3 2 1

For Josh

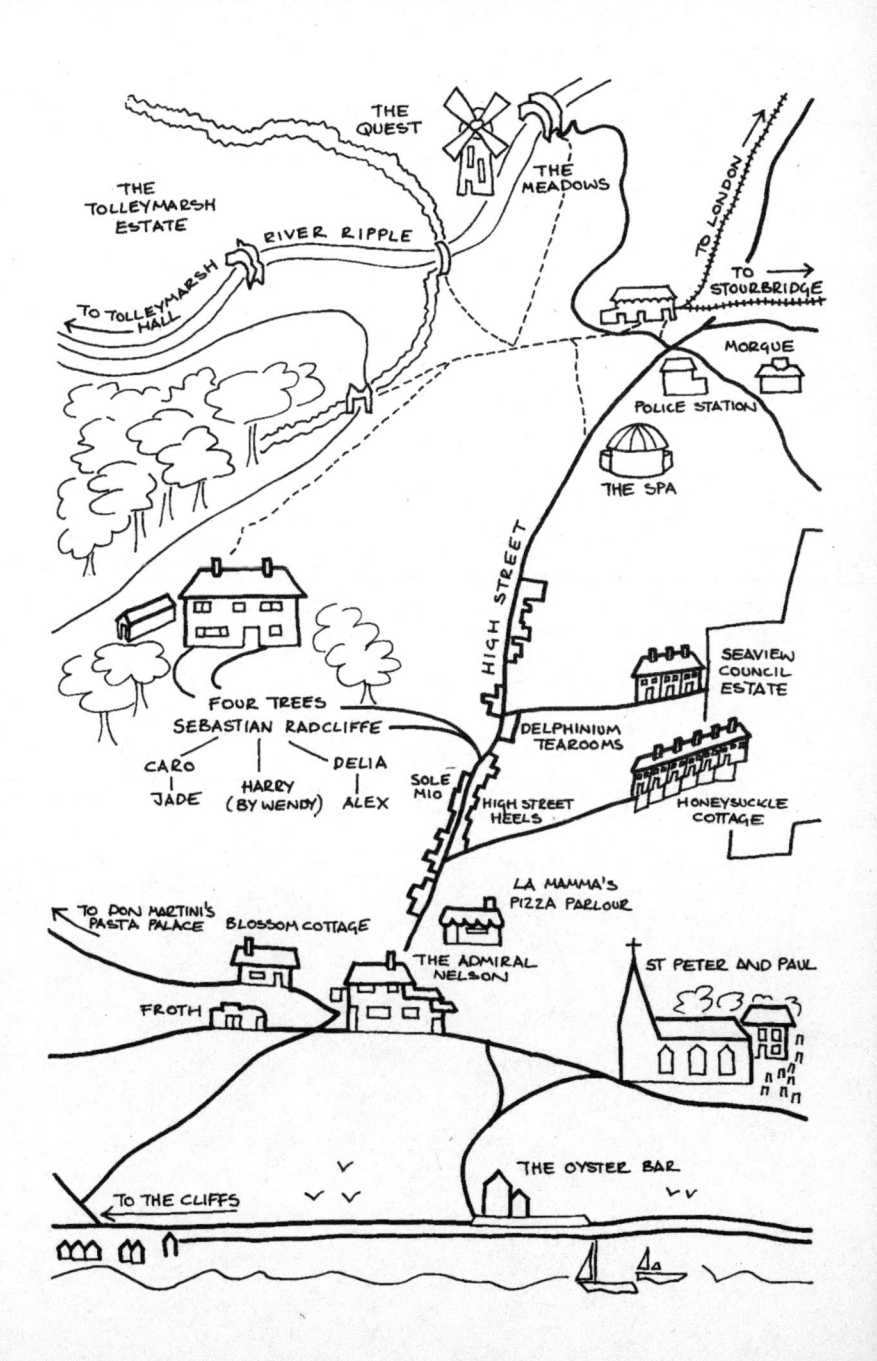
THE QUEST
THE MEADOWS
THE TOLLEYMARSH ESTATE
RIVER RIPPLE
TO TOLLEYMARSH HALL
TO LONDON
TO STOURBRIDGE
MORGUE
POLICE STATION
THE SPA
HIGH STREET
SEAVIEW COUNCIL ESTATE
FOUR TREES
SEBASTIAN RADCLIFFE
CARO
JADE
HARRY (BY WENDY)
DELIA
ALEX
DELPHINIUM TEAROOMS
SOLE MIO
HIGH STREET HEELS
HONEYSUCKLE COTTAGE
LA MAMMA'S PIZZA PARLOUR
TO DON MARTINI'S PASTA PALACE
BLOSSOM COTTAGE
THE ADMIRAL NELSON
ST PETER AND PAUL
FROTH
THE OYSTER BAR
TO THE CLIFFS

PROLOGUE

The night was very still. The bitter wind that blew in from the sea had died down, and looking out from the bedroom window Delia could see no movement in the four trees which gave her home its name. The only sounds were the occasional shrieks of night predators and the distant ebb and flow of the tide, caressing the shingly beach with the tenderness of a lover.

Four Trees was on a high wooded slope, and from the bay in which she stood Delia could see the whole of the little town laid out beneath her. Lights still beckoned here and there in the narrow cobbled streets though, as it was late, the Admiral Nelson was in darkness. Further out, she could see the sodium blot of the council estate and on the jagged cliffs the clear beam from the lighthouse. Its white shaft scanned the waves, turning them liquid pearl, fanning over flirtatiously bobbing fishing craft and more solid, dependable dredgers. The steeple of St Peter and Paul's was lit in sepulchre green, like a pantomime bad fairy. Delia well remembered the row over it. Though she was a relative newcomer to Warfleet life, she had swiftly been drawn into its eccentricities.

There was a blank coldness in the room, despite the central heating. Delia put out a finger, drawn by the condensation on the sash window panes. She traced some letters, S, e, b, smiling at her own absurdity. Behind her, in the big brass bed, Sebastian stirred. She turned to him as the church clock struck two-thirty.

A sudden unpleasant buzz from the word processor brought Caro Radcliffe back to life. She stretched to ease the crease in her back and reached out to switch off the computer before the wasp in the machine became insistent. She glanced at her luminous watch, a present from Zo on her last birthday, and thought for the umpteenth time how inconvenient it was to have a timepiece bearing more resemblance to a ship's compass. With a struggle she made out that it was a quarter to three. Suddenly she knew Sebastian was dead. She was coldly certain. She stared at the telephone expecting it to ring, and after a moment it did, with the shrill clarity that could only mean bad news.

Delia's voice on the other end was small and childlike. 'He's gone,' she said briefly.

'I know,' said Caro. 'Are you all right?' There was a short silence. Then a short sob. Then a short silence.

'Fine,' said Delia eventually.

'Do you want me to come down?' asked Caro, hoping Delia would not.

'No-o,' said Delia, 'except for the funeral. But will you tell Jade? I can't face it.' Caro agreed that she would and after murmuring the usual condolences, informed on this occasion with genuine, albeit mixed, feelings, she replaced the receiver. How odd, she thought, to be offering sympathy to another woman over the death of your husband.

ONE

It was difficult to obtain a plot for Sebastian Radcliffe's grave. Delia had to use most of her charm plus several jars of home-made jam to sweeten up Kevin Souter. He kept saying of course it wasn't really up to him, but she knew well that the Reverend Pepper, like most other Christians in Warfleet, was in thrall to the Gothic churchwarden.

It had not occurred to Sebastian to book a plot any more than it had occurred to him that he was going to die. Certainly not so soon. And not in Warfleet. Now, Delia stood in the slate-grey February churchyard, hugging her duvet coat around her plump, shivering body. Although slightly irritated with Sebastian for making so little provision, she had no intention of leaving until she got what she wanted.

Kevin Souter gave no sign that he noticed the cold, though his breath billowed white into the sleety air. Like dry ice, thought Delia, thinking of corpses. She was reminded of the hollows in Sebastian's face as she'd kissed him her last goodbye. Eventually she played her trump card, which was to offer the use of Four Trees for the bellringers' AGM – coffee and sandwiches to be provided – on the understanding that none of the mad artistes who came there in retreat would be visibly in residence that Friday.

The allotted place was under a large chestnut tree. Though it was now starkly leafless, Delia could visualize its summer splendour. She let her mind drift over the possibilities of arboreous picnics, horticultural triumphs, even graveside siestas. Would she, like Dante Gabriel Rossetti, fling herself headlong into the earth when it opened to receive the coffin? She shook her head to clear the poetical debris and stamped her booted feet, indicating that, the business having been transacted, she would like a return of warmth and feeling. It was hard to imagine that Kevin Souter had much of either. His long face was as gloomy and pitiless as those of the carved saints on the church façade. He took the hint, however, and led the way back to the vestibule.

There he handed Delia a form to fill in, which she did with trembling fingers, whilst he laboriously locked the big oak door with a set of keys the size of which indicated his own importance. He was not displeased with the afternoon's outcome. He had always intended to grant Delia's request. Sebastian Radcliffe was, after all, one of Warfleet's great and good, but it was gratifying to have another of their number begging.

Delia handed him back the form, hoping her contemptuous shudder would pass for mere physical coldness.

'And the funeral is . . . ?' queried Souter, though he knew perfectly well, since he was also the keeper of the Reverend Pepper's diary.

'Thursday,' said Delia shortly. Sebastian had died the previous Friday, but in this weather . . . 'So many people to notify.'

'Quite,' agreed Souter, a gleam coming into his pebble eye. He relished the prospect of exercising his powers of crowd control.

Delia, now thoroughly out of charm, stumped down the path, her moon boots carelessly dislodging Kevin's meticulously laid chipped gravel. Much as she loved Warfleet, she found its petty politics insufferable. Already many people had rung demanding invitations to the funeral. It was not so much that they had loved Sebastian as that they loved an occasion. 'Le tout Warfleet' would insist on being present at an event provoking such media attention.

There had been so much of a practical nature to organize since Friday that Delia had barely had time to think about her feelings. Seb's illness, though short by oncological standards, had been long enough to recognize death before it happened. 'Coming to terms' with it, whatever that meant, was quite another matter.

Seb's face as it had been in his last hours haunted her. The skin was transparent; stretched tight across jutting bones, yet baby-soft to the touch. She had spent many hours stroking it, watching the tiny veins throbbing with desperate life beneath its surface. She would brush his still thick, now white, hair from his forehead and lean over him to catch the occasional opening of his deep dark eyes. They still seemed to glow with love for her but perhaps it was the drugs. He might just be seeing a mysterious presence. A visitor from the other world hovering insistently above him. He used to call her his angel. Tears rushed into her eyes at this point, hot in contrast to the freezing air. She let them spill down her frosty cheeks, until they too turned cold, then brushed them away with a mittened hand, quickening her pace towards Four Trees.

The funeral morning, unlike the previous two days, was dry and bright. The service, at St Peter and Paul's, was at eleven o'clock, then the graveside ritual, then everyone back to Four Trees for a fork and finger reception. Jean Plummer, Delia's housekeeper, had been readying the fine old house for days. This morning she had arrived at eight, her concession to the funeral a black skirt four inches above her bony knees instead of her usual shocking pink one, and was still clacking from room to room in her high-heeled mules, straightening, sidening, polishing.

Toni and Rumer, friends from the Quest Natural Healing Centre, had insisted on helping with the food. Their holistic beansprouts and brown rice dishes sat rather incongruously with Delia's platters of smoked salmon and sides of ham garnished with intriguing dips and sauces. She was glad of their presence, though. Caro had arrived from London the previous evening but seemed helpless with catering. She had wandered from room to room as though tracing her former life. Now she stood, gaunt and svelte in a Joseph suit, warming herself by the ancient Aga. Delia could not suppress a dry smile; Caro seemed completely out of place in the kitchen that had once been her centre.

Jade, Caro and Sebastian's daughter, would arrive, as usual, at some point convenient to herself. Delia hoped that her reputation as one who would be late for her own funeral did not extend to that of others. Delia's own children, Harry and Alex, were being dealt with by Anthea, the Australian nanny. Alex was too young to understand what was happening but Harry was insisting he wanted to throw earth on Daddy. There were no artistic residents currently at Four Trees. Delia had closed the retreat for the last two months of Sebastian's illness. She would have to open it again soon, though. She needed the money.

Delia dressed in a hurry. Her only good dark suit, a relic from her days in publishing, was more than a little tight on her, but she applied a generous coat of lipstick to her wide mouth. Lipstick at least she insisted upon. She ran down to take a last look in the wide stone-flagged kitchen. The kettle steamed gently on the Aga, ready for all emergencies. The refectory table, which usually accommodated assorted writers, painters, poets and was used to fielding conversations of dramatic intensity, now stood ready to feed the literary lions of Warfleet. It looked, thought Delia, nobly resigned.

The hearse drew away down the drive, its roof stately with white lilies. Delia followed in the limousine with Caro and Jade, who had erupted from a taxi moments earlier.

'Sorry, sorry. There was a man on the train who only had one leg, and . . . oh, it's a long story.'

Mrs Strongitharm, once Caro's cleaning lady, had come in an appropriately bucket-shaped hat to pay her respects. As the cortège drove by she remarked that it was very peculiar to have the wife and the mistress in the same car, but then she supposed people had got used to the strange goings-on at Four Trees. Standing next to her, hatless, Jean Plummer bridled. As the current factotum of the household, she was fiercely loyal to Delia. Just because Sebastian and Caro had never actually *divorced*, she returned, and he and Delia had never actually *married*, there was nothing peculiar about it. People had different standards now. These were the nineties.

Mrs Strongitharm sniffed scornfully but said no more. Jean smoothed her orange hair, from which she had recently snatched rollers, and hurried back to the house. She wasn't going to the funeral but preparing the hot food and drink for the wake. Mulled wine, with cloves and spices, she thought, on this bitter winter morning. It would serve a double purpose, having the faint odour of sanctity about it.

Inside the limousine there was silence apart from Jade's occasional snuffles. Caro stared out of the window and Delia straight ahead. Delia was always single-visioned.

The cortège moved slowly down the hill and into the winding streets of the town. People stopped and stared, one or two doffed their hats, others hurried indoors as though proximity to death might make it catching. The trinket shops were closed and shuttered at this time of year. Their faded boards announced last year's two-for-the-price-of-one bargains. Other buildings were derelict. This part of the country was eternally in recession. Even the amusement arcades were empty of people to amuse. The machines ping-ponged relentlessly luminous colours and emitted screams and bangs across a void. The cafés gave notice that they were 'Closed until April'. Only the Delphinium had its doors open 'All day and all weathers'. May, the proprietress, stood on the steps untying her apron in deference.

They passed the Admiral Nelson which had its blinds down this early. Outside, the sign advertising 'Jumbo Sausage' spun in the wind. Above it Nelson swayed as he stared out to sea. Much as he must have done in life, thought Caro. A sole seagull followed the procession down the promenade. It skimmed the coffin wailing pitifully. Caro was reminded of the Ancient Mariner.

Jade's sobs became more pronounced as they neared the churchyard, and with a slight click of her teeth Delia handed her a tissue. Though Jade carried a Prada bag of cabin-trunk size, it contained, apparently, nothing essential.

Along the dry-stone wall on either side of the lich-gate were ranged many uninvited well-wishers who saluted the cortège as it passed through. The occasion was Warfleet at its most feudal, thought Caro, the gentry warm inside the church, the peasants freezing outside it. In many ways the town was still medieval. Visitors to it noted not only its ruined battlements, but also a curiously timeless feel. It was as though the little town was in a bubble, resistant to all development.

The hearse came to a halt outside the church door and the bearers made ready to take the coffin. Among them was Jeremy Taylor, one of Caro and Sebastian's oldest friends, and Darryl Willoughby, his lover, incredibly dapper in Armani.

Caro, alighting and helping out the now convulsed Jade, was relieved to see them. She had worried that the send-off, peopled as it would be by media associates from Sebastian's former life, might be impersonal. Even unfriendly. She flashed Delia a grateful smile for having recognized and subverted this. Delia nodded and, falling in behind the now shoulder-high coffin, permitted herself a slight choke. She and Sebastian had had such a short time together. Barely four years since they had found each other and a love, for them both, unique and revelatory.

Inside the church, however, her spirits rose. There was indeed a good turnout and for once she looked to right and left, nodding to people and half smiling. The smile became a little rigid as she spotted a team of people from Talk TV, the company where Sebastian had once been a high-flying producer. The execrable Briar, who had taken his job, was present. But of course she would be; Jade now worked in her department.

Caro, following arm in arm with Jade, also looked around and was pleased to see many familiar faces. There was dear Toni, Jeremy's sister and another old friend. Next to her Rumer, her business partner at the Quest, then Marsha Snelgrove, Laurel Hopcraft, Jim and Peggy Bacon ... As they neared the altar she was touched to see Warren Peabody in the Tolleymarsh pew. Jade saw him at the same moment and stiffened beside her. They entered the family pew, hearing its familiar oak creak as Reverend Pepper bade them kneel to begin the service.

The reception was talked about for some time afterwards by 'le tout Warfleet'. Everyone agreed the food was excellent, though Laurel Hopcraft complained the mulled wine had given her a migraine. 'Serves her right for drinking too much,' opined Rumer, though Laurel's explanation was that Jean Plummer had been over-liberal with the nutmeg.

Warring Warfleet factions were at either end of the long, light living room. The Warfleet Players hobnobbed near the drink, their leading light, Marsha Snelgrove, demonstrably dramatic in a long black cloak and Shakespearean tiara. Near them were grouped members of the Poetry Society. Laurel Hopcraft, both playwright and poet, hovered uneasily between the two, her velvet jacket increasingly speckled with Gauloise droppings.

'Trade' – Jim and Peggy Bacon, Teddy Forbes from the B & B, and Sergeant Plummer of the local constabulary – mingled with 'antiques', Jeremy and Darryl, at the other end. Toni, in flowered kaftan, and Rumer, resembling a bear rather than a leopard in mottled fake fur, fetched and carried between the two. The media folk, for once oblivious to politics, ate, and drank intemperately, in the middle.

Jade Radcliffe and Warren Peabody had been observed having a warm exchange in the otherwise chilly conservatory. A small fire had broken out in the bedroom serving for a cloakroom. Briar had thrown herself, or perhaps fallen, on top of it, extinguishing the flames with her considerable body weight. She did herself no damage, but several coats were left smouldering.

Delia sailed through it all apparently calm and clear-eyed. Whatever grieving she was going to do, she would do, or had done, in private. This attitude was admired by some as properly British. Others said it was cold-hearted and besides she was American. One or two members of the Warfleet Players felt the occasion lacked 'passion'.

For Caro there was passion enough, though of a subtextual variety. She was very aware of Jade and Warren and watched covertly as they circled each other, eventually ending up amongst Delia's wintry geraniums. It was their first meeting since they had parted – was it four years ago? – and they did seem uneasy. She made a note to ask Jade later. Jeremy, in funeral attire of aubergine velvet with a spotted cravat, was well, though Darryl looked rather peaky. Jeremy was cheerfully dispensing drinks as was his habit. Darryl was drinking them as was his. 'Guy died, you know,' said Toni *sotto voce*; she was referring to an ex-lover of Darryl's whom the couple had been nursing.

Caro too lowered her voice. 'Yes,' she said. 'How was it?'

Toni shook her head. 'Very upsetting. I did a lot of yoga with him.' She passed on with a plate of ham vol-au-vents, holding them at arm's length as though they might be contaminating.

Jeremy refilled Caro's glass and said, 'Darryl and I are moving back to Warfleet. There's a nice little house near the

Admiral Nelson.' Caro smiled. That at least would be handy for Darryl. 'You don't miss it?' said Jeremy. The question was almost rhetorical. Caro had made her home in London and was very happy there. Or, if not happy, satisfied. London with its global angst suited her writer's head better.

'No Zo?' continued Jeremy on a more probing note.

Caro looked aside. 'She's very busy. Quill and Pen's been sold, you know, along with the rest of StrongFellows.'

'I read,' said Jeremy. 'Charlie Fong, isn't it?'

Caro rolled her eyes skywards. 'Zo's fighting tooth and nail for her job. She daren't be away for a minute.' She took a gulp of her wine; there was more to the story of her love affair but this was not the time to go into it.

Jeremy's plump face registered concern. He changed the subject, saying brightly, 'And Cynthia? The same?'

Caro grimaced at the mention of her mother. 'The same,' she confirmed. 'She wanted to come but I dissuaded her. The weather and so on . . . besides, there's nowhere for her to stay. She forgets I no longer own Four Trees.'

'It's still a lovely house,' said Jeremy, glancing round the room. It was old pine, William Morris, clever modern pictures.

'Umm,' said Caro. Some of the objects had been her wedding presents but her tastes were more minimal these days. 'Come on, Jeremy,' she said, wanting to lighten the mood, 'tell me all the gossip.'

Jeremy fluttered a plump, ring-heavy hand. 'Well . . .' he began. Jeremy lived to gossip.

In the conservatory Warren picked a dead head from a geranium. It was, they were both aware, displacement activity. 'You're very successful,' he said to Jade. 'I see your name on programmes.'

Jade made a dismissive gesture. 'What about you, anyway,' she said lightly, 'not only managing the Tolleymarsh estate but married to the Marquis's daughter?' A slight malice entered her tone as she continued. 'What does that make you? A baron or something?'

Warren smiled reassuringly. 'No. Still a jumped-up peasant.'

Jade acknowledged their past inequalities with a careless laugh, then said more graciously, 'How many children is it?'

'Two,' said Warren, looking her in the eye. He was aware that in their previous life he would have been blushing and stumbling by this point. 'You?'

Jade laughed again and shook her expensive haircut. 'Jesus. No. No time. Can't remember what sex feels like.' There was a short silence after this. Warren dead-headed another geranium.

'But you're happy?' he said when they had both recovered.

Jade shrugged. 'Who's happy? These are the nineties.' She put out her hand, the wrist, Warren saw, still much bangled, and laid it on his arm. 'You are, I take it?'

Warren smiled and his eyes crinkled and turned sherry-gold. 'Yes,' he said directly, as though laying a ghost. 'Yes. I'm happy.'

Jade dropped her arm and turned her face aside to stare through the frost-traced windows. Beyond the conservatory the garden was bleak. The promising sun of the morning had been overtaken by cloud and the day was already darkening.

Warren touched the fall of thick shiny hair that shielded Jade's face from him. He had once loved to plunge his hands into her long, many-beaded locks. 'It suits you short,' he said. She turned back to him, her head close. They were both still for a moment. Then she brushed his cheek lightly with her lips. 'I'm glad you came,' she said. 'Let's go back in. It's cold out here.'

'... And Laurel Hopcraft's book's been turned down ... too much story, apparently ... the Quest is doing frightfully well; they got a donation to start it up. Darryl and I go frequently ...' Jeremy turned to search for his partner. Darryl was propped against the wall talking to a pretty youth, and judging by his angle was three sheets to the wind already. 'Yes,' sighed Jeremy, turning back, 'tomorrow's aromatherapy.'

If Toni and Rumer's remedies could take care of an excess of alcohol, thought Caro, they had a certain future in Warfleet.

'Jade?' queried Jeremy.

'Oh. OK.' Caro shrugged. 'She's a producer now. Following in Sebastian's footsteps.'

'Let's hope not quite,' said Jeremy. Sebastian had been a maverick in the television world. A thorn in the side of his company. He'd be honoured more now, safely dead, than he had been in life by the industry. 'He would have loved this,' said Jeremy, indicating the turnout.

'The two worlds meet head on,' smiled Caro. 'Subject for a programme.'

Jeremy nodded. 'Or a book?' They both laughed a little, a note of sadness in their voices.

Caro saw Jade and Warren re-enter and waved to them. Warren picked his way through the crowd and gave her a hug. 'Warren,' said Caro, truly glad, 'how very nice to see you.'

'You too,' said Warren, holding her arms wide. 'You look . . . different.'

'It's the clothes,' said Caro. 'I have to keep up my image.'

Warren grinned. 'The lady writer.'

'Shush,' said Caro, smothering a laugh. 'Don't let Laurel Hopcraft hear you. She's the only lady writer in Warfleet. I'm just a pretender.' Laurel, having already had 'words' with Marsha Snelgrove, was back with the Poetry Society, but her pinched face with its beady black eyes was indeed turned towards Caro.

Warren drew her into a corner. 'Are you staying long?' he said. 'I'd like you to see what I've done with the estate.' Warren had revived the Marquis of Tolleymarsh's declining fortunes by making a huge success of the safari park. His marriage, too, was successful, Caro had heard. He'd come a long way from that other estate, the unappealing council ghetto.

Now she said, 'I'm going back to London this afternoon, but I'll be down again when Delia opens for business. I've got a novel to finish.' At the thought of work and the attendant publishing upheaval, Caro's frown-lines deepened.

'Make sure you call,' said Warren. 'I'll show you round. It would be good to . . .' He paused as though uncertain of his ground.

'To what?' asked Caro.

'Oh. To talk to you.'

Caro nodded, slightly puzzled. She and Warren had never exactly 'talked', though she did feel very close to him. 'I'll call,' she promised.

*

'. . . And that's Caro Racliffe,' Jeremy was saying to the pretty youth, Ashley, whom he had rescued from Darryl's attentions. 'She used to be married to the deceased, but now—'

'Never mind her. Who's he?' interrupted Ashley, rather rudely.

'Ah,' said Jeremy, in a special tone. 'We're all in love with the beauteous Warren.'

'Is he gay?' asked Ashley eagerly.

Far from it.' Jeremy giggled. 'He had a torrid affair with Caro's daughter Jade . . .' He searched the room and pointed to Jade, posed scornful and beautiful by Talk TV. 'Rumour has it she had an abortion, but Caro doesn't know it.'

'He's gorgeous,' said Ashley. 'I wouldn't mind having his baby.'

'Too late, alas!' bemoaned Jeremy. 'Annabel Trenche has stolen him. Not that her family is without its looks. My sister Toni was involved with her brother years ago, but that's another story. Now . . .' Jeremy looked around for Harry who was skateboarding hazardously between forests of legs, 'Warren used to look after Harry when he was little. You see, Harry is the child of Sebastian and Wendy . . . Wendy? Well, it doesn't matter, but she was Delia's best friend and when she died Delia adopted Harry. Then she hunted down Seb and they fell in love and settled here and had Alex. And Caro . . . Caro had it all in her lap because she and Seb were still married. See?'

Ashley rolled his eyes slowly.

'It's obvious,' cried Jeremy. 'Warren stepped in to help Caro out by becoming Harry's nanny. That's how he got involved with Jade, and the rest, as they say, is history.

'I need another drink,' said Ashley.

*

Toni bustled up to Caro and Warren collecting plates and glasses. 'I'm going to give Delia a hand clearing up,' she said. 'Dishwashers welcome.'

'I guess that means me,' said Caro, as Toni took hold of her shoulder. ''Bye, Warren.'

'How do you feel?' said Toni.

'Fine,' said Caro. 'Am I expected to behave badly?'

'You know how this crowd love a scandal.'

'I wouldn't give them the satisfaction.' Caro rolled up her silk sleeves.

'Good girl,' said Toni, bracing her old friend's shoulders. The entire gathering turned to watch as she propelled Caro towards the kitchen.

TWO

The March day crackled with bright frost and the piercing sunshine of a ski slope, yet Caro felt her spirits sink as she approached Charlie Fong's stronghold, somewhere in which grubbed Quill and Pen Books. The grotesque cube of Tesco-style red brick reared out of the surrounding debris of an industrial estate in Fulham. It looked, she thought, like a millennial abattoir. Some kind of dying room, anyway. She missed the cosy offices in Mayfair and the casual grace that had attended them.

There was nothing graceful about Charlie Fong's empire. It had been built in the eighties on the Hong Kong property market: presumably buildings with no more style than this one. Charlie had swiftly strayed into global communications. He now owned a cable network, a record company, a girlie magazine chain, an airline or two and a large chunk of mainland China. He was rumoured to be turning it into a Fanshen-style theme park. It was joked, cynically, in the trade, that Charlie still had a few floors to fill. Buying up the StrongFellow group, which included Quill and Pen, was his latest piece of whimsy.

Charlie must feel like Gulliver in Lilliput, thought Caro as she negotiated spillage from the shrapnelled cars strewn across the wasteland; looking down from his domed penthouse at the little people spinning in a vortex of paranoia. They must seem easily crushable.

In appearance Charlie was far from Olympian. He was short and fat with no discernible neck. It was the odder that he chose to draw attention to this deformity by displaying it garlanded in airport-style jewellery. Caro had only met him once, when StrongFellows' move to the castle colony was marked with a 'celebration'. It had been held in the monstrous atrium of the building. Teeth had clattered against champagne glasses, though whether from cold or terror was unclear. It certainly gave new meaning to the phrase 'the chattering classes'.

Charlie appeared briefly, flanked by skinny young women and fat young men, the whole posse exuding a faint air of menace. He was introduced to people in his path, one of whom happened to be Caro. He had taken off his dark glasses and his eyes, small and pouchy, sent out cheery beams. He looked charming. The Chinese equivalent of a garden gnome, not out of place on willow-pattern. This, Caro was assured, was deceptive; he was definitely underworld, but more troll than harmless pixie.

Noelle, Caro's agent, had taken her out to lunch to discuss the situation. 'I think it's a case of watch this space,' said Noelle, reaching for the red wine. 'It could be good. StrongFellows has been staggering for a decade.'

'He might have bought it as a tax loss,' said Caro gloomily.

Noelle shook her head. 'Charlie likes success,' she said. 'He'll want to turn it into a money-spinner.'

Lottery more like, thought Caro, sipping her pellegrino. 'But,' she said, 'surely he'll get rid of Quill and Pen. Their sales are minuscule.'

Noelle shrugged. 'Could plough in cash. Make it their

literary flagship. Get you a better advance off your bloody editor.' She cackled at this point and Caro joined in, rather more tentatively. The editor referred to was Zo, who was also Caro's lover. 'Don't worry, love. I've got an idea this year's going to be good for you.' Caro surveyed her agent's battered face and tufty greying hair with something like despair. Noelle was on her second bottle of house red and it was only lunch time. Could her ideas be depended upon?

She had inherited Noelle from Sebastian. When Zo had commissioned Caro's first novel she had advised her to find an agent. Noelle was the only one Caro knew. She had represented Seb for his entire career and was almost a family member. Caro was the one who provided the ashtrays and vodka for the weekend visits. She couldn't complain she hadn't known Noelle's habits.

Now as she picked her way towards this meeting – twice postponed by Zo through pressure of other meetings – she reviewed the year ahead. One novel, her second, coming out in the summer and another to finish. Her first had done modestly well. Been entered for, but failed to win, several prizes. Sold five thousand in hardback and six thousand in paperback and prompted a slightly better advance for her second. It wasn't exactly a living and Caro was only too aware that without Zo's salary to fall back on her life would be much less comfortable.

The new novel was good, however. It had, Noelle assured her, a 'global' theme, though it stopped short of the sort of thing usually made into a Major Motion Picture. The problem was Zo didn't like it.

The electronic door slid silently back, ushering Caro into a world of echoing footfalls and dangerous talk that cost lives. She crossed to the massive reception desk, where an immensely haughty girl flicked disinterestedly through *Vogue*, and in a small voice explained that she was here to see Zo Acland. The girl – Semolina, her badge claimed, though it seemed unlikely; perhaps Caro needed glasses – now flicked her hair in a similarly disinterested way and pressed a series of buttons. 'I've got a – sorry, what did you say your name was? – a Caro Radcliffe here for Zo Acland,' she announced to the cavernous atrium. The words clashed against the frozen marble, almost eliciting sparks. Caro winced with embarrassment.

She sat watching the flux of couriers, models, photographers, journalists and less distinct suspects in middle-management suits, until eventually footsteps clanged down a metal spiral and Zo's secretary, Milly, appeared. 'Hi,' she said. 'I've come to collect you.' Rather as though I were a parcel, thought Caro. But she followed Milly's pert bottom docilely enough, wondering how much shorter her skirt could get and whether the fat young men noticed.

Zo's office was several floors up amongst an incomprehensible warren of open-plan 'Japanese-style' corridors. Zo, at least, had a door. She paced behind it ceaselessly. There was no smoking in castle Fong and Zo's nails were bitten to the quick. This was only one distracting habit; others were chewing gum, tugging at her bristle-cut hair, foot-tapping, desk-tapping and sipping endless cups of coffee. Caro found her intimidating in the office.

Zo rose – her rangy form, suited to the T-shirt and blue jeans optional on a Friday, still gave Caro a thrill – and kissed her briefly on the cheek. Caro was aware of Milly's stare, but, 'Sit,' said Zo, dismissing Milly with a command to bring more coffee. The pert bottom wriggled through the door which shut rather noisily.

Caro saw her manuscript spread out on the desk. 'Needs a lot of work,' said Zo, shoving it aside. 'I want to talk to you about a new scheme Charlie's instigating.'

Caro raised her eyebrows. Charlie was famous for his schemes; often a mixture of American and Japanese business practice, but with a spin all of his own.

'It's called "David and Goliath",' Zo went on.

Caro was reminded of her vision of the pigmies. 'Goliath's the market place and we, Quill and Pen, are David. He's sending us on assault courses.'

Caro shook her head, bemused.

'It's very simple,' said Zo with slight irritation. 'It's doubled circulation on the magazines.' This, Caro thought but did not say, was hardly surprising; most of them were pornographic.

Zo was now pointing to a complex wall chart. 'We handpick books that are promotable. Then work in a team on strategy.'

The coloured dots danced before Caro's eyes. 'But . . . isn't that going to be expensive?' she ventured.

Zo laughed drily. 'Strategy's got to be cheap. God knows what the assault weekends are costing.' Probably, thought Caro, as much as her three advances put together. 'Never mind the nuts and bolts,' said Zo, 'the point is your new book's perfect for it.' Zo had certainly changed her view.

'You mean . . . you like it now?' stammered Caro.

'No,' said Zo, 'not that one. The one I want you to write. Greed . . . crime . . . sudden death. In other words high concept.'

Caro took a deep breath. 'You're saying I should abandon this one?' She pointed at the hapless manuscript.'

'Put it in a drawer,' said Zo unsentimentally. 'Not appropriate. Genre-less. Marketing can't handle it.'

They might if they were given a budget, Caro thought. The phone rang and Zo snatched it up and snapped briefly into it, 'What? The bastards! Offer two-fifty.'

Caro wondered how many noughts were attached. At least three, judging by the colour that had risen in Zo's cheeks. Zo slammed down the phone, unconsciously twiddling a pencil in her hair, then seeing Caro's stricken face said more kindly, 'Look, I know what you're trying to do in this, but the marketplace is too narrow. Trust me on this one.'

Caro shrugged; she was beyond words.

'Go down to Warfleet,' said Zo. 'At Four Trees you can think about it. Remember, greed, crime, sudden death. I want you to write a bestseller.' She shuffled the manuscript together and glanced at her watch.

Caro stumbled up, gathering her coat and bag. She stopped herself asking Zo if she would be round to supper that evening. There was a rule, unspoken but rigid, that they did not discuss personals at the office.

Outside, charted peaks and troughs still zigzagging through her head, she attempted to flag down a taxi; black cabs were suspicious of the area and tended to drive past quickly if they strayed at all into these blighted suburbs. She finally found one on the Fulham Road and sank back into it gratefully. How much Zo had changed, she found herself thinking. Once they had been like-minded about work, feeling it should come from the heart, indeed the soul. Now Caro had been dismissed, heart and soul, in less than ten minutes. Zo seemed to have completely embraced Charlie's corporate values. Of course, the takeover had resulted in promotion for her – Caro looked for reasons to excuse her lover – and Zo had always been ambitious . . .

About one thing she was right: Caro needed time to think. Greed, crime, sudden death were not normally her subjects. She had better call Delia tonight and see if she could take sanctuary at Four Trees.

THREE

'Lordy lord,' said Delia, banging down a tray of cinnamon bagels fresh from the Aga. Caro, seated at the long refectory table, breathed in their comfort gratefully.

'The worst of it is,' she continued, 'Zo and I don't seem to talk any more. We used to share everything.'

Delia nodded. 'Tell me about it. I miss the talking terribly.'

There was a silence, during which they both thought of Sebastian, and Caro felt guilty because until now she hadn't.

'I'm so glad I'm out of it,' said Delia at length. 'The world's gone mad.' She glanced round the comfortable kitchen. 'The angst people bring down here with them.'

Caro laughed, thinking of the current residents: a local historian researching the wrecks and wracks of Warfleet who appeared wrecked and wracked himself; a brat-pack novelist with bad teeth and writer's block; an arts presenter who stomped about in wellies and large intimidating glasses and a theatre producer, apparently on the edge of a nervous breakdown, who paced for hours chain-smoking in the flint-frozen garden. In the night there was sometimes the sound of weeping. Though of course, that could have been Delia. She said generously, 'You're our haven. Our Goddess of the Aga.'

Delia gave a shout of laughter. 'Sounds like one of those hideous books!'

'Sorry,' said Caro. She did sometimes become fanciful.

Delia, still chuckling, said, 'I guess I do have the figure for it.' It was true that Delia, though not yet forty, had acquired a shape as round and wholesome as her bagels. And it was wonderful what she had accomplished at Four Trees. It *was* Delia; Sebastian, though dotingly supportive, was little help practically. He had become very involved in Warfleet community affairs and was always at some meeting or society. He had also written a couple of frightful novels about life in a small seaside town, which Delia had carefully edited.

Recently she had bought the barn and land next door and had it converted into further rustic dwellings. She ran her empire, at the heart – or at least the gut – of which was the Aga cooker, with the same staggering efficiency she had brought to Quill and Pen as its senior editor. The difference was she had put on thirty pounds and seemed to enjoy her life more. She split and buttered two bagels, pushing one towards Caro. 'You're too thin,' she said. 'Not eating?'

Caro said, 'I cook when Zo comes round.' Which isn't so often, she added mentally.

'What about an afternoon at the Quest?' suggested Delia. '*Mens sana in corpore sano* and all that. Toni'd be glad to see you.' Caro knew that to be true. Last year Toni and her associate, Rumer Petulengro, benefiting from a large and, according to Jeremy, anonymous donation, had opened the Quest Natural Healing Centre in an old mill on the River Ripple. Toni had previously made a sporadic living as an artist. Rumer, also known as Janice Wainright, had run a wig boutique in Stourbridge and done tarot on the side. Whatever their healing skills, their combined personalities would make any illness flee in terror. They lived in the covenous spirals above the Quest; a life, according to Toni, of holistic rigour and celibacy. Though Caro wasn't ready for that, Toni could be very supportive . . .

Toni's firm fingers bit into Caro's shoulder blades, then smoothed the aromatic oil around them. 'Oh,' groaned Caro. 'Mmm . . .'

'Lot of tension,' said Toni sternly. 'Things not going well with young Zo then?'

'It's not her,' said Caro defensively, although it was. 'Things aren't going well period.'

'At your age,' said Toni, 'you should be slowing down, not hurling yourself down stress chasms.'

Caro managed a laugh amidst the groans, which were anyway half pleasure. 'I feel like I've been on hold for years. Slowing down's not an option.' It was as though she had only recently found herself. Her true self. After years as an Aga-tending, dog-walking, jam-making, drain-clearing, one-woman service industry.

Toni turned her friend over, noting as she did so Caro's slender ribcage and muscle-toned stomach. 'Working out?' she asked with slight disapproval.

'Oh. Now and then,' murmured Caro, purposely vague. In fact she went to the gym twice a week and did vigorous weight training.

Toni smoothed back Caro's hair, well cut and shining copper, to expose her forehead to the oil. 'Dyed,' she said. It was not a question. She massaged Caro's face, noticing that although she had lines, the skin was still fine and firm. Caro looked younger than she had for some years. 'Zo's not been all bad for you,' she acknowledged grudgingly.

'Certainly not!' Caro sat up for Toni to chub her in a warm fluffy towel. 'It's not her fault,' she continued, almost thinking aloud. 'She's caught up in corporate paranoia. Hasn't got time for a private life. I just get the fallout.'

'I can recommend the celibate state,' said Toni with humour. Caro opened her eyes and surveyed her friend. Toni was wearing her habitual orange; in this case tracksuit bottoms and a sweatshirt. Her lined brown face reflected every day of her fifty-three years and her hair, grown a little longer than her summer shave, was naturally grey with flecks of blond, no youth out of a bottle. The two women were of an age, but had taken to it differently.

'Mm,' said Caro. 'Not yet.' She was thinking that the trouble with good sex was that you wanted more of it.

'I must admit you don't look your age,' said Toni judgementally.

'Just as well.' Caro was dry. 'Otherwise I'd have no chance. The world's not kind to fifty-something women.'

'The world isn't kind to women!' said Toni darkly.

'I've been thinking of doing the new book under a pseudonym,' mused Caro.

'Huh!' snorted Toni. 'Twenty-two and male?'

'Mm,' agreed Caro. 'And Scottish.' They laughed together, acknowledging everything about the position of women.'

Toni briskly towelled Caro's waxed legs. 'You could give men another whirl. You're in good shape for it.'

Caro shrugged doubtfully. 'I'm too old for men. Besides,' she pulled on her jeans, 'I've got to work. Zo's instructions. A high concept novel.'

Toni gave a derisive hoot. 'What the bloody hell is that?'

'I don't know,' said Caro grimly. 'But I'm down here on a hunt for it.'

The friends agreed to have dinner later in the week and Caro left the therapy room, descending the spiral stairs of the white tower to ground level. The mysterious donor, of whom Toni could only say 'must be someone holistic', had enabled the mill to be impressively converted. The walls throbbed with Toni's paintings; mystical subjects, suitably questing, with purple swirls and earthy New Age women. Shutting the brass-plaqued door, Caro decided to walk back to Four Trees through the wildish violet-skied day. Winter Warfleet was on the edge of spring and tossing madly at its tethers.

She headed down to the front, bent over against the gusts, which although cold seemed jovial, exhilarating. Out at sea breakers crested as high as the pier end, drenching the paint-peeled pavilion. Plastic-macked figures ran screaming and laughing, clutching the wrought-iron railings. A foolhardy windsurfer skiffed furiously across the far-out peaks. Above him guillemots and terns wheeled like reckless acrobats, occasionally diving headlong at the water. Others bounced like Barnes Wallis bombs from crest to crest of the foamy waves, apparently at home in the cracking peril. Even a capped swimmer's head, like a striped beach ball, could be seen now and then bobbing between the breakers.

Caro crunched down the pebbles to the high-tide mark. The sea had left its usual twisting path of eccentric debris: bottles, a shoe, plastic bags, bones, shells, tampax, streaks of winding kelp, and occasional bubbles of bladderwrack. She scuffed through it merrily, kicking up toecaps of soggy sand; postponing the moment when, having arranged desk, A4 pad and pens, she would sit staring at a blank sheet of paper.

There was another figure on the beach. Down near the water's edge. A man, she saw, as she got closer. He was city-dressed in a long dark overcoat. His expensive leather shoes, she thought, would not tolerate their salt staining. He turned towards her and his pale puggy face beneath dark glasses looked faintly familiar. He began to walk up the beach, and as he distanced himself from the crashing surf took a cellphone out of his pocket. Caro dawdled and watched him as he crossed ahead of her, grating up to the cement defences. He began to speak into the phone; above his head the aerial sprang, wavering in the wind, as though from his ear. From behind he looked like a Martian.

She forgot him as she turned her own steps inland. Work could no longer be ignored. With a lowering spirit, she marched back to Four Trees.

FOUR

Caro called Warren on her third day at Four Trees. He was delighted to hear from her.

'I'm staying a few weeks,' she said, adding firmly, 'working.'

'Good,' said Warren. 'Are you free this afternoon? I've just taken delivery of some koala bears.'

Caro, putting on her coat, thought who could resist a koala bear?

The Marquis of Tolleymarsh's estate was a couple of miles outside Warfleet. The original Norman castle had been destroyed but a fine seventeenth-century house had replaced it. It looked, thought Caro, as she drove up in Delia's car, as if this too was being renovated. Scaffolding clung to the Jacobean façade and men in white overalls sauntered about with paint pots.

The drive swung around to the left with signposts to the safari park. She left the car in a newly asphalted area and walked towards the white gate in the trees from which Warren was waving. He undid a huge padlock – the park was closed to visitors until the summer season – and ushered her to a khaki jeep parked nearby.

'I'll drive you,' he said. 'Can't have you getting lost.'

Caro laughed. 'I can just see the headlines in the *Warfleet*

Chronicle. Lady Writer Eaten by Lions. It would guarantee a bestseller.'

'Don't,' said Warren, grinning too. 'Wouldn't Laurel Hopcraft be furious?'

'She'd probably picket the park.' They giggled naughtily, reasserting their bond through Warfleet gossip.

The day was cold but bright and streaks of sunlight filtered through the trees, lighting up the occasional tiger stripe. 'The animals are mostly asleep,' said Warren.

'Oh,' said Caro, 'I just want to cuddle a koala.'

They drove through landscaped acres seeing copses of *Vogue*-elegant giraffes against the skyline and, later, wrestling schools of monkeys. Warren was proud of the estate and pointed out features he had introduced: the art gallery, the boating lake, the café, as well as improvements to the safari park. The koala bears were sleepy and surprised. Caro fed a grumpy one some eucalyptus leaves and was delighted when it put its sticky paws round her neck and rubbed her nose wetly. 'I want one,' she exclaimed as Warren lifted it from her. His gentle touch with the animal reminded her of how he'd been with baby Harry and she was filled with affection for him.

'Cup of tea?' he said. 'I'll take you back to my office.'

Taking her assent for granted he set off with his long loping stride. Caro, trotting behind, was struck by the grace of his body. He had lost the gawky angularity of early youth; seemed more solid, assured. His long hair bounced as he walked, the blond locks catching the sunbeams and creating a pale halo. He turned back to check her with a grin that turned his hazel eyes koala-brown, and she was reassured that in maturing Warren had lost none of his boyish charm.

*

Warren's office was in a converted stable block, not far from his home in the dower house. It was stylishly decorated with a casual ease about the bricks and beams and Shaker furniture. A contrasting bank of technology filled one wall. On Warren's desk was a photo of his wife and children. Caro scrutinized it as he made tea. The wife – what was her name? – was shiny with health: generations of good breeding showing in her hair and teeth. The children were blond pretty toddlers. Warren must be a natural father. He put a china mug in front of her and following her gaze said, 'That's Annabel, with Jasper and Dickon.'

'They're beautiful,' said Caro loyally. Though she spoke only the truth; the entire family seemed charmed.

She sipped her tea and said, 'You mentioned at the funeral that you wanted to talk to me?'

'Yes,' said Warren, his face losing some of its light. 'I wanted to ask you—' At that moment a car drew alongside the low latticed window in the bay of which they were sitting. It was a very long car, a Daimler, Caro thought, black with smoke-coloured windows. One of them slid slowly down revealing the face of a very beautiful foreign-looking woman. 'Bollocks,' hissed Warren. 'Look, Caro, another time . . .'

'Of course,' murmured Caro, wildly curious. A man in a dark overcoat and sunglasses got out of the car and circled to open the woman's door for her. Caro got a glimpse of long brown legs in elegant shoes and a coat that was surely not fake fur. It seemed they were heading for the office. 'Shall I go?' said Caro, standing. 'I can walk back to my car.'

'You may as well be introduced,' muttered Warren rather gracelessly. 'You're bound to meet sooner or later.'

The door opened and the woman came through it – 'swept'

was the word that came to Caro's mind – on a fog of perfume. The overcoated young man was holding the handle and also, Caro now saw, a small dog on a lead. It was a breed she could not name, but it looked expensive.

The woman strolled forward, her black eyes fixed on Caro. 'Darleeng,' she said, barely parting her dark red lips. Caro was startled. Had they met? But the woman suddenly veered away and it was clear she was talking to Warren.

'Hello, Viviana,' said Warren in a less than friendly tone. 'Can I do something for you?'

'Oh.' Viviana gave a gurgle of laughter. 'You are so formal een the offeece. I was showing Marcus around and we thought we would come and say ciao.' Her eyes slid back to Caro, who was now poised to make her exit. 'And thees ees?' She extended her hand, tanned and tipped with fine red-varnished nails. Caro took it, surprised at its hard clasp, as Warren said, 'Caro Radcliffe. This is Viviana Trenche, the Marchioness of Tolleymarsh.' Caro tried to stop her jaw dropping. She had no idea the Marquis had married again. And to a woman so much younger . . . Viviana was perhaps thirty-five, barely ten years older than her son-in-law. Warren was looking uncomfortable so Caro, having stuttered some greeting, extricated her hand and moved towards the door.

'I'll call you,' said Warren, a note of urgency in his voice.

'Do,' nodded Caro. 'Any excuse to stop working.'

She felt Viviana's gaze on her back as she reached the door and heard her say, 'Radcleeffe . . . don't I know that name?'

As she passed Marcus, Caro nodded to him briefly. She felt a flicker of recognition. He said nothing, however, and she went on quickly, glad to escape. The tension in the room was palpable.

Outside the window she fumbled for her car keys and stole

a quick glance at the office. Warren was turned away from her but she could see Viviana's red-tipped hand on his shoulder. She was looking up at him, smiling, mouthing something Caro could not hear. She saw Marcus watching her through the glass and realized with a slight shock that he was the young man she had seen on the beach. But even then she had felt that she knew him. She puzzled over it but came up with no answer, and turning away she walked briskly towards the car. The clouds had turned threatening.

FIVE

'She was a beauty queen,' said Delia, deftly juggling some lasagne slices. 'Colombian.'

'Goodness,' said Caro. She could only imagine what havoc that could wreak.

'Yes,' agreed Delia, as though Caro had spoken her thought. 'He married her a year ago and she's been nothing but trouble.'

It was the first time the women had had a chance to talk, though several days had passed since Caro's visit to the estate. Caro, as she doodled with her row of pens and stared out of the window, found time hanging heavy, but Delia shuttled from one domestic crisis to another in the running of Four Trees.

'What sort of trouble?' said Caro, seeing again the red fingernails on Warren's shoulder.

'Money,' said Delia bluntly. It was a subject much on her mind.

'You mean she spends it?' asked Caro rather enviously.

'Like it's going out of fashion,' responded Delia tartly. 'Did you see all that work going on at the house? That's for her birthday, if you please! The word is she's bankrupted the estate.'

'But why does the Marquis let her?' asked Caro, thinking of Warren.

Delia gave a snort of laughter. 'No fool like an old fool. He's potty about her. Thinks she's going to give him a son and heir!'

'No,' gasped Caro.

Henry Trenche had disinherited his first-born, Edgar, some years ago. He had gone to the bad with drink and drugs and was thought to be in South America.

'Oh yes,' continued Delia grimly. 'Think what that means to the rest of the family.'

Caro thought. In the absence of other sons Annabel would inherit, or rather Jasper, their angelic toddler, would. The Tolleymarsh line had no truck with feminism.

'But can he . . . ? Is he . . . able?' The Marquis was, after all, over seventy.

Delia shrugged. 'Who knows. But one thing's for sure. Viviana intends to get one somewhere.'

Caro fell silent, considering the possible targets for Viviana's conception plan.

'There's more,' said Delia. 'Warren's done wonders since he took over the estate, but last year he opened a club. Now the police have closed it down.'

'The police?' said Caro. This was alarming.

'I don't know the details,' said Delia, adding ominously, 'The Italians are involved.'

Before she could say more the kitchen door burst open and one of the residents entered tearfully. It was the arts presenter, apparently in collapse over her software. Delia popped the lasagne in the Aga and, wiping her hands, turned, with only a slight sigh, to deal with computer technology.

*

Back in her room Caro drank strong coffee and faced her A4 pad bravely. It was no good. Her curiosity was far more engaged by Delia's real-life gossip than by the fiction in her faltering paragraphs.

How, she wondered, were 'the Italians' involved? There were two Italian families in Warfleet. The Delgardos, to whom Warren was related on his mother's side, had been in ice-cream for years. One of the family, Dickon Delgardo, had been a poet of some Radio 3 renown, breaking many Warfleet hearts before he left to meet an early death in Greece, graveyard of poets. Sonny Delgardo, Dickon's surviving sister, had expanded the family firm, diversifying into pizza and property. Then, a few years ago, she had suddenly sold out, keeping only the Spa Health and Fitness Centre.

The family to whom she had sold were the Martinis. Or, more correctly, the Martini brothers. No one was sure from where they came, except originally Sicily. There were rumours of saunas in Margate and gaming clubs in Stourbridge. They were known to have international connections.

Although the Delgardos had been in Warfleet for several generations, they were still regarded as foreigners and approached with suitable caution. The Martini brothers, johnny-come-latelies, were treated with downright suspicion. The very names Ugo and Fabio had a soft menace about them. They were always referred to as 'the Italians'.

After half an hour of fantastic conjecture and growing anxiety, Caro gave up and rang Warren. Only his answerphone responded.

SIX

The following weekend Caro went back to London. She hadn't seen Zo for a fortnight and their phone conversations had been terse on Zo's part and apologetic on Caro's. The couple had fallen in passionate love four years ago. To Caro the relationship, her first with a woman, was both shocking and wonderful. They had braved much disapproval to be together but now Caro felt she was interrupting Zo's Important Life if she introduced anything personal.

The weather had turned pleasant and they took a walk on Hampstead Heath. Many eyes turned to the tall young woman with her ash-blond hair and long leather-clad legs, but Zo seemed depressed so Caro embarked upon the Warfleet story, turning it into a comedy. Zo, tramping through muddy stubble in her old Doc Martens, remained preoccupied and interrupted only to ask, 'So, with all this nonsense going on are you getting any work done?'

Caro shut up, feeling like a reprimanded child. They circled the ponds in awkward silence which Caro eventually broke by asking after David and Goliath. Zo gave a great sigh. Her shoulders sagged so much that Caro thought for a moment she was going to cry, though that would be most un-Zo-like. 'It's a disaster. Nobody knows what the fuck's going on. They're too busy looking over their shoulders.'

'Oh dear,' murmured Caro, wondering what that meant to her book, but wondering far more why Zo had changed her opinion.

'Bloody Charlie Fong and his bloody focus groups,' seethed Zo. 'He's sending a once great company down the tubes. StrongFellows isn't an airline!' She stopped as suddenly as she had begun, perhaps out of a sense of company loyalty, and after a brief sit in the sun suggested that they go home.

Jade was coming round that evening so, while Zo worked, Caro shopped and later, at Zo's flat for her convenience, cooked an excellent dinner. Zo came into the kitchen as she was adding the final touches and opened a bottle of champagne. She smiled at Caro over the glasses and some warmth came back into her expression. Perhaps she was thinking of the first glass they had shared. To Caro the picture was as clear as if it were yesterday: the tall girl, twenty years her junior, standing in the kitchen full of sure expectancy. The excitement. The anxiety. At least there was still champagne, she thought wryly.

Jade and Zo had struck up a friendship rather to Caro's surprise. She wasn't sure when it had started but Zo now treated Jade as though she were a younger sister, steering her career and advising her on her love life. They would fall to networking and cackle raucously over media titbits incomprehensible to Caro. At first she had been pleased but now she found herself rather resentful. They made her feel an outsider. The younger woman's intimacy underlined the lack of it in her own relationship with Jade. Since Zo, they had grown very distant.

Jade arrived late, as usual, and was picky about the food.

She seemed to live mostly on sushi and arugula, though she managed several glasses of champagne, Caro noticed.

She was entertaining Zo, as Caro came back and forward with plates, with some story of television corruption.

'... so apparently he'd taken this massive amount of money ... thanks, Ma ... to make sure a project got recommended. He said it was a loan but of course nobody believes him. Jed's furious. He'll have to sack him.'

'How is Jed?' asked Zo, in what seemed to Caro a knowing manner.

'Oh, fine,' said Jade, her eyes sliding about. 'We're going to MIP together.'

'Do you mean,' said Caro uncertainly, 'that you're involved with him?'

Jade snorted. 'You do use funny expressions, Ma. Yes, I'm *involved* with him.'

'Jade, really,' said Caro, suddenly annoyed, 'how can you? That ugly little man!' For some reason, Warren's face appeared mistily before her, making her doubly outraged.

'Ugly little man!' repeated Jade witheringly. 'You'll be telling me next he's unsuitable because he's Jewish.'

'He's unsuitable,' said Caro, controlling her voice with an effort, 'because he's your *boss* and because he's *married*. It has nothing to do with his racial characteristics.' Jade and Zo went off into peals of laughter at this and Caro got up and cleared the table. She stayed in the kitchen for some time toying with the dishwasher while she examined why she was so angry.

In the other room the talk had turned to business and as Caro re-entered with coffee Jade was saying, '... but everything's in upheaval because of the takeover.'

'What takeover?' asked Caro politely. She couldn't care less but was determined to restore friendliness.

'Talk TV,' said Jade, downing the dregs of her champagne. 'Honestly, Ma. Don't you read the trades?' Caro admitted that she did not. She occasionally tried but they left her feeling hopeless. 'Charlie Fong,' spat Jade. 'He's trying to buy us up. I suppose he's still got a floor empty.' The young women whooped humourlessly.

'But . . . what does it mean?' demanded Caro, suddenly engaged. Was there no end to Charlie's ambitions?

'If he succeeds,' said Jade, 'everyone's job will be on the line. There'll be a major reshuffle.'

'Tell me about it,' said Zo wearily. 'If there are any more revolutions at StrongFellows we'll all be taken to the nuthouse.'

'We're fighting it,' said Jade, 'but it comes at a bad time, what with all the scandals.'

'Is your job safe?' said Caro anxiously.

Jade shrugged. 'If Jed's is.' She grinned slyly at her mother. 'That's why he's suitable.'

Caro clicked her teeth but said nothing.

Zo said, 'Only death will stop Charlie. He's like the devil. He's got some scheme now to start a rival to Euro Disney.' Jade shrieked. Even Caro smiled. She had a vision of Charlie's gnome-like face in a pointed hat with a bell on it. 'It's not funny,' said Zo severely. 'He's abandoned StrongFellows completely.'

'Bored now,' said Jade.

'That's all very well,' continued Zo, 'but he won't relinquish control. He's a secretive bastard. We can't get decisions on anything.'

Caro recalled her conversation with Noelle. She had sensed

Charlie wanted a tax loss. She felt herself shrinking to pigmy size. She must talk to Noelle quickly. Feeling slightly disloyal to Zo, she began to stack the coffee cups.

Jade left, tottering out rather drunk into a taxi, and Caro showered and got thankfully into bed. One day in London was enough, she thought, to drain one's resources completely. She could hear Zo in the other room rustling papers. Surely she wasn't going to work now? It was past one. But when Zo eventually came to bed Caro had dozed off. She half woke as she felt Zo's chilly body slide in beside her, but was too sleepy to do more than give it a perfunctory cuddle. Zo lay still and straight, uninterested it seemed in lovemaking.

Caro called Noelle the next day, although it was Sunday.

'Darling,' said Noelle, already slurring her words at eleven-thirty in the morning. 'Can't talk now, I've got people here.'

'Um,' said Caro shortly. 'It's important.'

'Don't worry,' cried Noelle, and Caro heard the chink of bottle on glass. 'I'll come down and see you in Warfleet.'

Caro took an earlier train back than she expected. Zo was having a meeting so there seemed no point in hanging around. Zo was affectionate but distant as they parted. Gone were the days, thought Caro sadly, when she would have woken her with strawberries and kisses and zipped her down to Warfleet on the motorbike.

She stared moodily out of the train window as the urban sprawl gave way to the bursting green countryside. April had driven out roaring March and entered, eccentrically, as summer. That would be nice at the seaside, she thought, trying to cheer herself. Her heart remained heavy, however. So much had changed, it seemed without her noticing. Perhaps it was time to call it a day with Zo? It was hard to say what, except habit, still held them together.

She was overcome with grief at this thought and sudden tears spilled down her face. Was another relationship to end? Inevitably her thoughts turned to Sebastian, though her mourning for him had been over before his death. How like him Jade had become, in her brooding dark-eyed beauty. Her every gesture brought him back, to say nothing of her appetite for television politics. Caro dried her face and had a fond laugh at them both.

She wondered about Delia. Was she really satisfied with her role at Four Trees? She herself had once been a high-flyer. Caro remembered the anorexic American she had first met five years ago. Delia had been sharp, smart, successful. Her clothes were immaculate, as was her hair, and she never ate or drank in public. It was ironic that she now spent her days in a mess of batter, bread and puddings. Goddess of the Aga indeed! The female fate personified. Nevertheless, as the taxi drew up to the house Caro was profoundly grateful for its serenity.

There was a note in the hall for her. Warren had called to ask if she could have lunch with him. She mounted the stairs, her spirits rising with every step.

SEVEN

The weather continued warm, and although a stiff breeze blew as Caro set off to meet Warren the day was Warfleet gloriously at its best. The sky was the intense blue of lapis and the sea churned merrily beneath it, frothing into teasing kiss-curls and unfolding seamlessly to drag tiny pebbles in a dance behind it. Several windsurfers were at play, skittering across the choppier waves, and beyond them some sailing dinghies with bright pennants made stately progress in deeper waters.

Caro's heart filled with lightness. This was how she had first fallen in love with the town. She checked her watch, and realizing she was a little late for their meeting hurried towards the oyster bar where Warren would be waiting.

He was sitting on the tented terrace facing the beach. His long legs were stretched in front of him and his face, turned out to the sea, looked meditative and slightly sad. It lit up, however, as he saw her.

He pulled out a chair and filled a glass with white wine, rather a good Chablis, she noticed. 'Oysters?' he said, indicating the trestle tables on which were piled the fruits of the sea, some, alarmingly, still lively.

'Mmm,' said Caro, 'and lobster to follow.'

Warren rose, extending his graceful limbs and tossing back

his hair, unconfined in ponytail today and glistening streaky gold in the sunlight. He really was a beauty, thought Caro admiringly. No wonder Jade had—. She shut off that vexed area of her life. She didn't want to spoil the day's glad aspects.

Warren returned with piled plates and they applied themselves to the sensual oysters, occasionally catching each other's eye and smiling in appreciation. When the serious cracking of lobster claws had begun, Caro said, 'So, Warren . . . what did you want to ask me?'

Warren's face turned glum. He fiddled with a particularly difficult fishy tendril and said without looking up, 'Oh . . . some advice, I suppose.'

'Viviana?' said Caro, unable to restrain herself.

Warren's head jerked up. 'What have you heard?'

'Not much,' said Caro, slightly thrown. 'Only that she likes to spend money.'

Warren looked relieved. He grinned and said, 'She certainly does.' Caro thought he seemed almost admiring. After a moment Warren sighed and dropped the lobster pick. 'Things aren't great. The estate's in trouble financially . . . despite everything I've never quite managed to get it out of the red. It causes trouble between us.'

'Between,' Caro clarified, 'you and your wife?'

Warren nodded. 'It's understandable. As I manage it, Annabel gets anxious. And then there's her dad getting married . . .'

'Which seems to be the root of the problem,' said Caro with asperity.

'It's not all Viviana's fault,' Warren said, sounding defensive. 'Though it's true she hasn't helped.'

'What else then?' pressed Caro. 'I heard something about a nightclub?'

'Yeah,' said Warren, 'I opened it last year. I was hoping it would get us solvent . . . you can make a lot of money on clubs.'

So Caro understood.

'I'm so busy with the park, I leased it to a . . . friend. He's the root of the bother.' He stared darkly at his glass, then picked it up and downed the contents. 'Would you like another bottle?'

'No,' said Caro, laughing, 'I'll be totally gone. I've got to do some work this afternoon.'

'I wouldn't mind being totally gone,' said Warren, drawing the bottle towards him.

'Well, go on,' said Caro, wondering whether Warren had, like everyone else, become an alcoholic.

'Carl's using the club for raves . . . you know, techno music?'

Warren was checking her street credibility, Caro realized, and she said with a smile, 'I have heard of them. Drugs are involved, I suppose.'

Warren nodded briefly. 'The police bust a party a couple of weeks ago. They made fourteen arrests – not Carl, of course, just punters – they got spliff, E, a bit of coke . . .'

'Ah,' said Caro. She saw at once how that might reverberate on Warren.

'Now the police have shut the club. They're trying to put the finger on me as a dealer.'

Caro was startled. She said, 'Are you?'

'No,' said Warren, firmly. 'I'm not that daft. But Carl . . .' He'd said enough. Caro's mind flew instantly to Warren's

55

history with the law and previous involvement with the grisly Carl, a boy she had always thought generically related to the Kray twins.

'I'm so sorry, Warren,' she said, extending her hand to cover his. She was wondering whatever had possessed him to allow Carl back into his life.

'Thing is,' said Warren, 'I was never going to let Carl have the club. I got a great little company to run it. We'd done all the pre-publicity, set the opening date and everything. Then one of them broke his neck bungee-jumping and it all disintegrated.'

It would, thought Caro. Aloud she said, 'Is he dead? The bungee-jumper?'

Warren laughed. 'Only his brain. Must've been for him to do it in the first place.'

'So Carl stepped in,' she pressed, wanting to get to the bottom of the story.

'Yeah. Yeah ... to be honest, I had no choice. We'd already spent so much money ... we'd have lost face if we hadn't opened.'

Caro knew how important that was. 'But Annabel ... surely she doesn't believe you've done anything illegal?'

Warren looked away. 'Annabel's under pressure, with Viviana and everything.'

'Umm,' said Caro dryly, the picture both clouding and clearing.

'Shall we have a walk?' Warren said, suddenly changing the subject. He paid the bill with a credit card and tucked Caro's arm beneath his as they headed towards the strand. Caro's hand felt oddly tingly resting on Warren's tanned, well-muscled forearm. She was a little drunk, she realized, and glad of his support. They strode out towards the cliffs with the winking white lighthouse. They soon left behind the shops and stalls of the parade and reached the less bustly zone of serious swimming, the yacht club, and beyond that a thin straggle of beach huts.

Caro had a sudden vision of herself, the Lady Writer, wearing a large floppy hat, sitting on the veranda of a beach hut, pen poised over the wretched A4 pad as she gazed at the distant horizon. She gave a small self-mocking laugh. If the high concept novel didn't come, she could always fill her pockets with pebbles and walk into the sea.

Warren's mood lightened as they walked. He began to point out things of local fascination. The new spread of bungalows, an ancient oak cut down after being struck by lightning, the converted boathouse on the beach now for sale – Caro grew interested – the wooded hillside where the body of the barmaid from the Bun and Oven had been found. His talk was lively, even spiced with wit. The fun in him surfaced as the bright day gave comfort and Caro smiled encouragingly.

In a parking bay at the foot of the cliffs was a small tea shack with a few scattered tables and chairs. Warren bought two plastic beakers of faintly distilled Typhoo and he and Caro sat sipping in friendly silence. Caro watched a toddler pick its Penguin biscuit off the table and fling it on to the ground. His mother, barely out of childhood herself, retrieved it and moments later the toddler repeated the action. The third time he threw the biscuit at his mother. It hit her just above the eye and she let out a shout of rage. 'Jason, you stupid fuckhead! If you do that again I'll swipe you.'

Caro looked away, embarrassed for the woman in her primeval aggression. Warren too had been watching. He said, 'How's Jade?'

'Oh, Jade,' said Caro, rolling her eyes in mock despair. 'She's all right. She's one tough young lady is our Jade.'

Warren nodded though his eyes said he was uncertain.

'Does that sound hard from a mother?'

Warren laughed. 'You know better than me. Until the funeral, I hadn't seen her for years.'

'She's changed a lot,' said Caro. 'Believe me, Warren, you're better off out of it.'

Warren's glance told her he already knew it. 'But she's successful,' he said. 'It was what she wanted.'

'Who knows what Jade wants?' retorted Caro. 'She's only happy in some neurotic crisis.' They both laughed gently, then looked at each other and by mutual agreement rose to begin their return journey.

'So, what are you going to do about Carl and the club situation?' asked Caro finally, thinking Warren now cheerful enough to be constructive.

'I'm trying to open again,' said Warren, 'but without Carl this time.' He shrugged. 'He's furious. He wants to go on with it.' Of course he does, thought Caro, if he's in it for the dealing. 'There are other people involved,' said Warren, less philosophically. 'Backers. I borrowed from them to open the place.'

'The Martini brothers by any chance?' asked Caro, knowing she was pushing.

Warren's face tightened. 'They've got their toe in the door.' He gave an angry laugh. 'They'd like to get their whole bodies.' The mention of bodies gave Caro a jolt. Warren was in over his head apparently.

They had reached the beach huts again and Caro stopped to examine them more closely. She could hardly afford the converted boathouse, but a beach hut, surely . . . ? Warren said, 'This one's open.' He pulled at the shuttered door and it swung back, creaking on its sea-rusted hinges. Inside it was warm and dim, with a faint smell of creosote and barbecue charcoal. It was empty except for a built-in bench along one slatted wall.

Warren sat on it and pulled out his cigarettes. 'I reckon it's been abandoned. Quite a few were, when the council put up their ground rent.'

Caro sat next to him and accepted a cigarette. She said, 'I wonder if I could buy it.' She felt quite excited. Like a kid in Toys 'R' Us. The hut was so sweet. A little doll's house. But also, in the dark heat, sensual, womb-like.

Warren leaned over to light her cigarette. His hand was close and she noticed in the flame the fineness of it. The artist's hand, she thought, long, with shapely square-tipped fingers, better kept now than when she had known him.

They leaned back against the sun-warmed wood, drawing on their cigarettes. There was a silence. Suddenly Warren's body began to shake. Caro looked across, and saw to her alarm that his face had crumbled and tears were spurting down his cheeks. His mouth opened and hoarse gasping sounds came out. 'Warren,' she said with concern. His arms came up and hugged each other and his body rocked forward. Caro put out a hand and caught him. 'Warren,' she said again, 'what is it?' Warren lurched sideways so that his head collided with Caro's chest. She encircled his shoulders and held him tight, feeling at once shocked and moved. His sobs seemed so fundamental.

He wept into her breasts for a moment or two, then

stopped and lay quietly while Caro stroked his shoulder and murmured maternally, 'There, there . . . there, there . . . it's all right, love.' Her chin rested on his shining head. She could smell the freshness of his hair, shampoo mixed with sea breeze. It was frighteningly intoxicating.

In a moment a new tension arose between them. Caro held her breath as Warren's hand came up and rested on her damp breast. She sat rigid as he squeezed it gently then slid his hand into her open-necked shirt and down inside her brassiere, cupping her breast with his long fine fingers. He bent his head, nuzzling into her, nudging aside buttons and cloth until his lips found her nipple and opened over it. Caro gasped and struggled silently. She was gripped by a conflict of shock and desire. This was wrong . . . wrong . . . yet oh so lovely. Warren's head came up now and he faced her. His eyes were tawny in the sun-dappled light, and they gazed straight into Caro's wide blue ones.

He brought his face very close to hers so that their lips were almost touching. Now she wanted him to kiss her, she breathed in the scent of him and was filled with giddy longing. Warren grazed her lips with his, parting them gently and sliding his tongue between them. Caro held still, unable to respond until his teeth nipped her lower lip and she let out a small cry. Now his tongue was in her mouth, no longer gentle, and she let it take her, urge her along, as his hands moved down her body. A frantic haste overtook them. They clung to each other and scrabbled with buttons. Warren unzipped his Levi's and tugged up Caro's skirt. He lifted her until she sat on his lap, and eased his cock inside her. Caro gasped and wound her legs round his back as he braced against the wall and thrust deep inside her. She cried out and he withdrew, whispering, 'Am I hurting you?'

'No . . . yes,' she said, 'yes . . . but it's good.' Warren half smiled and pulled her close, moving inside her more gently.

She said, 'I want you on top of me,' and carefully he lowered her to the floor, keeping always inside her. As he let himself down on to her, she opened her legs wide and drew him in to her very centre.

Warren said, 'Can I come inside you?' And she breathed, 'Yes, yes,' as the orgasm overcame them.

She heard his cries very distantly as though her spirit had left her body and flown through the half-open door up into the radiance of the lapis sky.

EIGHT

A letter with the Tolleymarsh crest on it arrived at Four Trees a few days later. Since it was addressed to Mrs Radcliffe, Delia, naturally, opened it. It was an invitation, for Caro, to Viviana Trenche's birthday party. Delia was the angriest Caro had ever seen her. She stamped about the kitchen clattering platters and grinding the rubbish disposal unit. At one point Caro could have sworn she saw her kick the Aga.

'It's bloody disgraceful,' Delia spat. 'Just because I never *married* him. What am I? Some sort of *secret* woman! No, worse, I'm the *invisible* woman' – it was then that she kicked the Aga – 'here to provide for everyone else. Never mind *my* feelings.'

She sat down and put her face in her hands. Caro said tentatively, 'Coffee?' Delia nodded and a dry sob escaped her.

'Oh, Delia,' said Caro. She got up and put her arm round Delia's shoulders.

'This bloody little country,' said Delia, sounding her most American. 'Sometimes I just hate it!'

Caro felt a slight shock. It was one thing to criticize your native country yourself. Quite another if anyone else did.

'You're obsessed with status. Bowing and scraping and titles and position. It's all so . . .'

'Graceless?' offered Caro.

'Totally,' snapped Delia. 'If you ask me the more you decline in the world, the more you cling to your self-importance.' Delia was distancing herself from feudal England with every sentence. 'Look at your bloody silly royal family!'

Caro could only nod agreement.

'Viviana!' exploded Delia. 'Jumped-up tart. She's desperate to buy into it.'

And so, thought Caro, was Charlie Fong. To them England still meant something . . . or at least its past did.

There was a long silence full of Delia's heavy breathing. Her plump body trembled as she fought for control and at length subsided. 'I'm sorry, Caro,' she said, in a dull voice, 'it's not your fault.'

Caro made coffee and the two women sat in the conservatory with their cups, contemplating the newly sprung blossom. Caro said, 'Look, why don't you go instead of me?' It was generous as her curiosity was intense, but it was the least she felt she could offer.

Delia gave a short laugh. 'I'd cut a fine figure in my Oxfam clothes. And what would I have to talk about? No. You're the one she wants. Beastly little star-fucker.'

Caro said, 'I'm not the star. It's the connection to Seb.' Since his death Sebastian seemed to have acquired almost icon-status.

'Whatever,' said Delia and shrugged. 'I've got nothing to offer but kids and plumbing problems.' As if to emphasize this truth Alex's shouts were heard in the distance. Delia took a lipstick out of her apron pocket and drew a perfect red O on her mouth. She rubbed her lips together and fixed them in a smile and got up to attend to Alex.

*

Caro dressed with care for the party: a Nicole Farhi dress and some long bronze earrings. She and Warren had not communicated since the episode in the beach hut and she was extremely nervous about meeting him in public.

She took a taxi, expecting much champagne, and, as it followed a line of cars up the wide drive, saw the refurbished house in all its splendour. The stone had been washed and glowed ethereally in the floodlights; the terraces sparkled with fairy lights and the lozenged windows of the long wings were brilliant with candles. An Andean quartet, complete with harps and ponchos, was in residence at the top of the grand flight of steps. The great oak doors were flung wide and decorated with what appeared to be a small rain forest, and in the vaulted hall massive flares lit up the heraldry on the walls and fires leapt in the carved stone fireplaces. There were vast arrangements of exotic flowers, the chandeliers were strewn with vines, and at one end there was a crystal grotto of emerald green with a water-spouting dolphin. The theme was, apparently, Colombian. As she accepted a glass of champagne from a bowing waiter, Caro found herself already counting the cost and feeling anxious for Warren.

She could see no one she knew in the richly dressed crowd, though she recognized many faces from the magazines at her hairdresser's. Some minor royalty was present, the Kents of course and one or two she thought were foreign. The local MP, Scott Harvey-Dickson, who had crossed the floor just before the last election in anticipation of New Labour's triumph, was deep in conversation with a sinister-looking government minister – someone from Culture, Caro thought. Scott, wearing the tartan appropriate to his name, was waving his hands expressively.

Supper had just been announced and Caro edged her way

towards the banqueting room. It was cornucopian with food, the centrepiece an entire stuffed shark. She saw Laurel Hopcraft poking an experimental fork in it. Beyond her stood Jeremy, in mauve shantung, talking to Toni and Rumer. Relieved, she made her way through the swelling throng to join them.

Jeremy was saying, 'I don't know, darlings, but he's given her an Elizabeth Taylor-sized emerald.'

'Who?' said Caro. 'What?'

Jeremy smiled conspiratorially. 'They're over there ... look.'

Caro followed his finger and saw, surrounded by admirers, Viviana Trenche. She was wearing a tropically coloured, much-flounced dress with a headpiece resembling a bowl of fruit. She looked a little like Carmen Miranda. By her side was a small chubby man. His head was close to Viviana's and as he smiled at some vivacious remark he turned his face a little. It was, Caro recognized with a shock, Charlie Fong.

'Yes,' said Jeremy, his eyes on Caro's face, 'I thought that would surprise you.'

'What on earth is he doing here?' said Caro, astonished. It went through her head that she could beard him about StrongFellows.

Jeremy shrugged. 'Café society, darling. Viviana knows everybody.' He tapped his nose. 'I believe there's a Colombian connection.'

Recovering herself, Caro looked back at the couple. They were flanked by Henry Trenche, who was talking to a dark man, perhaps another Colombian, whilst looking with foolish affection towards his wife, and on the other side, slightly behind Charlie, Marcus, still in his dark glasses. Of course,

Caro realized in a flash, that was where she had seen him before: at the StrongFellows party in castle Fong, slightly behind Charlie and heading up his posse.

A little further from the group stood Warren. A sharp thrill shot through Caro at the sight of him, incredibly handsome in evening dress, his hair slicked into a ponytail. He, however, had his gaze fixed on Viviana and Charlie with an intensity that looked, to Caro, like jealousy. He turned away without noticing Caro, and after a moment when he was lost in the crowd she located him deep in conversation with two suavely suited men. Their dark skin and sleek black hair announced them as Ugo and Fabio, 'the Italians'.

'Shall we eat?' said Jeremy, looking longingly at the buffet. 'Caro, I'll get you a plate. You look as though you need one.'

Caro made her way rather dazedly to a table and sat sipping her champagne and grappling with her complex emotions. A sort of lustful shame had assaulted her at the sight of Warren. She had known it would be awkward to see him again but had not expected this powerful reaction. To add to her confusion, her worlds had collided and the shock was considerable.

Although the buffet was informal there was a large central table, and she saw suddenly that she was sitting only a few feet away from it. Annabel Trenche was already there. She had put on weight, Caro thought, since the photograph. Her face had a dissatisfied look which spoiled its prettiness a little, but she smiled fondly as her father sat down beside her. Whatever her feelings about his marriage, it appeared she was still close to him.

The others came back with loaded plates and put one in front of Caro. Toni had gone for kiwi fruit and rice salad, complaining that these functions never catered for vegetarians. Rumer had abandoned principles for an entire lobster. Jeremy's plate had fish, flesh and fowl, in keeping with his nature. The three of them tucked in while Caro fiddled with a piece of shark. It was apparently edible.

'Old Henry doesn't look well,' said Rumer, reaching for the butter, her African tribal bracelet dangling what appeared to be a shrunken head into the Marie Rose sauce.

'She's wearing him out,' said Toni.

'She won't rest till she's got a son.' Rumer shook her head prophetically. 'She's got to secure the succession.' It sounds like the court of the Borgias, thought Caro.

Jeremy leaned forward and said *sotto voce*, 'I hear she's not above trying other means.' They all looked at the central table. Viviana glittered in a throne-like chair, Charlie on her right and Henry on her left. Beyond were various crowned and uncrowned heads of Europe, along with the MPs, the Colombian ambassador, the mayor and his wife, and Annabel, Warren and Marcus. Viviana trilled with laughter, her bananas nodding this way and that. She waved her hands in extravagant Colombian gestures, displaying a large square emerald on her middle finger next to the more discreet Tolleymarsh diamond. As they stared, Warren looked up and caught Caro's eye. She went hot and then cold and dropped her fork, but Warren just smiled and nodded.

A salsa band struck up at the end of the hall and Viviana stood to lead the dancing. They all watched to see who would partner her. Caro tensed when the jewelled hand hovered over Warren, but in the end it fell upon Charlie. They rumbaed round the floor to applause; Charlie, though a foot shorter than the fruit confection, proved surprisingly dapper.

Caro turned away and choked down a prawn. She tried

hard to concentrate on the Warfleet conversation. Who was in and who was out . . . Darryl not there, not feeling well . . . Marsha Snelgrove furious not to be invited . . . Laurel Hopcraft already drunk . . . God knows how she'd wangled an invitation . . .

The dance floor began to fill up, and Caro's heart pounded as she saw Warren get to his feet. It slowed again as she saw him usher Annabel to the floor. She was grateful when Jeremy pulled her up and, despite her protests, propelled her towards the dancing. Jeremy had learned salsa at Warfleet's own Marcia Banks School of Dancing and his grip on the merengue was tenacious. As they circled and spun Caro caught sight of faces she knew. There was the bullet-headed Carl, Warren's bad angel, looking every inch the entrepreneur in a Paul Smith suit with a cellphone stuck in its pocket. He was talking to another youth she thought familiar. 'Who's that?' she asked Jeremy.

Jeremy completed a Marcia Banks Formation Team twirl and said breathlessly, 'Sidney Delgardo. Warren's cousin.'

Caro nodded. 'Oh.'

'Trouble,' said Jeremy in a lower voice. 'Caused the family a lot of heartache.'

Caro looked again towards the boy. He was thin and weasel-plain, though there was a slight family resemblance. He stood silently, staring sullenly at the dance floor. She half remembered stories about his childhood . . . torturing animals? Arson? Something vaguely psychotic.

There was a lull and the toastmaster stamped his staff and prayed silence for the Marquis. As people scattered to their seats Henry Trenche rose rather unsteadily and toasted Viviana. There was a chorus of 'Happy Birthday' followed by 'For She's a Jolly Good Fellow' and then a lengthy ode from

Henry on Viviana and the momentous changes she had made to his life. 'Certainly will be a change for him to be penniless,' said Rumer in a loud *tricoteuse*-style whisper.

Henry eventually sat down and Viviana stood, her pineapple towering, and in her charming accent thanked everyone for making her birthday so memorable and giving her such wonderful presents. 'But my greatest geeft,' she said, leaning towards Charlie, 'came from Mr Fong.' Caro stared at a circle of squid, embarrassed. Surely Viviana couldn't be tasteless enough to mention the emerald? But no, Viviana went on, 'Eet ees my greatest because eet ees also a geeft to us all. Some of you may know that Charlee has been looking for land for a major new development. A Millennium Theme Park. I am delighted to tell you that he has peecked Tolleymarsh as the site. I ask heem now to unveil hees plans, work on wheech will begeen een the autumn.'

She ushered Charlie to the wall, where he pulled a string attached to a drape of gold cloth which Caro had previously taken for decoration. It fell to the ground revealing a three-dimensional map of the Tolleymarsh estate. But not the Tolleymarsh estate as anyone had ever seen it before. The safari park had disappeared, as had the boating lake, art gallery, café and club. In their place was Ye Olde Worlde Theme Parke, the theme being Warfleet, complete with buildings targeted as leisure centres, therapy pools, museums, galleries, tearooms and crafte shops. There was a fully rigged windjammer on a simulated sea and even a strip of sandy beach around it. There were cobbled streets lined with chalet-like 'cottages' with thatch, and a village green with a pond and polystyrene ducks. The only thing missing was a ducking-stool. It could have been Warfleet a hundred years ago except that, as Viviana was now saying, the facilities would be 'state of the art'; even the fake steam engines connecting this fantasy town to the outside world were intended for high-speed operation.

There was a stunned silence. The inhabitants of Warfleet stared at the wall and like drowning men calculated the import on their lives of this development. At the high table Warren had gone white and Annabel looked close to tears. Henry's shifty expression betrayed that he had given his consent. Viviana appeared triumphant, Scott Harvey-Dickson was grinning maniacally, and even Marcus was smiling. Charlie, still standing by the edifice, cast in the hideous red of castle Fong, beamed with pleasure. As well he might. Everything except for the house and a few acres round it was soon to become part of his empire.

NINE

'The Italians are furious,' Delia said, as she dispensed toast next morning. News travelled fast in Warfleet. Caro was dealing with her hangover. She had, after all, consumed much champagne, though more in dismay than pleasure, and the home-made bread steaming with rich country butter made her heave slightly.

'I should think plenty of people are,' she muttered, drawing the coffee pot towards her. She recalled Toni and Rumer's shocked faces. Rumer practically broke into incantations. In the powder room, Sonny Delgardo had gone berserk and wrenched off a crested lavatory seat. She was certainly a good advert for her own power equipment.

And then there was Warren. He and Annabel had left, looking devastated, almost immediately after the announcement. There had been no opportunity to quiz him about his feelings. Delia and Caro were impatient for the arrival of Jean Plummer, formerly Peabody, Warren's mother, who would undoubtedly have more information.

When she arrived, late, her vibrant hair still rollered beneath a pink pearl-scattered net, she was tearful. With a snivel of distress she flung the *Warfleet Chronicle* upon the table. The front page had a huge photo of the planned park, under the banner headline: WELCOME TO THE WAR-FLEET EXPERIENCE.

The three women stood round the table staring at it in silence.

At last Jean got a piece of kitchen roll and blew her nose loudly. She lit the first of many cigarettes and said, 'Our Warren's ever so upset. He didn't know nothing about it.'

'Really!' said Caro. 'So this was all Viviana's doing?'

'I told you,' said Delia, with a certain smugness.

'As if he didn't have enough on his plate, what with Annabel and everything,' continued Jean.

'Annabel?' said Caro sharply, softening the enquiry with, 'Yes, it must be a terrible shock.'

'Hmm,' was Jean's only comment. She tied on a frilly apron and started gathering dishes. 'He's worked like a dog to get that place out of the dumps,' she went on, after a moment filled with running taps and clattering plates, 'and this is how he gets rewarded. They've never treated him like he belongs. Last night we weren't even invited!' It was hard to say which of these many slights was the main source of Jean's displeasure.

'But surely,' said Caro, rubbing her thudding temples, 'there'll be a job for him in it?'

'At a price,' said Delia, *sotto voce*.

'And as for this business with the club,' continued Jean, now on her own agenda, 'it's been that embarrassing for Bill.' Bill, Sergeant Plummer, the local community policeman, had married Jean a few summers before, thus becoming Warren's stepfather.

'Yes. Of course,' said Caro.

'Those blokes from the drug squad in Stourbridge,' said Jean in a tone of disgust. 'All fast cars and Bacardi. If you ask me they'd like to be the dealers.' Caro imagined a squad of roughnecks hung with medallions descending with sottish glee on Warren. 'Jealous,' said Jean with finality.

The residents began to erupt, demanding their mid-morning breakfasts, and Caro picked up her coffee and escaped before she could become embroiled in their tedious conversation.

On the stairs she encountered Deen Perry, the youngish boy novelist. 'Are the rumours true?' he demanded abruptly.

Caro nodded. Deen, like herself, was published by StrongFellows.

'Fuck it!' he snarled, clutching the banisters, 'I've got to get a new publisher.' Caro passed on, smiling wryly. Deen, at least, should not find it difficult.

She wondered if Zo had heard the news, which would confirm everything she feared about Charlie. She thought about calling her, but in the end could not face Zo's abrupt manner or being the bearer of bad tidings. Instead she phoned Noelle, who was, for once, in her office.

'I know, love. I know,' said Noelle, sounding reasonably sober. 'It was announced in the press this morning. Look, I'm coming down to see you. I could do with a day out of the office.'

They agreed she would visit in a couple of days' time, though to do what Caro wasn't sure. She, unlike Deen, would not easily find a new publisher. She was longing to phone Warren and stood staring at the coin box for some time as if willing it to ring. When it didn't, she took her thundering head back to bed for an hour. It was useless to think about work in the circumstances.

Later in the day Caro walked the streets of the little town. She was still feeling extremely delicate, besides which she had been seized with a great restlessness. Her world seemed to be turning topsy-turvy.

Her footsteps took her, almost at random, down the narrow High Street. Though the season was not yet in full swing there were a few signs of regeneration. She passed the shop that had been Jeremy and Darryl's Euro Antiques. It was now photographic and the window was full of bravely smiling spring brides. She peered into Jim and Peggy Bacon's High Street Heels, and saw Peggy dressing the window with trainers and stripy plimsolls. The fish and chip shop, Sole Mio, owned by Ugo and Fabio, was open, as was their pizzeria, La Mamma's, and in a side street Froth, their ice-cream parlour. This had a genuine espresso machine and Caro was drawn in by the liquoricy smell. As she drank the hot bitter thimbleful, she thought there was coffee at least for which to thank 'the Italians'.

The day was overcast and inclined to rain. It didn't favour the promenade and Caro hovered, uncertain where to turn. She knew, but could not admit, that her wanderings were really in search of Warren. After a further desultory meander down alleys full of still boarded second-hand shops and depressed-looking charity outlets, she found herself close to the hanging baskets of Jeremy and Darryl's new house, Blossom Cottage.

'Well, it's not all bad, you know,' said Jeremy, handing Caro a cup of tea, the cup fine, hand-painted bone, the tea also China. Darryl lay on the chaise longue looking Dorian Grayish, in a striped silk dressing gown. He stretched out a languid hand, thin now, Caro saw, and took the proffered cup and saucer.

'It sounds immensely tasteless,' he said. It was the worst

Darryl could say about anything. The pretty youth, Ashley, leaned forward to take a cup. The brittle China looked dangerously vulnerable in his blunt tattooed hand. Though Ashley was gay, he wasn't fey, as his butch denim shirt and jewel-punched face indicated. He was, surmised Caro, a tasty bit of rough from Stourbridge.

Blossom Cottage was in need of a facelift, explained Jeremy, and Ashley was helping with the decorating. Ashley snorted. Plans perpetually broke down as Jeremy and Darryl argued over shades of pink and Liberty or Osborne & Little fabric. The room in which they sat, with a pretty bay window giving on to the street, was rather over-crammed with furniture. Jeremy, having given up his antiques business, was beginning to dabble again. He couldn't resist a bargain.

'How is it good?' said Caro.

'Work, of course,' said Jeremy. 'I mean look around you, dear. It's thin on the ground in Warfleet.'

Ashley looked interested. 'I might get a job brickie-ing.'

'Now, now, you're spoken for,' said Jeremy. Ashley pulled a face and subsided.

Caro nodded. 'It's true. The town's very empty.'

'We used to have mining, the naval college, ships . . .'

'We used to have tourists,' cried Darryl, livening up. 'Festivals, parades, tea dances . . .' He poured a little whisky into his tea as if in homage to the good times.

Jeremy sighed. 'They go abroad. Like the antiques. Now all we have is fishing.'

'And smuggling,' said Ashley with a leer.

'I doubt a few illegal immigrants make much difference to the local economy,' murmured Jeremy.

'Dope, I mean,' said Ashley. 'Still the best place of entry.'

Caro thought of Warren. Carl and 'the Italians' could well be involved, Warren's club a handy outlet.

'Warren looked furious,' said Jeremy, as though reading her thoughts. 'It must be awful for him, with her pregnant—'

'Pregnant?' Caro's head snapped up, 'Who?'

'Annabel. Who did you think?' said Jeremy, looking at her archly.

Caro felt as though a large writhing octopus had taken possession of her stomach. 'Excuse me,' she mumbled, and blundered towards the stairs.

'Second on the left,' called Jeremy. 'Oh dear, *somebody*'s got a hangover.'

In the bathroom, semi-tiled and chilly, Caro stared into the art deco mirror. The sepia glass made her face look sick and sallow and her eyes seemed overwide, with huge black pupils. So Annabel was pregnant and Warren hadn't mentioned it, hadn't thought it necessary, or perhaps conducive to seduction. What other lies or half-truths had he told her? She leaned her forehead into the mirror, her breath making a misty pool on the cold glass. She felt angry. Humiliated. But after all, it was ridiculous. She was old enough to be his mother. Besides, Warren was married. He had a perfect right — She must stop this before it got out of hand. What was she expecting?

Jeremy was calling from below, 'Caro, are you all right, dear?'

Caro wiped the cold sweat from her face. The sense of betrayal she could not wipe away so easily. As she flicked a comb through her hair, she heard Zo's voice saying, 'All men are prats.' And then Delia's words about Henry Trenche, 'No fool like an old fool.'

TEN

Judging by the colour of her agent's cheeks when Caro met her at the station, Noelle had availed herself freely of Southern Region's hospitality. 'Lunch,' she muttered, swaying slightly. 'Is there a local hostelry?'

Caro led the way to Delia's car, in the back of which sat Deen Perry. He'd asked if he could tag along, wanting to know, as he put it, 'the bloody starting price'.

As they entered the public bar of the Admiral Nelson – Deen had vetoed the lounge as 'poncey' – Caro immediately saw Warren. He was sitting on a bar stool, talking to his cousin, Sidney Delgardo. Their heads were close together and in profile their resemblance was more pronounced, though whereas in Warren the prominent cheekbones were beautiful, in Sidney they were merely bony. So engrossed was Warren that he did not at first notice Caro, though the bar was only sparsely peopled. She regained her composure by finding a suitable seat for Noelle – backless was out of the question – and taking the drinks order. Deen said a pint of 'the local brew', and Noelle a Bloody Mary.

At the bar Caro could not avoid Warren and she nodded to him curtly. He looked surprised and then pleased. His warm smile bathed her and she found it hard to stop the corners of her own mouth lifting. He excused himself from

Sidney, who turned upon Caro a hard stare, and came over to her. 'I've been meaning to call you,' he said. 'It's just . . . everything's been crazy.'

'I can imagine,' said Caro, aiming for icy politeness. 'How's Annabel? And Viviana?' Without waiting for an answer, she gathered her change and was about to turn from the bar.

'Are you angry with me?' Warren looked puzzled, wounded.

'Why should I be?' Caro gave a carefree laugh, though she spoiled it a little by spilling the Bloody Mary.

Warren gave her a long look, his cat's eyes narrowed against the sunlight shafting into the bar. 'I've got the club going again,' he said. 'It's open tonight. Will you come?' He put a hand on her arm and Caro's resolve melted.

'I'll see,' she stammered. 'I must go.' She indicated her table. 'I've got people waiting.' Warren released her and watched her go. She held her head high and carried the glasses carefully.

At the table Deen was whining about StrongFellows. 'Bunch of sad bastards. Serves them right. If it was up to me I'd nuke them.'

Noelle said, 'You're having trouble with your latest book, I gather?'

'Who gives a toss?' Deen shoved his greasy fringe out of his eyes. 'My editor's a turd. Hey. How many editors does it take to change a light bulb?'

Noelle stared at him, unsmiling.

Deen assumed an earnest editor's voice. 'Does it have to be a *light bulb*?' He laughed loudly, then, when they did not, repeated the punch line.

Noelle and Caro exchanged a look. One of Noelle's eyebrows had drifted to her hairline. Caro said, 'Zo tells me they know nothing except what's in the papers.'

Noelle nodded. 'If I was them I'd be thinking of a hitman.'

Above Noelle's head Caro saw Carl enter the bar and cross to join Sidney and Warren; despite his sharp clothes he still had the bouncing walk of a geezer. The bright sun lit up his scalp, bluish-white, through his number one hair cut. The three men went into a huddle and Caro dragged her eyes away. Deen was monologuing on deconstruction and the state of the modern novel. 'What's yours about?' Caro asked, forcing herself to concentrate.

'Sex and death,' said Deen without pause. Caro wondered if that was high concept.

They talked over and around the StrongFellow situation for some time, though they arrived at no conclusion. Deen claimed most of the attention. There was something almost attractive about his egocentricity, thought Caro. Indeed, despite his long unwashed hair and snaggle teeth, there was a kind of glamour to him. They had many rounds of drinks which Noelle generously paid for, perhaps losing track after her fourth vodka. At some point Caro noticed Warren and his associates leave the bar. He raised his hand to her briefly.

Noelle was poured back on to a London-bound train, promising to 'look around, love. Seriously.'

Deen lay in the back of the car, picking crisp flakes out of his ragged teeth and chortling, 'Does it have to be a *light bulb?*'

Caro took the car when she left at ten o'clock that evening. The Aga needed cleaning, but Delia resolutely ignored its reproachful gravy stains and sat at the kitchen table with the *Warfleet Chronicle*. Now the house was quiet she could steal her own moment of peace before going to the big empty bed. She shuffled through pages announcing births, deaths, marriages, sales, charity functions, boot fairs. At the lonely hearts column, here called coyly 'Meeting Place', she stopped. After a moment she put her head down on the paper and wept. Her own heart was so terribly lonely.

There was a slight scratching at the door and it opened a crack and Harry's teddy bear came through, followed by Harry. He stood blinking in the fluorescent light. 'Mumma?' he said uncertainly.

Delia could not answer and turned her head aside. She didn't want him to see her crying.

Harry came across, padding in bare feet to the table. He dangled his teddy bear on the stone flags behind him. When he reached Delia's side, he nestled against her and wound his hand through the crook of her arm until he found her fingers. 'Mumma,' he said again, more urgently.

'It's OK, Harry,' said Delia, sniffing. 'Mummy's a little tired is all.' She sat up and wiped her nose on a tissue from her pinny. Harry looked at her with anxious eyes. They were pale blue and his hair was pale blond like Wendy's. He looked a little like Sebastian only more fragile and nervous. He had had a strange beginning. She was glad Alex favoured her. He was a robust, straightforward child, not given to Harry's bursts of imagination.

'I had a dream,' said Harry. 'A big man came and saved us all. He was a bit like Daddy.' Delia smiled at the child who, though not her own, seemed prescient of her feelings. Harry struggled on to her lap and put the teddy bear between her breasts. 'And we were on a beach. No, on a raft, and there were waves . . . and a huge monster . . .'

'Harry,' said Delia warningly.

'A small monster,' he conceded, 'and the man came out of the sea, a flying boat . . . I think it was.'

'Mmm hmm. I suppose he was a Dutchman?'

'No,' said Harry. 'American. He was American like you, Mummy.'

'Bedtime,' said Delia, burying her face in the child's silky neck. She breathed in, filling her heart with the scent of him.

They went upstairs and Harry, without asking, climbed into Delia's bed. There he rocked and made swishing wave noises until they fell asleep together.

The music came before the lights as Caro drove the winding road through the estate. Drum and bass with an irresistible beat. She found her own foot involuntarily tapping. The club appeared suddenly round a bend, like a ship out of the darkness. 'Caro Radcliffe,' she said to the youth on the door, one she remembered having seen at the party. 'I'm a guest of Warren Peabody.'

He looked at his list then gave a grudging nod and ushered her through wordlessly. There was security on the door. Her bag was searched and so were her pockets.

Inside the dim, laser-lit room, she saw the golden youth of Warfleet. They were dancing, or sitting at the bar, or shouting above the sounds, or just standing staring. Caro glimpsed Anthea, Delia's nanny, in the centre of an animated crowd. She was wearing flesh-crunching Lycra, which revealed things about her Caro had not previously noticed.

The place was filling up and she wondered how to find Warren. Then she saw him, above the crowd, in a giant coruscating sphere on which the word *Bliss* was lit up in purple neon. The lights glanced off his hair, turning it red, purple, green, silver. Caro stared, entranced. He looked like a young god, Dionysus, Bacchus, as he deftly spun the decks. The music became more frenzied and the crowd danced wildly. Caro hovered near the wall, watching everything. Though Zo, who loved to dance, had often described these clubs to her, they had never been to one together. Caro had resisted, feeling too old, not wanting to embarrass her lover. The sound and movement reached a peak then died away to more gentle trancey music. Warren left the DJ egg, which she now saw had quite ordinary steps to the floor, and she followed his head, higher than most, as he moved through the dancers towards her.

'I saw you come in,' he said. 'What do you think?'

'Oh,' said Caro, still touched by his magic, 'I think it's terrific.'

Warren bought her a Coke and they went outside where they could talk. The dense blackness gave way to shadowy shapes as their eyes became accustomed to it. Caro could make out trees, and then stars. Somewhere in the wood an owl hooted. They lit cigarettes and leaned against the warm brick of the building. It had once been a barn, destroyed by fire. Warren had reclaimed it.

Caro said, 'So you managed to get it open?'

'Viviana fixed it,' said Warren, adding ruefully, 'the booby prize.'

Caro wanted to ask about Carl and the meeting in the pub, but as neither he nor Sidney was in evidence she resisted. 'I'm sorry about all that's happened,' she said rather stiffly. Now that they were out of the sensual glow, she had remembered she was cross with him.

Warren gave a shrug. 'I knew it was coming. I just wasn't expecting it that evening.'

'You knew?' said Caro, surprised.

'Yes,' said Warren. 'She offered me a deal.' He shifted away. 'I didn't find it appealing.' It did not take much for Caro to guess what the deal was. 'Would you like a spliff?' said Warren hospitably.

'Here?' said Caro. 'What about security?'

Warren laughed. 'I can leave now. The other DJ's taken over. Let's go down to the beach.' He looked at her, holding her glance with his lids half lowered. She knew he meant the beach hut.

'I . . . I can't,' she stammered, her mouth dry.

'Why not?' Even in the dark his eyes were hypnotic.

'I know . . . about Annabel.'

'Oh,' said Warren, dropping his hand.

'You should have told me,' said Caro.

'When?' he said. 'Before? Or after? I didn't plan for it to happen.' She saw he had a point. 'I would have told you. The next time.'

She said dryly, 'News travels fast in Warfleet.'

There was a burst of noise as a group of dancers came out of the club and stood about chattering and laughing. Caro shrank into the wall as she recognized Anthea among them.

'Look,' said Warren, 'we can't talk here. Let's go down there anyway.' He put a hand on Caro's shoulder and her whole body shuddered. She was quite unable to resist him.

The beach hut had had a padlock put on it. It was small and Warren wrenched it away easily. 'Someone knows we were here.' Caro was not sure why, on the empty beach, she was whispering.

Warren shook his head. 'They lock them up against vagrants.'

They pulled the door to behind them, grateful to be in out

of the damp misty air. It was still only April and the seashore reverted, at night, to winter. It was pitch dark in the hut. Warren struck a match and the flare lit up their questioning faces. They stared at each other until the flame burned down and Warren yelped and dropped it. The next moment they were in each other's arms. Warren caught hold of Caro's head and his lips searched out her mouth and his tongue sank deep inside it. She strained him to her, feeling his cock harden against her stomach. Her hand slid to his belt and he held her away and undid it. She dropped her skirt to the floor, wanting his warm flesh next to her. They stood naked, clasped together, kissing and murmuring. Something about the hopelessness of their case made their desire greater. They lay down on the wooden boards, Warren pulling her on top of him and sliding into her wide open wetness and moving her with his hands on her waist, while she gasped and cried out and clung to his shoulders. And at last a long slow orgasm began that caught them up in its spiral and whirled them this way and that, until they were gone and lost to everything but each other.

They must have slept because the next thing Caro saw was pale grey light filtering through the wall slats. She was cold and sat up and pulled Warren's sweatshirt towards her. He was sleeping soundly, a regular escape of breath from his parted lips lifting strands of blond hair where they had fallen across his face. She looked at him and a great tenderness overwhelmed her and made her want to laugh and shout. 'Oh my God,' she whispered to herself, 'oh my God. This is crazy.'

She shook Warren and he sat up looking fluffy and boyish. He seemed not to know where he was, but after a moment smiled at her. 'We never even had that spliff,' he said teasingly. They pushed open the door and sat smoking and looking out to sea. The sky was dawn-pink, shading to lavender at the horizon. Even at this hour a little boat was out, heading for a day's fishing.

'We must go,' said Caro. 'It's five o'clock.'

'Mmm,' said Warren unwillingly. He pulled Caro back down and they lay quiet for a moment. Warren stroked Caro's breast. 'I want to make love again,' he said, 'but you're right. The club will be finishing.'

They dressed quickly, shivery in the light breeze, and left, pulling the door shut and replacing the broken padlock. 'They'll never notice,' said Warren.

Delia's car, in which they had come, was some distance away in a parking bay, so they walked along the beach. They stayed silent, as if there was too much to say. Their hands hung by their sides and once Warren caught Caro's and squeezed it. The sea was quiet, lapping the shingles gently. A thin mist lay over them, promising heat later.

As they neared the bay, Caro made out something at the water's edge. A large dark object.

'What's that?' she said. 'A fish?'

Warren looked and frowned. 'Too big. Perhaps a seal.' They did sometimes beach on this coastline.

'Oh no!' said Caro. 'Quick. Let's look. We might be able to save it.'

Warren looked grave, but he followed Caro down the beach to where the object lay, with small waves breaking over it. When they got closer, the mist cleared and they saw it was not a fish. Nor a seal. It was a dark-suited body.

The head was turned away from them, face down on the beach. Blood had seeped into the water pooled around it and soaked into the rough sand, turning it the colour of treacle toffee. Caro and Warren stood very still. Then Warren stooped down and heaved the body over. The face that rolled into view looked mildly surprised. The small eyes were open and stared at the sky, but Charlie Fong's twinkle was gone for ever.

ELEVEN

The dream hovered and finally came to rest with a dark thud, waking Caro to a sense of present panic and impending disaster. It took a moment for her to collect her sleep-scattered thoughts; to remember with dread that only three hours ago she had leant against the desk in the barren police station, shiveringly recounting to the startled boy behind it her discovery of a body.

She and Warren had stood for what seemed like hours staring at Charlie Fong's upturned face, whilst the slow realization of what this find meant to them both corrosively invaded their consciousness. During this endless nanosecond they had also looked wildly round as though checking for other observers. Witnesses to their guilt. The beach was deserted save for a couple of casually circling seagulls. There were no houses overlooking this stretch and the beach huts, locked and shuttered, had petered out some yards before. The sandy pebbles gave way to a steep green bank above which was the parking bay. The top of Delia's Clio was just visible. No other cars were evident. All this they took in whilst seemingly not moving their eyes from the neat black hole, surrounded by congealed blood, in the middle of Charlie's forehead.

'He's been shot,' said Warren.

'What shall we do?' asked Caro in a small, childlike voice. It was as though, in primitive circumstances, the man should take the decision.

Warren expelled air slowly. 'We'll have to report it,' he said.

They both focused on what that meant. Warren shrugged. 'We could have been out for a walk.'

'At five o'clock in the morning?'

'Well . . . after the club . . .'

'Did people see us leave?'

Warren shrugged again and they both fell silent.

Caro shook her head violently. 'I'll report it. I'll say I was by myself.'

'I can't let you do that,' said Warren quickly.

'It'll ruin your life if this comes out.' Caro was vehement. 'Charlie's had enough of a try already.'

'My God,' said Warren softly, 'what will this mean to the Millennium Park?'

'Rough justice,' said Caro, astounded at her own callousness. But it did not seem as if the body was real. The whole scene was from some movie.

Eventually Warren agreed. He would cut up through the woods to the Tolleymarsh estate. It was not unusual, on a club night, for him to get home with breakfast. Caro would take the car to the police station, claim early morning walk, sleepless night, writer's angst, etc. Warren could take care of his people at Bliss, if they had noticed his absence.

It was cold, now, on the beach and with a quick brush of their passionless lips they parted, each hurrying to their allotted stories. They moved swiftly, slyly, with heads down, as befitted conspirators.

Caro sat on the edge of the bed, shuddering. She thrust her feet into her worn sheepskin slippers for comfort and pulled the hefty hand-woven coverlet around her. She stared at the sharp, blue sky through the ivy-framed window and tried to dismiss Ruth Rendell-ish visions of the ugly modern police station, with its bright light blanching the terrified face of the young police officer.

There was a knock on the door and Delia entered with a tray. 'Well,' she said, setting it down with a bump, 'seems you got more from your night out than you bargained for.'

Caro nodded, speechless.

'Drink this. You're in shock.' Delia thrust a mug into Caro's trembling hands. Caro sipped the hot sweet tea, amazed, yet again, at the speed of Warfleet networking. 'Sergeant Plummer's down below. He wants to talk to you.'

By lunch time the entire town was on red alert. A crowd had gathered at the beach to watch the Special Operations team, called in from Stourbridge, seal off the area and erect a forensic tent around the plastic-sheeted body. Sergeant Plummer, as community liaison officer and known Warfleet man, carefully dispersed it. His leave had been cancelled at seven-thirty that morning, which was irritating as he and Jean had planned a visit to the DIY superstore followed by two days (for him) of building cupboards and shelves in the kitchen.

The Delphinium café did an exceptional trade in all-day breakfasts (£2.95 including tea or coffee) and the Admiral Nelson opened its doors half an hour early. By then several policemen were on their first break and the public bar had the air of a Masonic day trip as it filled with the burly urban crime squad, a handful of Warfleet's own CID amongst them.

'Viviana had a fit of hysterics when she heard,' said Laurel Hopcraft, licking fingers buttery from toast in the Delphinium. 'She's had to be sedated.'

Nobody doubted her words. Laurel's sources, usually from the staff, were always impeccable.

'Feverfew,' said May, setting down another plate of eggs, bacon and sausage. 'Good for hysterics and migraine.'

Laurel touched her fingers delicately to her temple, as though the mention had prophetic power. May was known to be a witch, albeit a white one.

Marsha Snelgrove addressed the eggs and bacon with enthusiasm. 'Shock makes you hungry,' she said, by way of defence. Marsha fought a constant battle with her body which, apparently on its own agenda, was capable of ballooning out of costumes once a first night was over.

'Umm,' said Laurel disparagingly. She pushed aside a third cup of black coffee and flicked her Gauloise ash perilously close to Marsha's plate.

Jeremy bustled in, rubbing his hands against the raw morning. He headed for the fireplace where real coals smouldered, giving a smoky warmth to the blue room. 'I've been asked to billet some of the Stourbridge officers,' he said. 'The Admiral Nelson is full already.'

Laurel's beady eyes turned sharp. 'Do they need other volunteers? I've got the boxroom.' The boxroom was indeed full of boxes, mostly containing Laurel's unpublished novels, but she was never slow in pursuit of a bargain.

'Talk to Sergeant Plummer,' said Jeremy. 'He seems to be in charge of it.'

A couple of young, uniformed policemen entered and a hush fell on the company. The newcomers nodded and smiled awkwardly, as though they had been instructed to make friends with the natives.

'Can you tell us what's happening?' demanded Jeremy boldly.

The policemen shook their heads. One, laughing slightly, said, 'They don't even tell us.' They had come for takeaway teas and coffees. The natives turned back to their own conversations. The coppers were too low level to be of more interest. Teddy Forbes murmured that he had the senior investigating officer booked into his B & B. Any crumbs, other than toast, dropped at the table he would be sure to circulate.

Peggy Bacon stuck her head round the door, looking for her husband, Jim. 'I've got a shop full of people,' she said distractedly. There had been an unprecedented run on wellingtons and waterproof trainers. Most of the policemen had left Stourbridge before the shops were open. 'We'll have to restock. Big sizes.'

Rumer pushed past her and briskly began to distribute flyers for the Quest Natural Healing Centre to the handful of empty tables. The flyers, fresh off Rumer's computer, advertised Stress Management. 'You never know,' she said. 'These days the police have counselling for everything.'

'Have you seen what the Italians have done?' said Ashley, coming in with pots of paint. Jeremy had instructed him to get the spare room ready.

'No. What?' chorused his audience.

'Only set up a beach stand for coffee and sandwiches.'

'Trust them,' said May, clicking her teeth. She was one of the few independents left in Warfleet.

Ashley shoved through the wicker chairs to stand at the

fire with Jeremy. He was garbed in denim with massive bike boots which Peggy eyed speculatively. His shirt was open to the waist despite the biting wind outside. He had heard rumours of a gay clique within the Stourbridge constabulary.

As May and her niece, Angie, came in and out with plates, coffee percolated, cups chinked, there was an almost celebratory air to the gathering. It was certainly true that more than one participant could benefit from the increased trade. Beneath that was a relish for the drama and the gossip and speculation that went with it. Events of such magnitude were rare in the town (at least since the sixteenth century) though it had its fair share of ordinary violence. This was on another scale. Forgotten Warfleet would now be a byword. But for what? As each inhabitant pondered this, the buzz of chatter fell away. When Fabio Martini, in dark glasses and leather jacket, passed by the chintz-curtained window, he left in his wake a shiver of anxiety. The diners sat, as if waiting for release, in slow confused silence.

Caro spent an uncomfortable morning. Sergeant Plummer had invited her to the police station to give a further statement to the detective superintendent in charge of the case. It was unthinkable, once Charlie's international status was identified, that the small Warfleet force could handle it. Detective Superintendent Cooper of the Stourbridge division was pleasant and polite, but his slightly reddened features had a tough uncompromising look about them. His eyes, behind his rimless glasses, were blue and hard. Caro felt he could detect a lie at a hundred paces. Charlie Fong, he told her, had now been officially identified, in the absence of next of kin, by his closest associate Marcus Croft. Had Ms Radcliffe anything to add to what she had already told them?

He swayed slightly on the swivel chair behind the shiny black desk, occasionally tapping his fingertips together as Caro went through the story again, trying hard to stick word for word to what she had told PC Armitage at six o'clock that morning. Fortunately the shock had sent him witless and he had made only sketchy notes for his superior. Besides, it wasn't as though she lied, except for saying it was she who had turned the body over, only omitted.

As she left the police station, scuttling past posters on domestic violence and lost dogs, shaky with exhaustion, she remembered the horrors forensic could uncover. What if some jacket fluff or a hair from Warren's head had landed on the body? Her action on the beach now seemed quixotic. Stupid. But a fierce, almost animal, instinct had made her want to protect Warren. The escutcheon of the lion and unicorn proclaiming '*Dieu et mon Droit*' stared censoriously at her as she hurried through the door. Too late now for regrets. Perhaps they would be lucky.

The day, though blindingly bright, was cold after all. Caro's own body felt deathly chilled as, bent against the wind, she struggled back to Four Trees. But it was not the wind, she knew, that froze her blood. It was almost as though one of them was a murderer.

TWELVE

Caro kept to her room for the rest of the day. When she did emerge, desperate for caffeine, it was to encounter, as she imagined, suspicious looks and whispers. Deen Perry passed her in the hall and snarled, 'Some people will do anything to get a better advance.' He followed this with a loud cackle and, as Caro scurried back to her room, shouted after her, 'I'd have shot him myself given half a chance.'

Delia popped in every half-hour or so with bulletins fuelled by Jean Plummer, who had dealt with her disappointment over the loss of a new kitchen by making herself the surrogate centre of the drama and was holding court by the Aga, surrounded by gaping residents. The police pathologist had established that Charlie had been shot in the head by a .38 handgun, at approximately three a.m. Just at the moment Warren and I were—. Caro instantly banished the blush-raising picture. Death would have been instantaneous.

'Of course,' opined Jean, drawing on her assumed knowledge of criminal behaviour rather than anything strictly factual, 'he could have been shot elsewhere and dumped on the beach. That's what often happens.'

The town was already swarming with journalists; a press conference was expected. Delia brought Caro a cup of tea and said Glyn Madoc, editor of the *Chronicle*, was on the phone, begging Caro to speak to him. 'Oh God,' said Caro, visualizing the headline.

Reluctantly she took the call, wresting the receiver from Jean Plummer; she didn't want to put Delia to more trouble than necessary. She answered Glyn's questions politely, confirming nothing she had not said to Detective Superintendent Cooper. No, she had not heard of any FBI involvement; no, no mention of a conspiracy; no, in fact, no clues at all. She did admit that earlier in the evening she had been at Bliss. 'Writer's research,' she added tersely. When Glyn, disappointed, had rung off, Caro dialled Zo's office number. It was engaged as it had been all day. In the circumstances, hardly surprising.

Delia called her to watch the local news on which a Stourbridge press officer made the statement Jean Plummer had pre-empted. He followed it by asking anyone who could assist to come forward and gave out a Warfleet telephone number. A large crowd had assembled outside the police station to hear the announcement. Few people in it were recognizable. Presumably it was composed of international media representatives; Caro saw many flash cameras and at least two video units. There was a handful of residents hovering on the outskirts looking shell-shocked at the onslaught. Caro wondered desperately what Warren was feeling. Was he, like her, consumed with terror? One thing was certain, she could not communicate with him.

As the news bulletin ended, Jade called to speak to Caro. She was coming down on the morrow, she said, delegated by Jed to cover the story.

'But why?' stuttered Caro, horrified. 'You're Arts and Entertainment.'

'Oh, Ma,' said Jade pityingly. 'This investigative stuff's

right up my street. Besides, I *come* from there, I'm the obvious person.'

Caro marvelled at the alacrity with which her daughter had embraced her provincial connection. She generally behaved as though she had sprung, fully formed, from a bar in Soho.

'Look,' said Jade, 'he was trying to take us over. Naturally we've got an interest.'

Perhaps, thought Caro with further alarm, more than an interest.

'Tell Delia to save me the attic.' Jade slammed down the phone before Caro could explain that Delia, overwhelmed with requests for temporary housing, had already reassigned Caro to the attic. Even now she was turning out the laundry room to make way for extra beds.

Caro stood for a moment contemplating the frightening implications of Jade's arrival. She stared at the faded William Morris wallpaper above the phone but saw only Jade finding herself and Warren *in flagrante*. Charlie's dead face swam before her, followed by Warren's, white and strained as he'd kissed her goodbye.

Feeling a shuddering need for security, she rang Zo's home number. This time Zo's answerphone responded with a burst of techno music followed by a brief instruction to leave a message or call back later. No message seemed appropriate so Caro said lamely, 'Hi, only me,' and replaced the receiver.

She wandered into the kitchen, empty now Jean Plummer the walking website had left, and placed the kettle on the murmuring Aga, the only thing complacently unmoved by events. It occurred to her that she hadn't eaten all day and she put a couple of slices of bread to toast on the plate.

The back door was open letting in the bright, chilly

evening and Caro pulled her cardigan closer as she looked on to the cobbled courtyard Delia had created. Across it, the old outhouse had been converted into a state-of-the-art launderette and it was this Delia was clearing. Occasionally her head could be seen bobbing past the new plastic-framed windows. Caro rather missed the ancient metal ones, but the area had a homely, reassuring feel to it and she crossed the courtyard thinking she should give Delia a hand. Really what she craved was company.

Delia straightened wearily from erecting a camp bed and put her hand to the small of her back. 'Phew,' she said, 'as if normal business weren't bad enough! Feeling better?'

Caro shrugged and picked up a pile of duvets to avoid Delia's glance. She suspected that Delia knew she hadn't told her everything. The women worked in careful silence, putting pillows into cases and laying sheets and under-blankets.

'Shouldn't be too uncomfortable,' said Delia at last. She looked round the room, satisfying herself that its neat order had humanizing touches; here a pile of books, there a bowl of garden primroses.

'Jade's coming,' warned Caro, 'but really, I don't see why Talk TV can't pay for a hotel.'

'Oh lord,' sighed Delia. 'To save my life I couldn't cram so much as a cat in.'

They went out into the courtyard, now grown dim, with thin wisps of bluish mist floating. 'What's that smell?' said Delia, sniffing.

'Bonfire?' said Caro, though it seemed a little early in the year. As they approached the house, the mist became a dense fog and through the back door came the unmistakable smell of burning.

'We're on fire,' cried Delia, rushing ahead.

'Oh shit, the toast,' muttered Caro, hurrying after.

The kitchen was cloudy with smoke and as they beat a clearing a bulky figure emerged at its centre. A tall broad-shouldered man stood with a piece of charcoaled bread in each hand.

'Looks like I arrived in the nick of time, ladies,' he drawled in an accent from somewhere in the American south and grinned a slow, charming grin. 'I was just stopping by to see if you had a bed for me.'

Craig O'Connell, for that was his name, and yes, indeed, he was proud of his Irish ancestry, was professor of medieval history at Austin University, Texas. He was researching the correlation of ley lines and eleventh-century battle sites and his sabbatical tour had taken him across Europe and from Agincourt directly to Warfleet. He had also – and here he looked persuasively at Delia – heard many tales of the excellence of Four Trees and Delia's cooking. Delia made a gesture of almost coy despair at this; the most she had been able to rustle together after the smoke had died down was an international cheese board and a delicious pesto rice salad, accompanied by one of Sebastian's remaining vintage clarets.

Craig had been astonished at the activity in the town; no idea until he got in that anything had happened. He'd had to fight his way through the thronged streets to the Admiral Nelson (original building, sixteenth century) where he had sought news and directions. Arriving at Four Trees, he had found the back door open and smoke billowing about. Why, it was almost like a medieval battle. At this he laughed uproariously, and after a moment Delia joined in.

Caro looked at her wonderingly. Delia threw back her head and opened her mouth, lipsticked Caro noticed, revealing her American-white, pointed teeth. Ripples of merriment ran up and down her throat. It was the first time Caro had heard her laugh, really laugh, since Sebastian's death. Perhaps relief, after the stress of this extraordinary day, had something to do with it.

Taking a second glass of wine with her, Caro went to her attic. Much as she feared sleep and its attendant nightmares, she felt completely exhausted. Delia had discovered reserves of energy and sat on at the crumb-scattered refectory table looking relaxed and entertained. Craig's large shaggy head was propped on one broad hand and he said something in his low drawl that made Delia again trill with laughter. He was more lion than cat, thought Caro, but, crammed or not, no doubt Delia would find a space for him.

THIRTEEN

'And guess what the contents of his stomach were?' Jean Plummer looked around the breakfast table, arms folded in expectant triumph.

'Champagne, I imagine,' said Delia dryly, 'if Viviana had dinner with him.'

'Spaghetti!' announced Jean, as if producing a rabbit from a hat. 'The last meal he ate was *Italian*!'

There was a silence after this and Delia began putting coffee cups into the dishwasher. Deen Perry had three ranged before him as well as an ashtray overflowing with butts. Caro, who had come down early hoping to avoid the other residents, had reckoned without Jean Plummer. She had hurried in, hopping with new storylines, and swiftly assembled an audience whose appetite for this fascinating soap had overcome even its late drowsing habit.

'Course it's difficult,' continued Jean, 'what with the tide having washed over him. You lose a lot of clues in salt water.'

Caro, unaware until then that she had been holding her breath, let out a little puff; perhaps she and Warren were safe, then.

'I suppose he was meant to be carried out to sea,' said Deen, 'but when the tide went out it left him stranded.' He was making notes as he spoke. Caro wondered if he was intending to abandon the literary novel for blockbusting crime fiction.

Jean shook her head vehemently, unwilling to concede theory to a novice. 'More likely he was dumped off a boat. Or left as a warning if it was, say, a Mafia killing.' Jean was keen on the Italian connection, it seemed. There was no love lost between the Delgardos and the Martinis.

Miriam, the arts presenter, who was reading the *Financial Times*, said, 'StrongFellows will be sold, I suppose. Fong empire stocks are plummeting.'

Deen lit another cigarette and drew on it anxiously. 'Wonder who's the beneficiary?' It was well known Charlie had no immediate family.

'If I were you,' said Miriam, gathering her things and smiling cruelly, 'I'd worry more about what it meant to my work. Whoever buys StrongFellows's bound to pare down.'

Deen stubbed out his cigarette furiously.

Delia said, 'Jean, we must get on. I'm going to move Anthea out of the boxroom and in with the boys. Then I'll have her bed and Mr O'Connell can have mine. Last night he had to sleep on the sofa.' She glanced towards Caro as she spoke, as if to check she had absorbed this information.

Jean reluctantly abandoned centre stage and tied on her pinny. There was no one left to impress anyway. Craig had gone out early to 'examine the ramparts'; Harold, the Warfleet historian, had accompanied him. Neil, the theatre producer, had not yet descended – Caro, lying sleepless, had heard him pacing in the night – and the two journalists who were staying in the laundry had arrived late and left at crack of dawn for the television studios in Stourbridge. They were making an instant response programme on the local economy and what Charlie's loss would mean to it.

Deen Perry said, 'Fancy a walk?'

Caro looked up, startled. Deen was never seen to walk anywhere except to the bar if no one else was buying. Since the others had left the room, it must be she he was addressing and she nodded, thinking Deen's spin on the situation could be interesting.

She had finally managed to catch Zo in that morning. She had answered the phone sounding alert and tense at seven-thirty. 'Oh, Caro,' she said with relief, 'thank God for a real person. Thought it was another fucking journalist. Look, darling, sorry, are you OK?'

'Mmhumm. It's a bit bizarre.'

'Tell me about it. You're all over the press this morning. Maybe we should bring forward publication, what the hell. What on earth were you doing out at that time in the morning?' Without waiting for an answer Zo went on, 'I'm holding the fort. Marcus is still down there, helping the police with their inquiries. Hah! Seems he was the last person to see Charlie alive. They were at Tolleymarsh finalizing plans for this fucking theme park.'

Caro had read as much in the *Warfleet Chronicle*, where that morning's jarring headline had been: WARFLEET WOMAN FINDS TYCOON'S BODY.

The paragraph which followed – 'Caro Radcliffe (58) ex-wife of TV celebrity Sebastian Radcliffe (deceased) was walking on Warfleet strand at 5 a.m. yesterday when she stumbled across the body of media tycoon Charlie Fong' – had infuriated her. Fifty-eight! Stumbled! She sounded drunk or infirm. However, that was the least of her problems.

'Shall I come up?' she said, thinking Zo could use moral support.

'No, no. I'm on the phone twenty-four hours. I'd never have time to see you.'

Despite herself, Caro felt a treacherous relief. 'What will happen?' she said, meaning at StrongFellows.

'Fuck knows. I'm instructed to tell people business as usual, but the shares are falling like rotten apples. Look, love, I've got to go. I'll try and call you later.' Zo had rung off, leaving Caro more confused than ever. What did Zo mean about Marcus 'helping the police'? Was he then under suspicion? The *Warfleet Chronicle* had made no mention of suspects.

The day was blustery and cold, as though recent events had driven out all prospect of summer. The seafront was vetoed by Deen, who was already shivering in his greasy anorak, so they set off through the more sheltered woods which linked Four Trees to the edge of the Tolleymarsh estate. Deen walked, or rather shuffled, head down into the gusts, chewing on a smouldering cigarette, while Caro, used to the vagaries of Warfleet weather, strode out, taking the blasts on the chin and almost rejoicing as they tugged her hair vertical. Being out always made her feel better. Above their heads the trees swayed and crashed, occasional branches pitching to the root-veined path before them.

'Christ,' muttered Deen, gripping his anorak at the throat.

He looked like a seedy derelict, thought Caro, mystified again at the attraction he held for media people. They must imagine they were in touch with the cutting edge through Deen's sorry appearance and rumoured drug habits.

The path eventually came out into a calmer clearing. The

sunlight brightened the mossy boles and they stopped for a moment to breathe easily. Deen sat on a stump and discarded the dead cigarette he'd been sucking for a fresh one. 'Smoke?' he said, offering the battered pack to Caro.

She shook her head though the offer was tempting. Instead she leaned against the broad trunk of a sun-warmed sycamore and breathed in the swirls of secondary smoke. She'd given up smoking, again, at New Year.

Deen said, 'So, who do you think killed him?'

Caro shifted, her comfortable moment spoiled. 'I've no idea,' she said. 'Who do you?'

'Make sense if it was his heir. Marcus bloody Croft was being groomed for that honour. Christ knows why, he's bloody useless at StrongFellows!'

This tallied with what Zo had said earlier. Caro tried to recall what else she had said of Marcus on the rare occasions they talked business. Something about meteoric promotion? That was it: before the takeover he'd been her boss at Quill and Pen, but had swiftly risen to MD of StrongFellows. There'd been muttering at the time about his relationship with Charlie, but Zo had been happy enough. It meant promotion for her too and she'd always got on well with Marcus. As to his being Charlie's heir, of that Zo had mentioned nothing. 'Isn't it a bit obvious,' she said, 'the heir? Why not just wait to inherit?'

'Charlie'd never relinquish the power,' sneered Deen. 'Besides, he's notorious for turning against people. Maybe he and Marcus baby fell out.'

Over Viviana, thought Caro. It was quite possible, flirt that she was, that she was playing them off against each other, though to what purpose Caro could not imagine.

'Well,' Deen gave a snarling laugh, 'two writers ought to

be able to come up with the plot. What does your girlfriend say?'

Caro turned her head sharply.

'Don't look so shocked,' said Deen, baring his evil teeth. 'Everyone knows about you and Zo Acland.'

So much, thought Caro, for Zo's extreme caution in the workplace.

'Doesn't bother me,' shrugged Deen. 'I've toyed with the idea of bisexuality.'

I bet you have, thought Caro. These days it was practically de rigueur for devotees of street credibility.

'She used to be my editor at Quill and Pen,' Deen gave a self-congratulatory smirk, 'until I went big time.'

He approached her, tossing away his cigarette, 'Actually, I still fancy her. Those long legs. Very tasty.' He leaned against Caro's tree, his frail body trembling in the wind. 'Don't suppose you'd consider a threesome?'

He was close enough for Caro to smell the tobacco on his breath. His lips were drawn back in an unpleasant but strangely hypnotic grimace. Caro focused hard on the wings of his nose, embedded in which she could see several blackheads, but before she could gather herself for the obvious response Deen lunged at her, folding her lips beneath his own and forcing a sloppy tongue between them. Caro wriggled away, gasping. Deen's mouth travelled across her cheek, leaving a slime trail, and buried itself in her neck, slavering aside her rollnecked sweater. Caro felt a violent energy rising from her gut and, grateful for her years of weight training, shoved Deen so hard he fell sideways into a small bush. Before he could right himself she took off, flying through the clearing with her coat flapping. Behind her she could hear Deen's crowing laughter. 'Just testing!' he bawled as she dived between hair-snagging branches, oblivious of brambles, mud, boulders, everything except flight.

She came to a breathless halt as the woods thinned out and dwindled to a fringe on the meadows of Tolleymarsh. She dropped her head to her knees and crouched sweating and panting, one swift crane round telling her Deen was not in pursuit. His physique, or perhaps libido, was obviously not up to it. No doubt he felt obliged to make a pass at any woman he encountered, if only to maintain his reputation.

Ahead, she could see buildings belonging to the estate. The long low barn looked familiar and after a moment she realized it was the one housing Warren's office. Her heart leaping, she set off towards it; whatever the cost, Warren represented sanctuary.

As she neared the barn, however, reason took over from instinct. They'd agreed not to meet. Other people might be about. It was foolish to tempt fate in this manner. So, instead of approaching boldly through the front entrance, Caro ducked around a side building from where she had a view of it. The place looked deserted. Perhaps Warren wasn't in. There was no sign of his jeep, nor of any other vehicle. It was impossible to be that close and not make sure, though. Caro slid on stealthily, keeping close to the wall with its overhanging eaves, until she could make the short dash across the flagged paving to the side of Warren's bay window. Immediately, she heard voices coming from inside the room. She edged forward, camouflaged by the heavy honeysuckle clinging to the old stone wall, and, separating some fronds, peered through the lattice. Inside the room stood Warren, his shirt half off revealing his naked chest. Viviana was on her knees before him with her arms locked round his thighs. She was crying theatrically, rolling her eyes and throwing her head from side to side. Warren, apparently unmoved by her emotion, looked stonily ahead, occasionally patting her in an automatic fashion.

Viviana began beating her fists against Warren's waistband. She was screaming something, but Caro could not make out the words; the combination of hysteria and Colombian accent obscured everything but the glass-endangering pitch. Caro drew back, her heart bouncing so wildly it threatened to make her sick. Several thousand explanations for the scene jumbled through her head, none of them appealing. She flattened herself into the honeysuckle, smelling, incongruously, its sweet, crushed scent, her one rational thought to escape before she was discovered.

She heard a vehicle drive up to the other side of the barn, then footsteps and voices. She quickly shifted to the end of the building, then cornered it briskly as if she was on legitimate business. The two overalled workers who had descended from Warren's jeep nodded to her, then watched her go. She felt their eyes trained on her back as, head held stiffly, she crossed the gravel to the road out of the estate.

It wasn't until she got back to Four Trees and caught sight of herself in the hall mirror that she realized why they'd been staring. Bits of woodland attached to various parts of her clothing and about her head waved tendrils of honeysuckle. She resembled the Queen of the May, or worse, the mad Ophelia.

FOURTEEN

'It's not me that's late, it's the train,' Jade said aggressively, attack being, as Seb had taught her, the best means of defence. Caro, who had waited at Warfleet station in Delia's Clio for over twenty minutes, knew better than to say anything. She reversed the car out of the car park and set off along the road into town.

The wind had died down a little and been replaced by fitful sunshine. The chalky lane, bordered by blossoming hedgerows, was lit in sudden brilliant patches.

'Zo sends love, by the way. Saw her last night.'

'How is she?' said Caro, slightly miffed. Zo apparently had time for her daughter.

'Frantic,' said Jade. 'It's all fallen on her shoulders.'

'She thrives on stress,' said Caro, keeping her tone neutral. 'I'm sure she'll rise to the occasion.'

'Mmm,' said Jade. 'Don't know. The bank may send the receivers in. Turns out Charlie was arbitraged up to his eyebrows. And he was the sole shareholder.'

Caro, whose grasp of financial matters was not great, had not got beyond Charlie's arbitraged brows when Jade's cellphone bleeped, leaving her dangling. Zo had said nothing about receivers.

Jade's conversation on the phone consisted of shouted

monosyllables, some of them in Spanish. At length she snapped it shut with the words, 'Barking mad researcher.'

The road dipped down into town and soon they were passing familiar landscape: the farm where they had got Cindy, their Labrador, now deceased, as a puppy; the swimming pool where Jade had learned the breast stroke; Jade's favourite old-fashioned sweet shop; a hoarding advertising the Spa Leisure Centre, with a photo of a leotarded Sonny Delgardo, bearing a wide smile and a dumb-bell in each hand. A large van was parked outside the police station at the junction with the Stourbridge road, and several uniformed policemen were unloading boxes. Jade twisted round to look and said, 'Could be computer equipment.' Caro gave a small shudder and averted her eyes. She didn't want to think what that meant. 'There's rumours,' said Jade, 'the FBI are involved.'

'What!' said Caro, swerving slightly. Now she understood the reason for Glyn's question. She had assumed he was just fishing.

'Yeah,' continued Jade airily. 'They were already on Charlie's case about something or other.'

'How on earth did you find out?' said Caro, fearing the worst about her daughter's investigative powers.

'Oh, Jed knows the American embassy legal attaché. They were at Cambridge together.'

Enough said, thought Caro. Global information, it seemed, was still manipulated by the Oxbridge brotherhood. 'How is Jed?' she said, trying to steer clear of irony.

Jade's beautiful brows drew together. 'We're on hold,' she said shortly.

'No use to you any more?' Caro could not resist.

'If you must know,' said Jade crossly, 'I don't like his behaviour over this corruption business. I think he knew about it all along.'

'But is Talk TV safe now Charlie's dead?' asked Caro, wondering if Jed's involvement stretched to murder.

Jade shrugged. 'Safe from Charlie. But its reputation's in tatters. I've come down here to get away from it.'

How like Seb she was, Caro thought again. No matter how outrageous his personal behaviour, he had to have the high moral ground in the workplace. Anything less he couldn't tolerate. 'Oh,' she said. 'I thought you'd come to follow the story.'

'Yes,' said Jade, with more enthusiasm. 'I'm planning an in-depth examination of Charlie's life. People will be screaming to buy it. Now, Ma, let's start with you. Describe *exactly* how you found him.'

Caro wiped a hand across her forehead, wishing fervently she hadn't raised the subject.

The High Street was so lively it was shocking. They were caught in a traffic jam, normally unheard of except during the oyster festival, and saw many natives mixed with the unfamiliar faces. Jeremy went by loaded with Sainsbury's bags. A counselling caravan had been set up by Toni and Rumer in the car park of the Admiral Nelson and Rumer sat outside it waiting for customers, her exotic clothes creating a carnival atmosphere. A bed came out of the furniture shop, followed by Laurel Hopcraft. All the Italian premises had new advertising banners. None the less, there was a queue outside the Delphinium Tearooms and Caro saw Craig O'Connell join it.

'Who's that?' asked Jade, catching his smile and wave.

'A professor of history. Texan,' said Carl. 'He's staying at Four Trees.'

'Mmm,' said Jade. 'Dishy for a professor.'

'Jade,' said Caro, warningly.

'I'm drawn to older men.' Jade gave a laugh, cynical beyond her years. 'Anything's better than TV moguls. Fat, woman-hating alcoholics.'

As they headed up the lane to Four Trees, passing the sign to the Tolleymarsh estate, Jade said with studied unconcern, 'Seen anything of Warren?'

It was the question Caro had been dreading. 'Not really,' she began, concentrating hard on the road she could navigate in her sleep. 'I was at the party where the theme park was announced. I believe he took it very badly.'

'Not surprising,' said Jade. 'Snatched the ground from beneath his feet, so to speak.' She gazed speculatively across the fields. 'I wonder what he knows about this business.'

The scene of the morning, Warren crushed in Viviana's python-like embrace, came back to Caro so vividly she almost closed her eyes and had to brake hard to avoid a rabbit. She too was keen to find out what Warren knew about 'this business'.

'So, if we take them out, sarge, who's going to pay for it?' PC Armitage put down the last heavy box and wiped his pink freckled face with a grubby handkerchief.

'I wouldn't worry too much about that, son,' said Sergeant Plummer. 'I don't think the odd takeaway'll break the bank.'

'No, but, sarge, I've heard the Bureau are really hospitable. You don't want to lose face, like.'

'It's not our responsibility, Keith,' said Sergeant Plummer sternly. 'CID'll take care of it.'

PC Armitage, disappointed, sloped off to the new water cooler. He'd been looking forward to a few rounds courtesy of expenses.

Sergeant Plummer surveyed the mountain of technology in the office now designated 'Major Incident Room' and sighed. He was too old for this caper. Urged by Jean, who wanted more of his time around the home, he'd been thinking of putting in for early retirement. Now, suddenly, the backwater police station with its ration of domestics, rapes and petty thievery was to play host to the FBI. As community liaison officer, he'd be responsible for housing their agents and smoothing their passage through the often unpredictable turbulences of Warfleet life. The detective sergeant and detective constable assigned from Stourbridge were nice enough blokes, if a bit brash for his taste, but they didn't know the town. Why, oh why, did Charlie have to get himself murdered on his patch?

He drew closer to the assemblage of equipment. The bright blue screens blinked, awaiting instruction. It was hardly likely he'd need to use the computers, his job was more old-style policing, door to door stuff, but they did have a certain fascination. Of the five children he'd inherited on his marriage to Jean, the four still at home were all computer literate. He sometimes joined in their savage techno games which, he had to admit, could be fun. But his favourite game was still patience. There was an eruption of ebullience as the Stourbridge officers returned from their liquid lunch and the sergeant sighed again. He'd certainly need it for this job.

FIFTEEN

Almost twenty people sat down to dinner at Four Trees that night. It would have been twenty except that Delia hardly sat, so busy was she ferrying trays loaded with food from Aga to miraculously expanding refectory table. Caro and Jade offered to help, but Caro, clumsy under stress, burnt her hand on a casserole and Jade's mobile phone rang every three minutes, so she was really more of a hindrance.

Craig O'Connell stepped, with Southern grace, into the breach and good-humouredly balanced trays on each plate-sized hand, while a flushed Delia, perhaps feeling the Aga-heat, filled them with dishes and smiled at him encouragingly.

Caro placed herself as far as possible from Deen, whose only acknowledgement of the morning had been a mocking leer as they'd passed on the landing. At the table, though, he barely took his eyes off Jade; she rewarded him with an occasional, disdainful flick of her hair, implying she was not an admirer of post-modernism. The journalists she regarded with slit-eyed intensity until they breathlessly revealed that their interest in Charlie was purely headline deep. In fact they spoke entirely in exclamation marks. They had arrived back from Stourbridge with the whole of their video team: several youngish media types of uncertain sexuality, who all seemed to have ginger hair and answer to the names of Steve and Dave, even the women. Harold, excited from a day out with Craig amid Warfleet relics, was unusually sociable, and Neil, the theatre producer, had for once come down. Normally he dined in his room, or returned the food uneaten.

The talk, of course, was of Warfleet's crisis, though mostly as it affected the life of each individual. Miriam said if the disturbance went on she would have to return to London. She simply couldn't get any work done. She and Jade fell to discussing the status of arts programmes in the new television world and agreed it was negligible.

'I'm thinking of diversifying,' said Jade. 'I'm bored with making programmes about self-inflated artists.' She shot Deen a sideways glance at this point, to which he responded with a shameless snigger.

'Yes,' said Miriam, 'it's tragic. Nowadays it's all PR. No content. I'm hard pressed to find questions they can answer. If it gets any worse, I'll have to start coaching them.'

They both laughed then sat back, congratulating themselves on the pitiless picture they had created.

Craig said, 'Well, Harold and I had a great day.'

'Oh yes!' interjected Harold.

'Your town is extraordinary. Did you know that in 597 BC another international marauder was killed here?'

A blank-eyed silence greeted this.

'Yes,' enthused Craig. 'Thor-axe the mighty. He'd looted and pillaged most of the known world.'

The diners nodded. The comparison with Charlie was irresistible.

Harold said excitedly, 'It may not seem it until now, but Warfleet's got a very violent history.'

'I guess it didn't get the "war" part by accident,' said

Craig genially. 'It's on a ley line linking several major battle sites.'

'Where does it run?' asked Caro, curious.

'Right through the Tolleymarsh estate,' said Craig.

A chillier silence fell at the table. Delia broke it by murmuring drily, 'Talking of looters.'

'OK,' said Tiffany, one of the journalists, 'but the theme park would have been a way of giving something back. It'll be devastating to the local economy if it doesn't happen.'

'Rubbish,' said Miriam. 'This whole bloody country's being turned into a theme park. I blame you.' She turned to Craig. 'Americans come here wanting quaint oldie worldie. Since we don't have any left, we have to invent it.'

Harold checked with Craig before nodding his agreement. Deen laughed and Delia, still American enough, looked rather angry.

'Well, you have a point,' drawled Craig, without losing his smile. 'It's difficult in post-industrial societies unless they develop other skills.'

'Arms trade?' suggested Deen. 'Drug-running?' He went off into a chortle at his own wit, while Craig turned a sudden hard look on him.

'Oh, excuse *me*,' said Deen. 'Forgot we live in a moral dictatorship. We're not allowed guns or drugs any more.'

Neil put an end to that line of conversation by bursting into tears and rushing from the table. There was a short pause, during which even the Daves and Steves stopped eating, then Miriam muttered, 'Nervous breakdown.'

'Too much coke if you ask me,' opined Deen. 'By the way, anybody got some?'

Delia rose to pick up the scattered cutlery and napkin but

Craig was there before her. 'Finish your supper,' he commanded gently. 'You've hardly touched it.' Delia did as she was bid, which was unusual.

Neil's departure had broken the mood and the chat became scattered. Miriam asked Caro about her new novel, due out soon. Gratified, Caro began to describe it, only to realize midsentence that the upheaval at StrongFellows might prevent its publication. Something else Zo had not confided. Jade mentioned the receivers again and Deen turned from mirth to instant neurosis. 'What have you heard?' he demanded, taking the opportunity to move his chair closer to Jade's.

'Only that Charlie was in mega financial difficulties,' said Jade offhandedly. 'It's not unheard of. Look at Donald Trump.'

'Yes,' said Deen darkly, 'but look at Robert Maxwell.'

Craig, though engaged in an obscure conversation with Harold, which necessitated the drawing of complex grid-lines on a paper napkin, was, Caro noticed, listening intently.

Delia, helped by Caro, cleared the plates and brought dessert; towering lemon meringue and fresh fruit. The video team fell with grunts upon the pie. Miriam had a large slice, which she attacked with the venom she usually reserved for her interviewees; Craig a small slice, which he pronounced 'American as momma made', causing Delia to glow modestly; Caro had an apple, Jade a grape, and Deen lit another cigarette.

As they were finishing, Anthea, the nanny, entered with Harry in her arms. Harry was white-faced with tiredness but completely alert. Anthea looked shattered. 'Can't git the li'l bigger to slape,' she said. 'Wants to know what's goan on down here.' Harry had always preferred the company of grown-ups.

'Too much excitement,' said Delia, coming forward to take him. 'Sit down, Anthea. Have some pudding.'

Anthea did so, gratefully. Normally she ate with the children then went out after putting them to bed, but the new sleeping arrangements made that impossible.

Harry quickly wooed the company with his adult manner, his only concession to childhood his tightly gripped teddy. He sat on Delia's lap and fed himself meringue from her plate. After a couple of spoonfuls he said, pointing at Craig, 'Who's that, Mumma?'

'That's Mr O'Connell,' said Delia. 'He's staying here.'

'Do I know him?' enquired Harry. 'He looks very familiar.'

There was a ripple of indulgent laughter at his use of the word. Craig too laughed, then said, 'Come and sit here and get acquainted.' He offered his broad knee and Harry, to Delia's surprise, scrambled down and on to it.

'Well,' she said, 'I hope you're flattered. Harry never goes to anyone like that.'

'Oh, I think Harry and I will understand each other,' said Craig and looked at Delia over the child's head. She returned his glance until a blush rose in her cheeks.

Harry nestled into Craig's chest and sucked his teddy's ear. 'I know who he is, Mumma,' he murmured sleepily, 'he's the man on the raft. In my dream. The man who saved us.'

SIXTEEN

Neither Caro nor Jade slept well that night, Jade because she was in a sleeping bag on Caro's floor, which was, as she made clear, inappropriate to her status, Caro because she was tormented by visions of Warren and Viviana. Besides, the two hadn't shared a room since Jade was a baby and the intimacy it implied was uncomfortable. At about five Caro slipped out of bed and without fumbling for clothes tiptoed out of the room and down to the kitchen. There was a crack of light under the door, but she wasn't surprised. Delia often left a lamp on for nocturnally wandering artistes.

When she pushed open the door she saw Neil sitting at the table, staring morosely into a mug. 'Hemlock?' she was tempted to ask, but not wanting to provoke another outburst merely whispered gently, 'Can't sleep either?'

Neil stared dumbly on, so Caro made herself tea and they both sat, silent, at the table, companions in misery.

After a while Neil began to speak. 'My wife's left me.'

'Ah,' said Caro. Such revelations seemed commonplace at five o'clock in the morning. But it certainly explained Neil's distress.

'It's not that,' Neil continued, catching her thought. 'It's why she left. She went off with an actor in one of my shows.'

Caro shook her head. 'Actors.'

'He's a prat, of course,' agreed Neil, 'but it closed the show and now my company's bankrupt.'

That did seem worse than losing a wife, but from her years with Sebastian Caro understood that thespians thrived on this roller-coaster existence. It was odd though that Neil had chosen to go into retreat. Shouldn't he be up in the city trying to retrieve his fortunes?

'I went a bit mad,' said Neil, as if in explanation. 'Couldn't stop calling people and faxing. Sometimes in the middle of the night. Hour after hour of nonsense. Eventually my friends – huh, those I had left – said I should get away. One of them recommended Four Trees.'

It was the most Caro had ever heard him say, but presumably this was the hour at which the need to communicate bit him.

'It was all the backer's fault,' said Neil, suddenly stabbing the table viciously with a spoon. 'If he hadn't pulled out we'd have been fine. I'd've got a new lead. I was talking to Simon Callow, but the bastard pulled the plug on me.' His voice tailed away and he dropped the spoon, reverting to his former unnatural stillness.

Caro shivered, aware that she was wearing only a flimsy nightie, a present from Zo when such things had still been important. Neil was hardly in a state to notice, but still she said, 'I think I'll go back up. Hope you get some shut-eye.'

Neil did not seem aware of her departure. He was staring dully at the table as though his clockwork had run down.

Jade was sitting propped against the wall, smoking a cigarette.

'Sorry,' said Caro. 'Did I wake you?'

Jade shrugged. 'Awake anyway. This floor's bloody hard.'

'Want to swap?' Caro felt obliged to offer.

Jade shook her head. 'Thanks, though.'

Caro got into bed and, cold now, hunched her legs up to rub her feet. Jade's smoke was torture. She was dying for a cigarette.

'Anything happening downstairs?' asked Jade.

'Neil Kenton's monologuing in the kitchen.'

'Him. He's loopy,' said Jade dismissively. 'His show got terrible reviews. Closed in a matter of weeks. I saw it. Ghastly.'

'He reckons it was all the backer's fault.'

'Oh yeah? In his dreams,' said Jade derisively. She paused to drag tantalizingly on the cigarette, then said, looking at Caro, 'Zo's worried about you, you know.'

'Really?' Caro shrank down the bed to cover her suddenly over-exposed flesh.

'She asked me if I thought you were having an affair.'

'Ridiculous!' squeaked Caro, her heart leaping to her throat and strangling her vocal chords. Warren's long torso with its golden-brown skin floated before her; could she hear a cock crowing?

'That's what I said,' continued Jade. 'We had quite a laugh about it.'

'Really,' said Caro, rather huffily. The disbelief in Jade's tone was nettling. It was one thing to keep a secret, quite another to be deemed incapable of having one. She had an insane desire to shout Warren's name. It would serve Jade right with her assumptions about age and desirability. But no, that way madness lay. Jade's reluctance to see her as a sexual being was just the cover she needed. Zo was another matter, though. What had prompted her to make the comment? What clues had Caro given?

'I think I'll go to Tolleymarsh Hall tomorrow,' said Jade. 'Night, Ma.'

'Sleep well,' said Caro, knowing that, after that information, *she* certainly wouldn't.

SEVENTEEN

The FBI arrived bearing gifts. The two agents, urbane men in their early forties, brought ashtrays, pens, embroidered cloth badges. PC Armitage, catching Sergeant Plummer's eye at the inaugural meeting, raised an 'I told you so' eyebrow. There was much hand-shaking and apparent goodwill. Agents Benson and Hedges, unaware that their names caused hilarity at each introduction, toasted the constabulary in Bureau Jim Beam and declared themselves delighted to be in England. Their purpose there remained mysterious, at least to the lower ranking officers.

They spent a long time closeted with Detective Superintendent Cooper, emerging to be driven, with their neat leather luggage, to their lodgings. They were to stay with Jeremy and Darryl. The uniformed coppers had been demoted to a lower calibre B & B, much to Ashley's distress. He was convinced one of them was gay – something about the way he wore his whistle. The whole thing had given Sergeant Plummer a bit of a headache.

After they were safely despatched, Sergeant Plummer was called into the Super's office. 'Er . . . Plummer,' said Cooper, regarding his notes. 'Warren Peabody.'

'Yes?' prompted the sergeant, anxious to know if another headache was pending.

'He's your stepson, right?'

'Right,' agreed the sergeant.

'Thing is, we've received a tip-off.'

'From the FBI?' said Bill Plummer, alarmed.

'No. No,' said his boss, with a brief smile which did not reach his eyes. 'They are pursuing their own lines of inquiry. This has come anonymously. A phone call. From a woman.'

Sergeant Plummer felt a tightening in his chest.

'She alleges Peabody knows something about Fong's murder.'

'No way,' said the sergeant vehemently. 'He's had his troubles has Warren, but there's never been violence.'

'Wait a minute, Plummer,' said his boss in a reasonable tone. 'He has got previous, and I gather this takeover rankled.'

'It would rile anybody,' asserted the sergeant. 'But not to kill. I can't believe that. Who is this grass?'

The Super shrugged. 'Hard to say. Local call. Disguised her voice with an incredible accent.'

'Is Warren under suspicion?' demanded the sergeant, beads of sweat appearing on his temples.

'He's got plenty of access to guns on that estate,' warned the Super. 'But, phone call like that . . . probably malicious. I thought a friendly word? Check his alibi. You're the obvious person to do it.'

Sergeant Plummer didn't feel that at all to be the case. He could just see Jean's expression. But Superintendent Cooper's eyes had condensed into sapphire-bright chips.

'Where shall I start?' he said wearily, corrugating his brow. He could already feel the headache.

'Try the wife,' said the Super, tapping his teeth with an FBI pen. '*Cherchez la femme*, eh, Plummer?'

*

Jade's taxi stopped short of the grand entrance to the Hall, as though the driver felt a peasant's reticence. As she was paying, Jade saw two trench-coated, middle-aged men emerge and head for a car parked nearby. Their preppy haircuts announced them as American and their chauffeur, though not in uniform, was clearly a policeman, so Jade concluded they were the FBI agents. She was a little annoyed they had got there before her, though it was to be expected they would interview those closely connected. Still, Jade had her own suspicions.

She was greeted in the high-ceilinged hall by a small barking shih-tzu. It snapped at her heels as she passed coldly glinting armour and musty robber-baron escutcheons, rather spoiling her studied saunter. The double doors to the drawing room were open, and despite the mugginess of the afternoon gas flames gambolled in the Adam fireplace. Announced by the dog, Jade entered.

Viviana was standing by the French windows, watching the departing car. She turned as Jade came in and the slight frown on her brow was instantly replaced with a glittering smile of official welcome. Though she had seen many pictures of Viviana in magazines, this was Jade's first face-to-face encounter, and as Viviana's cool, manicured hand brushed hers she could not help but blink at her style. Viviana was wearing a violently pink Chanel suit and much heavy gold costume jewellery; her eyelids were bordering on puce and her hair was piled into a flossy dome, reminiscent of Madame de Pompadour.

'So, Mees Radcleeffe,' said Viviana, drawing closer to the fire and rubbing her jewel-laden hands, a large emerald particularly prominent, 'Talk TV wants to make a documentary on Charlee?'

'Yes,' said Jade, adding hastily, 'as a benefactor to the arts,' for this had been her ploy on the telephone that morning.

'Ah,' said Viviana, her large eyes glowing moistly, 'he was so good. So beeg-hearted.'

'Yes,' murmured Jade. 'His offer to the shareholders of Talk TV was more than beeg-hearted.'

If Viviana detected any irony in the remark, she ignored it, continuing with, 'He would have been the saviour of life een Warfleet.'

'Mmm,' said Jade. 'Always assuming it needed a saviour.'

'Of course eet does,' snapped Viviana, showing a sudden likeness to her dog. 'Thees town ees pathetic. Resort, ha! Eet has nothing except your terrible Eengleesh weather.' She waved her hands perilously close to the fire. Possibly hexing Warfleet, thought Jade, as the flames bounced higher. She could see how Viviana's dreams of a splendid aristocratic life had been somewhat dashed by the reality.

'I wonder,' she said, 'if you could give me a little background?'

Viviana was all smiles again. 'Eet ees seemple. When I came to leeve here, I realized I could help. But we needed a beeg cash eenvestment. I contacted Charlee and he was pleased to asseest. Eet was only because of hees fondness for me—' She broke off to give the emerald an intimate fondle. 'He was planning to make hees park in Milton Keynes.'

Where, thought Jade, it would barely have been remarkable. 'So Charlie was an old friend?' she queried.

'For many years,' sighed Viviana, her eyes threatening to brim again.

'From Colombia?' pursued Jade. 'I believe he judged' – she consulted her pad – 'a competition in which you were crowned beauty queen of Bogotá.'

Viviana's eyes dried. 'Eet was not for *beauty*. Eet was for *talent*!' she said icily. 'I had to seeng, play the bombardeeno, answer questions on politics. Thees theengs are always meesreported!'

'Of course,' agreed Jade, wondering what, or who, was a bombardino. 'Perhaps it was also misreported that drug money was behind the event. There were accusations of laundering.'

'That was a deesgraceful allegation!' spat Viviana. 'Eet was never proved. Eet ees just how people like to see Colombia!'

'It was certainly hushed up,' continued Jade, unabashed, 'by Charlie's own newspapers.'

'Are you eenseenuateeng he was eenvolved?' said Viviana, her eyes growing huge with incredulity. 'Thees man who was a patron of so many theengs, theatres, films, art galleries . . .'

'Quite,' said Jade.

'He was a saint,' said Viviana with ferocity. Jade almost expected her to fall to her knees, such was her display of conviction.

'Well, we'll try to get that view across,' she said, putting her pad away. 'I'm sure many people will see it your way. By the way,' she threw in as a parting shot, 'did you know Charlie was being investigated for fraud? I saw the FBI leaving.'

'They are crazee,' said Viviana, sweeping her arm in an arc, as though the FBI were so many skittles. 'As eef he would need to defraud anyone. He was the reechest man een the beezness.'

'So it seemed,' nodded Jade. 'But many of his companies aren't doing well. People wonder where the supply of money was coming from.'

'I am een mourning,' said Viviana, putting her beetroot-red nails to her eyebrows. 'I'm afraid I must conclude our conversation.'

'Fine,' said Jade. 'Thanks for your time. You understand, I'm sure, we have a duty to our viewers to present all sides.' The look Viviana gave her made Jade doubly glad Charlie had not had the chance to buy Talk TV. She had a strong suspicion he would not have made duty to the viewers a priority.

Viviana gestured her towards the door and followed to make sure she went out of it. As Jade crossed the hall, Henry Trenche meandered by. He nodded a vague greeting then turned eagerly to his wife. Jade's last view was of Viviana jerking her cheek away as Henry, with an abject look, attempted to land a kiss on it.

Jade fairly skipped down the drive, not minding even the long walk back. Barking her Colombian researcher might be, but she had certainly struck pay dirt on this one!

It didn't take Bill Plummer long to find Annabel Peabody. He leaned his bike on the wicker fence that surrounded the handsome dower house and, opening the rose-covered gate, saw Annabel in the greenhouse of the kitchen garden. She was pricking out seedlings; dill and basil, she told him. 'Warren's not here,' she said. 'He's probably at the office.' As the afternoon was warm, if overcast, she asked if he'd like a glass of home-made lemonade and he followed her into the house, pondering how to begin the conversation.

Relations between the two families had never been easy. Jean complained constantly of Annabel's coldness. She tended to see her grandchildren when Warren brought them round. The Plummers had, of course, been to the house, even the Hall, on visits; awkward occasions in which food was involved and Jean monitored him over the cutlery. She scoured *Hello!* magazine for clues on etiquette. But since Viviana, all invitations to the big house had ceased, much to Jean's annoyance. Bill soothed her by remarking that, as she knew very well, class divisions died hard in Warfleet.

Annabel was always polite, however, and having seated the sergeant in a comfortable armchair, and served him a glass of frosted lemon, she waited for him to state the purpose of his visit.

'Er,' said Bill, gazing at the ceiling, a pleasant shade of pistachio, 'I was hoping you could help me . . . unofficially, of course . . . with the night of the . . . er . . .'

'Murder?' said Annabel helpfully.

'Yes.' Relief made the sergeant sweat and he ran a finger round his collar.

'I've already told Detective . . . Malton, is it? all I know. We had dinner at the Hall . . . well, I did. Warren was at his club. It was just Daddy, Viviana,' her lips tightened a little, 'Charlie, Marcus and me. I left about ten-thirty and Charlie and Marcus walked me across the park. I was home in bed by eleven.'

'And . . . er . . . Warren? What time did he get to bed?'

Annabel laughed, but not happily. 'He didn't. He never does on club nights. He was making breakfast when I got up. That was about six-thirty.'

'Right. Right,' said Bill. 'And he didn't mention anything unusual . . . that he'd been somewhere else, for instance?'

'No,' said Annabel. 'Why? What's this about, Bill?'

The sergeant sighed heavily and, to give himself a moment, sipped the lemonade. 'Probably nothing, love. But we've had a call from . . . someone, alleging Warren's involved in some way. Now, don't get me wrong. *I* don't believe it. But these . . . hoaxes have to be checked on, you see. And I was thinking . . . hoping . . . you might be able to . . .'

'Provide an alibi,' finished Annabel flatly.

'That's it,' said the sergeant, grateful to her again.

'Well I can't.' Annabel's tone was blunt. 'I don't know the half of what Warren does, and what's more' – her face twisted and Sergeant Plummer feared she was going to cry – 'I don't want to.'

'I'm sorry, love,' he said gruffly. 'I didn't mean to upset you.'

'It's not you,' she said, regaining her composure, 'it's the whole situation. I'm worried about Daddy.'

'Course you are, love.' Jean frequently opined Henry had bitten off more than he could chew. 'And in your condition' – Jean had also railed against this new pregnancy – 'very difficult for everybody.'

There was nothing more to be said, so, finishing his lemonade – very good, he noticed – the sergeant rose and made his goodbyes. As Annabel showed him to the gate, the nanny came through it with his step-grandchildren. Jasper immediately demanded a piggyback, whilst Dickon held up his arms from the pushchair. The sergeant was rather good with young children. He swung Jasper about, panting a little in the sticky heat, and noticing again a slight pain in his chest. He should do as Jean ordered and remember his indigestion tablets. He was pleased to see Annabel lift Dickon from the pram and cuddle him, looking happier and quite her old, pretty self. Unlike Jean, he was fond of his daughter-in-law.

Cycling back, he had to stop once or twice to get his breath. Jade Radcliffe swung jauntily by and gave him a wave. He wondered what she was doing on the estate and, remembering her past involvement with Warren, felt his spirits sink further. He shook his head. Jean had spared the rod with that young gangster.

EIGHTEEN

A slab of May's date and walnut cake went a long way towards assuaging the gnawing pain in Caro's centre. It was mostly, she knew, the product of thwarted lust. Among the many anxieties created by the last few days, the fear that she might never make love with Warren again had emerged as by far the strongest.

The Delphinium was full, mostly with strangers. May had had to take on extra help, though, as she said herself, she wasn't complaining. Teddy Forbes bustled in, demanding at Warfleet Players pitch, 'A dozen of your fruit scones, May, luvvie. My officer's got *such* a sweet tooth and I haven't had a *second* to make them.'

He was followed by Laurel Hopcraft, who was desperate for cookery hints. She now had a paying guest for B & B and, though she had acquired a bed, had no idea how to make breakfast. 'It's the timing. This morning the sausages were raw while the bacon was burning!'

Caro had arranged to meet Toni in the café. They had not seen each other since the recent alarming developments. When Toni arrived, wafting with her a strong odour of geranium oil, she too was in a state of excitement.

'Rumer wants to dowse you for clues. Pick up on your aura. She's thinking of holding a séance.'

'Oh no,' said Caro. She had experienced Rumer's séances before; they could be uncannily accurate.

'Don't be such a spoilsport,' scolded Toni. 'I can't say too much, it wouldn't be professional, but Rumer's got reason to believe' – she lowered her voice – '*certain things* about the murder. It would be marvellous for the Quest if she got it right. Think of the publicity.'

Caro did and shuddered. 'What,' she said, 'Rumer as the next Mystic Meg?'

'Don't be silly,' said Toni, though Caro saw a flicker of temptation cross her face. 'It would put us on the map as a healing centre. The media types down here'd tell everyone about us.'

'Count me out,' said Caro. 'The idea is appalling.'

'Suit yourself,' said Toni sulkily. 'But I don't see what you've got to lose. The publicity would be good for you too. You're not exactly a bestseller.'

Her remark mirrored that of Zo earlier, thought Caro despairingly; did everything now bow down before publicity? She said shortly, 'I can do without that sort of notoriety.'

They ordered more tea and Toni, pique forgotten, said, 'Well anyway, Jeremy's having a dinner party tonight for the FBI. You know they're staying with him. Le tout Warfleet will be there. You're invited. No, *commanded*.'

Caro felt a flutter of fear mixed with curiosity. The knowledge of the FBI's presence had swept through the town within minutes of their arrival. Like everyone else, Caro was intrigued. Would the agents say anything revelatory? Then again, perhaps, as in detective novels, they would get a 'hunch' that she was guilty.

'Oh, I don't know,' she said warily.

'Of course you'll come,' said Toni with finality. 'Dinner's at eight. I'm going to help, so you can arrive early.'

At seven Caro was still undecided. For a start, what costume was appropriate? Was it Lauren Bacall tailored suits and a lot of lipstick, or something Burberry-ish with a trilby? The thought of another evening at Four Trees, though, was dispiriting. When she'd come in from town, Caro had witnessed Delia and Craig bending over the Aga together. Delia was apparently showing him how to riddle it. Their mild flirting was unsettling, as was that between Deen and Jade. The latter's flouncing in from Tolleymarsh full of cryptic glee – 'Let's just say, I got a result' – finally drove Caro to fling on her Joseph leathers and order a taxi for Blossom Cottage. It was, she had to admit, her competitive instinct.

Jeremy was still up to his elbows in marinade at seven-forty-five and the kitchen looked as if a small warhead had hit it. Toni was chopping vegetables with the speed of a Chinese chef. Ashley, wearing a frilly pinny over his studded jeans, was arranging steaming cornbreads on a platter, stuffing every third one into his mouth. 'Mm,' he said, spitting crumbs. 'I'm bloody starving.'

'I thought American food was supposed to be simple,' fretted Jeremy. 'Ashley, stop that and set the table! It's oak-smoked ribs with grits and black-eyed peas,' he directed at Caro. 'I wanted to make them feel at home.'

'Where do they come from,' said Caro, 'Kentucky?'

The dining room had been transformed into a cross between a fertility festival and a presidential campaign rally. Fairy lights and ribbons festooned the picture rails and swags of stars and stripes billowed from every surface. The sideboard was a study in fruit and vegetables; as a still life, it only lacked a dead pheasant.

'Good, innit,' grinned Ashley, entering with a tray of glasses, then with pride, 'I done it.'

In the front room Darryl was mixing cocktails which required frequent sampling. 'How's this?' he asked, thrusting the shaker into Caro's hand. 'It's called a Hairy Navel. Or perhaps that should be Hairy Nav*a*l, ha ha. Mm. Not enough vodka, I think.' His speech was already slurred and Caro despaired for the end of the evening.

Laurel Hopcraft, Gauloise-speckled as usual, was the first to arrive. She eyed Caro's Joseph suit suspiciously. 'Did you buy that in the sale?' she said. 'I meant to get something for Hay-on-Wye, but I've been so busy.'

Caro suppressed a snort. In one sentence Laurel had reduced her to poor, unknown, under-commissioned. She was nothing if not blatant.

The room started to fill. Marsha Snelgrove made an entrance, bursting out of a see-through lace shift, which Darryl remarked, in a loud aside, she had last worn in *Blithe Spirit*. She was followed by Sonny Delgardo, looking stringy and sunbedded; Rumer, in stripes, splendid as a circus tent; and Glyn Madoc, in his habitual leather-elbowed tweed jacket, who made a beeline for Caro.

'Anything new?' he demanded, with journalistic disregard for manners.

Caro shook her head. She was certainly going to part with nothing to the *Chronicle*.

Ashley, still pinafored, circulated with canapés, shrimp boats with parasols on top – another of his own touches –

but there was a tension in the room that could only be allayed by the arrival of the agents.

'Now no jokes about their names,' giggled Darryl, 'and no waving fag packets under their noses.'

By the time the smiling Benson and Hedges entered the room, full of apology for their lateness, Darryl's cocktails had taken effect and the company was glassy-eyed and babbling. As Jeremy was still in the kitchen and Darryl slumped sideways on the sofa, Rumer took it upon herself to make the introductions. Caro was presented as 'our star', though she soon realized Rumer was alluding to her discovery of the body rather than her literary credentials. She was grateful to agent Benson for taking that in his stride, no hunch apparent, and beginning a conversation about her books.

'What do you write about?' he asked, looking genuinely interested.

'Oh,' said Caro, thinking, 'I don't know . . .' It occurred to her that this was why marketing found her so difficult. 'Death, I suppose.'

'Really,' said Laurie Benson, regarding her closely. 'Fascinating subject. Particularly murder.' He passed on with a quizzical twinkle, to discuss Californian wine with Laurel Hopcraft and golf with Glyn Madoc.

How different they were from English policemen, with their well-cut, expensive suits, club ties, discreet aftershave, thought Caro. They seemed more like businessmen, suave and civilized, with an air of the campus around them. It crossed her mind that, conversely, Craig, the real academic, might be mistaken for a policeman.

Eventually Jeremy, pink and agitated, a smear of mashed

potato on his Moroccan smoking jacket, announced that dinner was ready. Ashley showed everyone through to the table, propping Darryl, who was now incapable of standing, and waited for the congratulatory cries over his decor before beginning to serve the soup, which Jeremy referred to as 'gumbo'.

There was a clacking of spoons as the guests fell upon it. 'Damn fine,' said Laurie Benson, and Frank Hedges nodded agreement.

When the first hunger was appeased, Glyn Madoc lit a cigarette – both Benson and Hedges declined – and said brashly, 'So come on then, what have you uncovered?'

There was a ripple of uncomfortable laughter, but Laurie Benson said smoothly enough, 'Now, Glyn, you can't expect me to tell you that. Even off the record.'

'They've only been here a day,' chided Jeremy, the concerned host. 'They can't have had a chance to find anything.'

'My sources tell me your investigation goes back some months,' said Glyn, unrepentant. 'In fact I've had a report leaked to me' – he leaned back importantly – 'more or less accusing Fong of financial malpractice.'

'Is that so?' said Laurie Benson, exchanging a glance with Frank Hedges.

'Yup,' said Glyn, taking a deep pull on his cigarette. 'Definitely dirty business.'

Laurel, not to be outdone, said, 'My friends in the publishing world tell me StrongFellows books are likely to be impounded.'

'What!' said Caro, alarmed enough to rise to her bait.

'Yes,' said Laurel, giving her a pitying smile. 'Your novels may end up in a warehouse.'

Caro forbore to comment that that was generally where

they ended up anyway. She wished Zo had told her. This public discovery was embarrassing.

'Now, now,' steered Jeremy, 'that's enough shop. We want our guests to relax and enjoy themselves.'

'Ye-es,' cried Darryl. 'Ashley, where's the wine? Get in here, you silly fairy.'

Everyone looked at the table except Frank and Laurie, who smiled on benignly.

'I do hope you're going to have some time to embrace our local culture,' said Marsha, taking the cue to change the subject. 'We've got May Day soon. The Warfleet Players will be presenting a medieval pageant.'

'They'll have it wrapped up well before then,' said Glyn, unwilling to leave the subject. 'It's got all the marks of a Mafia-style execution.'

'Mafia! In lil Warflee! How exshiting!' said Darryl.

'It's obvious.' Glyn was sounding more Welsh with every word. 'Some gang he fell foul of in the subterranean world.'

He cocked an eyebrow at Laurie, who smiled humouringly and said, 'Our investigations may not be unconnected.'

'Ah hah,' pounced Glyn. 'Then you were after him for fraud.'

Laurie Benson said, 'No comment.'

'Have you met our very own Mafia yet?' put in Sonny Delgardo.

'I don't believe so,' said Frank, responding with a smile. 'Who would they be?'

'Ugo and Fabio,' drawled Darryl. 'The famush Martini brothers.'

'Ah yes,' nodded Frank. 'Froth.'

'A lot of people think they had a hand in this.' Sonny nodded eagerly. 'They're very territorial.' It was no secret within the group that Sonny had been hustled out of her businesses. 'Made an offer she daren't refuse,' was the way she'd put it.

'Gun s'not their style.' Darryl held up a knife. 'They're more Jacobean.' He stabbed the table cloth. 'Stiletto or poison.'

'Well,' said Laurie, 'they make a damn fine cup of coffee.'

Ashley trundled in a trolley loaded with ribs, peas and grits. 'I do hope this is all right,' said Jeremy nervously. 'I've never tried Native American before. It should be elk really, but Sainsbury's didn't have any.'

'That smells real good,' said Laurie, sniffing appreciatively.

'Sure does,' agreed Frank. 'Don't get food like this in Washington.'

'Tell me,' said Rumer, when only a pile of bones remained, 'do you go in for psychics at all?'

'We have used clairvoyants from time to time,' admitted Frank.

'You mean like the Exsh-Files?' giggled Darryl. 'That Foxsh Mulder is sho shexy.'

'Excellent,' said Rumer, quelling him with a look. 'I'd like to offer my services. There's something I could tell you . . .' she glanced meaningfully round the table and lowered her voice, 'but in private.'

'We run a healing centre,' Toni chipped in. She pushed a card across the table. 'Any time you need a stress-relieving massage . . .'

Sonny quickly whipped out a brochure for her gym, saying, 'I can see you keep yourselves fit. We've got state-of-the-art equipment.'

'Bugger that. More Chard'nay's what they need,' bellowed Darryl. 'Where's that dizz queen wiv bottle!'

Ashley, who was doing the washing up, stomped to the kitchen door in his Marigolds and shot Darryl a look of pure hatred.

'Darryl,' said Jeremy warningly.

'Oh,' said Laurie Benson, cutting through the atmosphere, 'Frank, we forgot our gifts.'

Frank Hedges rose and fetched a couple of bottles of Jack Daniel's from his briefcase.

'Ah,' said Glyn Madoc, smacking his lips. 'Very acceptable.'

'A wonderful evening,' said Laurie, when all Jeremy's crystal tumblers were full. 'A toast to our host. A great cook!'

Jeremy blushed with pleasure.

The party broke up soon afterwards, the agents declaring they were 'early to bed, early to rise'. Darryl had dispensed with bed and passed out on the table. The guests left, each clutching an FBI keyring, another gift from the agents, and Caro was home by eleven-thirty.

Feeling slightly unsteady, she went to the kitchen for a glass of water. Craig and Delia sat at the long table doing a jigsaw. As Caro hovered uncertainly on the threshold Craig said, laughing, 'No, no, that's sky. You're cheating!' His hand, Caro noticed, lingered on Delia's as he took the offending piece from her.

Delia looked up and said rather sharply, 'Caro, did you want something?'

'Glass . . . water,' mumbled Caro, crossing to the sink. 'Been to dinner . . . Jeremy's. Met the FBI agents.'

'What are they like?' said Delia, more interested now.

'Bank managers. G'night.' She saw, as she left the room,

that Craig was watching her intently. It was strange that the friendship developing between him and Delia made her so uncomfortable, she thought, as she dragged herself up the many stairs to the attic; after all, it was really none of her business.

NINETEEN

FBI USE PSYCHIC IN SEARCH FOR MAFIA KILLER read the headline in the *Warfleet Chronicle* next morning. Glyn Madoc must have been up all night, thought Caro grimly as she read it at the kitchen table. She swallowed a couple of Nurofen with her tea, marvelling again at journalistic powers of invention.

She was up early having slept badly. Jade's sleeping bag was empty when she'd climbed into bed, but this morning a tousle of hair curled on her pillow and when Caro got up Jade had stirred and opened one kohl-blackened eye.

'Want the bed? I'm getting up,' invited Caro.

Jade grunted sleepily and climbed out of the bag, looking so like a little girl in her pyjamas that Caro, with a rush of love, almost gave her a cuddle. Fearing Jade's appalled response, she contented herself with tucking her daughter in, remembering the many times Jade had appeared in her bed when she was a child.

'Where were you last night?' she murmured teasingly.

'Drink. Marcus Croft,' said Jade, muffling her face in the pillow. In another second she was asleep again and Caro left the room with her other questions unanswered.

Caro stepped into the garden, less overcast today, and wandered about, admiring the work Delia had done which built on her own careful tending. The *montana* var. *rubens* was in its full starry beauty and 'Albertine' only required a little more sun to reveal her scented blossom. Odd how the many years she had spent in this house as its mistress seemed irrelevant to her now, yet she could still feel glad to see her plants well grown, her pictures on the walls; still feel connected. The sun came out as she stood blowing greenfly off a rosebud and she decided, for a change, she would go for a jaunt to Stourbridge.

Delia was using the car, so Caro took the bus and got off in the centre of town, at the bus station. Without any particular plan, she meandered through the precinct, full of retailers you would find in any high street; stopped to buy some fudge; watched young women, single parents most probably, shoving pushchairs lingeringly past the cheap clothes shops. She crossed the town hall square with its pretty tubs of tulips and stopped dead in her tracks. There, parked on a meter, was Warren's jeep.

Her heart began to beat with teenage fury. She did not know whether to run, hide, or stand her ground and, as she dithered, saw Warren heading towards it with his familiar open stride. His name was out of her mouth in a strange croak, before she thought of the consequences. Warren turned, recognized her with an easy smile and waved. She almost ran to him and then stood, speechless. Warren didn't seem at all thrown by the encounter. 'What are you doing here?' he said. 'Shouldn't you be working?'

'With all this going on?' Caro squawked, angry at his manner. How dare he be so cool when she was consumed by consternation?

'Want some lunch?' he said, indicating a café across the square.

'But . . . is it all right?' said Caro, looking round as though expecting to be pounced upon.

'Why not?' said Warren smiling. 'We know each other, we met by chance . . .'

It was true. And after all this was Stourbridge not Warfleet.

In the café, Caro became tongue-tied. There were too many questions she wanted to ask. They tumbled about in her brain as she flashed on the scene between Warren and Viviana.

'Not hungry?' said Warren, watching her push limp chips around her plate. She looked up, meeting his golden gaze directly. His eyes held her as he said softly, 'I am.'

They went to a hotel. Warren checked them in as Mr and Mrs Truelove. The indifferent receptionist gave them a key and they sprang up the stairs as though a fire pursued them.

Inside the room, Warren drew the blinds and they were both still for a moment. Then he slowly came towards her and took her face in his hands. He looked deep into her fearful eyes, his own darkened to mahogany, and then bent his head and kissed her. His lips were warm and soft as they caressed hers and separated them. He slid his tongue in and she began to breathe more quickly, but Warren held her away and whispered, 'I want to take this one slowly.'

He kissed her face gently, her eyes, her nose, her ears, tantalizing her mouth by brushing across it, sometimes inserting the tip of his tongue. She stood with her arms at her sides letting him woo her, pleasure her. Carefully he undid her blouse, stopping to kiss every inch of new flesh, circling her nipples with his tongue until they stiffened almost unbearably. But still she stood without response except for involuntary murmurs. He slipped down her skirt and pants – thank God they were lacy, she thought ridiculously, had she somehow known this would happen? – and supported her as she stepped out of them. When he stroked her mound, then parted the lips and with swift strokes tongued her, Caro could resist no longer. She clung to his head and arched her back, forcing his tongue deep inside her.

'Warren, Warren,' she gasped.

He picked her up and carried her to the bed. She watched him strip off his clothes to reveal his long graceful body, and, as he lay next to her, bent forward and took his cock in her mouth, savouring its velvet saltiness. As he twisted and sighed, she climbed on top of him and took his whole length into her, up to the desperate ache that nothing else could pacify. She rode him until he groaned and cried out, letting him at last roll her beneath him and drive them, together, to their climax.

Still on his mission to find Warren an alibi, Sergeant Plummer made a second visit to the Tolleymarsh estate, this time to speak to Viviana. She received him, graciously enough, in the overheated drawing room; Bill Plummer, feeling bothered from the bike journey, was relieved to see the French windows open. He took his cup of Earl Grey over to them and breathed deeply; there was the sound of a lawn mower and the smell of new-cut grass was refreshing.

'So, Beel,' said Viviana, approaching with her cardigan clawed up to her chin, ''ow can I help you?'

'Er,' said the sergeant, off on another bumpy ride, 'I've

checked with security at Warren's club, and they tell me you were down there, you know, the night of Mr Fong's murder.'

He had eventually extracted this information from a surly youth, having gone down to Bliss earlier for a 'poke around'. It was clear he was told so he would go away. The staff were nervous of policemen.

'So?' said Viviana, raising her eyebrows until they disappeared under the fringe sprouting from her beehive.

'I just wondered if you saw young Warren?'

Viviana's eyebrows descended and drew together. 'No,' she said. 'And eet was strange. He had invited me there especially.'

That fitted, thought the sergeant. Viviana had smoothed the reopening of Bliss; a backhander, no doubt, to the drug squad.

'When, about, did you get there?' he said.

Viviana shrugged. 'I do not know. Perhaps two o'clock.'

'And where was Mr Fong at this time?'

Viviana adopted a sober expression. 'We would all like to know, Beel. I last saw heem after dinner. And no, before you ask, we deed not have spaghetti.' She said the word with distaste, as though the mere thought was a slur on her magnificent catering. 'Charlee and dear Marcus took my daughter-in-law home.' She sighed. 'I have told thees story many times now.'

Yes, thought the sergeant, but you left out one or two details.

'Right,' he said, 'right. And then Mr Croft came back to the Hall?'

'And went to bed,' said Viviana firmly. 'He told me Charlee had gone for a longer walk. Charlee,' she added, tearfully, 'was an insomniac.' She took a lace handkerchief from her sleeve and delicately sniffed into it.

'Do you have any idea where Warren was?' asked the sergeant, after a decent pause.

'No-o,' said Viviana, with just a hint of doubt, 'but . . .'

'Yes?' prompted the sergeant.

'I worry about the company he keeps. Carl and that horreed Seednee.'

Bill Plummer nodded. He worried about them himself. Warren's past had a way of catching up with him.

'Sometimes,' continued Viviana, 'they seem almost like conspeerators. Of course, Warren was very angry about dear Charlee's plans . . . and Seednee has so many guns . . . strange in leetle Warfleet . . .' She let the announcement die away provocatively. Bill Plummer stared at her. Sidney was an embarrassment to the whole family, but was Viviana seriously suggesting he was a murderer? She smiled sweetly, as though she had said nothing out of the ordinary, 'I must go now. I have a chareetee function to attend. Excuse me.'

Bill mounted his bike and pedalled slowly up the drive. He was convinced of only one thing: whatever her reasons, Viviana intended to implicate Warren. It was she who had made the anonymous phone call.

'Viviana knows I was away from the club that night,' said Warren.

'How?' said Caro, pausing with a scone halfway to her mouth; both hungry when they had awoken, they had ordered tea and now sat, naked, on the floor devouring scones with cream and strawberry jam.

Warren shrugged. 'I was supposed to go to the Hall. When

I didn't turn up, she came storming down to Bliss to find me. One of the security guards told her I'd left.'

'So, if someone put two and two together . . .' said Caro.

'Yeah. They'd know there were some hours missing.'

Caro put down the scone, her happy mood destroyed. 'Why were you supposed to go to the Hall?' she said, though her sinking heart knew the answer.

Warren pulled a face. 'It's a long story,' he said.

Caro stared at the busy carpet, though all she could see was Viviana crushed against Warren's thighs, weeping. 'I saw you,' she blurted, 'at your office. With Viviana.'

Warren looked puzzled. 'What were you doing there?' he asked; and when Caro mumbled some version of the story, burst out laughing.

'It's not funny,' said Caro, affronted. 'Anyway, explain!'

Warren too stopped eating. He spoke slowly as if testing how much Caro had seen. 'It was a business meeting. She wanted me to back her in getting the Martinis to take over Charlie's plans. I said I wouldn't.'

This didn't tally at all with what Caro had seen. What business meeting could ever be that desperate?

'Warren,' she said, 'I think you'd better tell me the truth. Don't you think you owe it to me?'

Warren fell silent. The afternoon sun glinting beneath the half-closed blinds fell on his blond skin and tangled locks, lighting him like a Renaissance angel. 'OK,' he said at last. 'I shagged her. Is that what you want to hear?'

Caro stared at him dumbly.

'It was nothing.' His voice sounded angry now. 'I slept with her once. It was stupid, I know. But Viviana . . . she's hard to resist once she's made up her mind to something.'

That Caro could imagine. She stood up and started to gather her clothes.

'Caro . . . Caro, please.' Warren caught at her as she passed, his eyes pleading. 'She was furious I'd stood her up. Begged me to begin the affair again.'

'She won't give up till she's got you back,' said Caro tonelessly. Really, in a way, she felt nothing.

'No,' said Warren. 'I made it clear that day. I want nothing to do with her, either personally or professionally.'

Caro pulled on her skirt, but before she could zip it Warren lunged across the bed and pinned her arms. 'Listen to me. I know it looks bad, but Annabel and I weren't . . . weren't . . . I'd never been unfaithful before. I'm not like that, I swear it. But Viviana . . . I don't know . . . she's a witch. Somehow, she just . . . got me!'

'And me?' said Caro, pulling away from him. 'What am I? A stupid old woman, another shag? A shoulder to cry on?'

'Stop it. Stop it!' cried Warren, burying his face in her neck. He strained her to him, biting at her flesh in a fury. Caro tried to hold him off, but her arms had lost their strength and in the end she let him hoist her on to the bed and push himself inside her. Despite herself, her body responded as, frantically, they struggled together.

'I love you,' shouted Warren, as he came, 'I love you, Caro, I love you.'

TWENTY

The search of Sidney's headquarters, a dilapidated hut on a stretch of allotments bordering the council estate, yielded a cache of arms worthy of an IRA hit squad. The Stourbridge detectives brought it in, rejoicing.

'Can we nick 'em now, guv?' said DI Malton. 'If we wait for ballistics, they could leg it.'

Detective Superintendent Cooper nodded briefly. There was a certain pressure to make an arrest before the FBI came up with a suspect, no matter how superficially cordial the relations.

'All right, Malton,' he said. 'Collar Delgardo on illegal possession. The others on sus. Let's see what we get out of them.'

It was early evening by the time Caro, having parted from Warren at the hotel room, got back to Four Trees. Anthea, the nanny, was in the kitchen cooking supper. Caro had felt awkward in her company since the night at Bliss, but Anthea seemed oblivious. Delia, she said, had taken a night off, gone to the cinema in Stourbridge with Craig.

'Now,' she said, 'with shippud's pie, do you cook the munce meat furst or the pertaydose?'

Clearly Anthea's culinary skills did not extend beyond fish fingers.

Caro took over, glad of an occupation. The Aga had become a stranger in her years of absence and she would have to concentrate. As she was stirring the onions, soothed by their tangy succulent aroma, Jade breezed in carrying a bottle of wine, which she proceeded to open. 'Where've you been all day?' she flung at Caro.

'Oh,' mumbled Caro, 'just mooching about in Stourbridge.'

'I went to Warren's office at Tolleymarsh but no one knew where he was.'

'Really?' said Caro, hoping Jade would attribute her hot face to the onions. Fortunately, Jade was absorbed by her own concerns.

'That Annabel's a pudding. Wouldn't say a thing. But I had an interesting talk with Marcus Croft last night.'

'Ah,' said Caro, divided between joy at Jade's description of Annabel and concern that her daughter was about to embark on another unsuitable romance. Still, though Marcus might be a murder suspect, he was not, as far as Caro knew, married.

'What did you find out?'

Jade looked arch. 'Plenty,' she said. 'The FBI asked Marcus all sorts of questions about Charlie's finances. Marcus told them all he knew, which wasn't much, because even though he was sort of his heir, Charlie was very secretive. Apparently he wouldn't get out of bed without consulting a soothsayer, but he told his business associates nothing.'

'A soothsayer?' exclaimed Caro. This was not at all her vision of Charlie.

'Oh, you know, tarot, I Ching . . . all the stuff in his office feng shui-ed. The Chinese are very superstitious.'

Caro had never been in Charlie's office, but couldn't help wondering what feng shui expert had given a blessing to the vile StrongFellows building.

'What about StrongFellows?' she said.

Jade took a slurp of wine. 'Not good, Ma. It's going down the tubes. The bank are definitely repossessing.'

In the light of the other events of the day this news seemed hardly significant, but, 'Poor Zo,' said Caro.

'Zo'll be fine,' Jade assured her. 'Marcus's got all sorts of plans. He's gone back today to sort it.'

'And the police let him?'

'Why not?' Jade refilled her glass.

'Isn't he a suspect?'

Jade hooted with laughter. 'Marcus? No! He adored Charlie. He was the son Charlie never had.'

'But . . . if he was the heir . . .' said Caro, following Deen's line of argument.

'Actually he was quite uncomfortable with that. His only interest is publishing, but Charlie was insistent.'

And no one, thought Caro, said no to Charlie.

'Personally,' continued Jade, 'I think Charlie liked dangling him on a string. It was unofficial. No will or anything. Marcus had everything to lose by Charlie's dying.'

'What if they fell out? Over . . . for example . . . a woman?'

'You mean Viviana?' Jade was not one for hypothesis. 'Nah. She did have a go, daft cow. It's obvious Marcus is of the other persuasion.'

It was not at all obvious to Caro and she had to readjust her thinking. She recalled Marcus cuddling Viviana's dog. Perhaps there *was* something camp about him. At least she need worry no longer on Jade's account.

'What about Charlie?' she said. 'Was he gay?'

'Far from it. If he'd known about Marcus . . .' Jade blew out her cheeks explosively. 'The Chinese are funny about homosexuality. Now *he* and Viviana—'

Deen Perry entered the room and Jade stopped short.

'Anyone been arrested?' tittered Deen, snatching up the wine bottle.

'Help yourself,' said Jade sarcastically. She gave him a look under lowered lids, which he pointedly ignored, slouching across to the Aga. Caro jumped as he grabbed her, suddenly, from behind. She dropped the wooden spoon, splattering the Aga with tomato purée.

'Whoops!' taunted Deen, then turned a suggestive smirk on Jade. 'Fancy the Admiral Nelson?'

Jade wrinkled her nose disdainfully, but Caro saw she would agree. Jade could never resist a conquest.

'When they had gone, Deen exiting with the words, 'Drinks on me. Can you lend me a fiver?', Caro called the rest of the residents to supper. Not hungry herself, she decided to go for a walk on the front; she needed to get back her perspective.

The evening was still warm, the sky streaked with brilliant orchid from the sunset. The sea came in and out, lapping the speckled pebbles with the sound of a kiss. Watching it always made her feel hopeful. Swifts darted about with their piping childlike cries. A dog, straggly-wet from a dip, came bounding up and barked at her. On the promenade an old couple were trying to launch a kite, but the air was too still. How sweet, thought Caro, still together after all those years. She wanted to spend days and nights with Warren.

Warren. Had he told her the truth now? Particularly about loving her? She was no longer in any doubt she was in love with him, but had not, so far, told him so. They had parted in the fetid hotel bedroom with hardly a word. Made no other arrangements.

She walked on to the point where she had first seen Marcus. It seemed so long ago but it was just a few weeks. What had he been doing on the beach that day, she wondered. Checking up on the plans for the wretched theme park, or soaking up local flavour, pondering on his own future? The sun had finally expired, and, when the sky turned zinc and threatened rain, Caro quickened her steps back to Four Trees.

The kitchen was agog at Jean Plummer. She stood rain-drenched, crying loudly, having burst in and interrupted supper. When Caro, also caught in the storm, hurried in, shaking water from her hair, Jean leapt upon her and clung to her shoulders, sobbing and shaking.

'Jean. Jean! Whatever is it?' said Caro, trying to extricate an arm.

'Our Warren,' choked Jean. 'He's been arrested.'

'What do you mean?' said Caro, her whole body stiffening.

'They come for him an hour ago. We got a call from Annabel.' The diners gasped and began whispered conjecture.

'Jean!' Caro too was shaking now. 'Calm down. Tell us exactly what happened.'

Jean's sobs subsided and she released Caro. 'I don't know. I couldn't take it in. Bill's gone down to the station.'

Caro nodded, fighting for control. She rid herself of her sodden jacket and put the kettle on the hob. In a crisis ordinary actions counted.

Jean said, 'I couldn't think where else to go. The kids were out. I couldn't be on me own.'

'Of course not,' said Caro, attempting to keep her voice even. 'You did right.'

It was clear Jean had left in a hurry; her face was un-made up and she was still wearing her slippers. Caro thought, fleetingly, it was the first time she had seen her without blue eyeshadow and cyclamen-pink lipstick. 'Sit down, Jean,' she said. 'I'm making you some tea. For shock.' Her own hands trembled so much as she put the tea bags in the pot, she had to stop and grip the rail of the Aga.

There were not, fortunately, many witnesses to this unhappy drama. The video team was out on a night shoot, and earlier in the day Neil had left abruptly for London. Only Miriam, Anthea and Harold sat at the table.

Anthea, ever the nanny, said, 'Riskew rimedie. Jean. Sut.'

Jean did as she was bid and Anthea whipped out a small bottle and applied a few drops to her tongue. 'Wunnerful in a crysis,' she said. She gave the impression of having lived through many.

As Caro brought the teapot to the table, the back door opened and Craig and Delia entered. They were laughing and exclaiming about the rain but their merriment died away as they took in the atmosphere.

Anthea briskly explained, interrupted by a further burst of hysteria from Jean.

'Lordy lord!' exclaimed Delia.

Craig sat and put an arm round Jean, his large presence reassuring. 'The police are a little trigger-happy in cases like this,' he comforted. 'It may be nothing.'

There was the sound of a car drawing into the courtyard and a flashing blue light invaded the room.

'It's Bill,' hiccuped Jean. 'He said he'd come and get me.'

Delia opened the door and the sergeant came in, his normally pink face ashy grey.

'Bill!' cried Jean. 'What? What?'

'Bad news, love,' said the sergeant. 'They're charging him with murder.'

'No!' shrieked Jean, crashing forward on to the table.

The sergeant took a step towards her but stopped and did a spiral to the floor which would not have disgraced the Marcia Banks School of Dancing. He swayed, staggered, fell to a knee, a hip and full torso. For a moment no one moved. Then Craig sprang to the telephone and Anthea bent over the unconscious sergeant. She lifted his wrist and felt for a pulse.

'He's alarve,' she said, as the others crowded round. 'Ah think he's hed a hard atteck.'

TWENTY-ONE

Warfleet's cottage hospital was not one of Caro's favourite places; from Jade's childhood accidents to Sebastian's various sojourns, it spelled danger. Nevertheless she was there early next morning, carrying a bunch of tulips and asking whether Sergeant Plummer could receive a visitor.

'He's in intensive,' said the sister. 'I don't think . . .'

'Please,' begged Caro, 'it's very important.'

'Two minutes,' said the sister reluctantly. 'You're not to disturb him.' Caro was shown into a white room, where the sergeant lay, looking unusually small, with many tubes attached to him.

He was conscious and nodded groggily to Caro as she sat by the bed. 'Kind,' he said, seeing the flowers.

'How are you feeling, Bill?' said Caro, patting the freckled hand that lay motionless on the hospital-cornered sheet.

'Not too bad,' he said with an effort. 'It's Jean I'm worried about.'

Caro could understand why. Jean had arrived at Four Trees that morning in a state of collapse, the *Warfleet Chronicle*, bearing the headline WARFLEET MEN IN CONSPIRACY TO KILL, under her arm.

The article went on to report the finding of the firearms

and the arrest of Warren, Sidney and Carl. Glyn might be over-imaginative, but he was certainly not tardy.

'She blames me,' said the sergeant sadly. 'Thinks I shouldn't have reported what I found out. Should have talked to Warren first. Warned him, so to speak.' He moved his head hopelessly from side to side on the pillow. 'For Jean, family comes first. It's the Italian in her. She's never understood police work.'

'But,' said Caro, mindful of the sister's warning, keeping urgency out of her tone, 'what *did* you find out, Bill?'

The sergeant shifted painfully and said, 'Now, Caro, you know better than that.'

'Glyn Madoc seems to have been told plenty,' she could not help retorting.

'That Glyn,' sighed the sergeant. 'I'd like to know who he's bunging for information.'

There was a pause while they eyed each other, both knowing there was more. Then Caro said, in a small voice, 'I know Warren didn't shoot Charlie. I know, because I was with him.'

'It was you,' said Bill with something like relief. 'No offence, Caro, but I knew there was a woman.' He gave a mirthless chuckle. '*Cherchez la femme*, said the Super.'

Caro blushed and looked hard at her knees. Her silence told the sergeant everything.

'Well now,' he said, 'I won't ask why, or any of that. Just tell me, were you with him between one and five?'

Caro nodded.

'And you found Charlie's body together?'

She nodded again.

'Now . . . this is important . . . did anyone else see you?'

'I don't think so,' said Caro, reeling back the scenario. 'At the club perhaps . . . but at the beach . . . we were careful, you see, that they didn't.' It was terribly shaming to have to admit this. For the first time Caro saw her affair as others would see it. Sordid. Sleazy. Sad, even.

'That's a pity,' said the sergeant, 'particularly as you didn't tell the truth in the beginning.'

Caro said, almost whispering, 'I thought I could save him from exposure. It seemed so . . . innocent.'

'What a mess,' said the sergeant wearily. 'See, unless a third party corroborates your story, you could be lying now . . . just trying to help him. I don't think they'll buy it. There is other evidence.'

'What other evidence?' said Caro sharply. 'How could there be?'

The sergeant looked at her searchingly. 'I shouldn't tell you, Caro, but for Jean's sake I will. We had a tip-off, it doesn't matter who, which led us to the firearms. One may be the murder weapon – it's with forensic now. Sidney and Carl are definitely involved. We've had an eye on their activities.' He lifted a hand and let it fall heavily. 'I tell Jean, it's the company Warren keeps. It always catches up with him.'

'But even if the other two are guilty,' said Caro, 'there's nothing to say Warren is.'

'Nothing to say he isn't,' said the sergeant. 'His fingerprints are all over the gun crates.'

Caro fell silent, shocked.

'What the heck,' said the sergeant. 'It's worth a go. See Detective Superintendent Cooper, but my guess is they'll hold on to him.'

*

The Superintendent very much wanted to agree with Bill Plummer. His eyes fixed on Caro like a pair of knitting needles. He was clearly annoyed that she had come forward, complicating an otherwise open and shut result. He was already basking in glory headlines, Masonic rounds, the FBI returned to their rightful place and status.

'I could charge you, you know . . . perverting the course of justice.'

Caro had realized as much. But she had steeled herself for this meeting and, though the adrenalin pumped wildly from her heart, held her ground.

'Well,' she said, 'if you do you do, but I've told you the truth.'

'Pity you didn't in the first place,' said the Super tersely.

Caro knew he believed her. The question he was asking himself was whether he could hold on to Warren anyway. The same question had gone through her head, endlessly, on the bus. What if Warren *was* involved in a conspiracy? He may not have pulled the trigger, but he could have helped plan it. The scene in the Admiral Nelson came back to her over and over. The three young men in a huddle. Warren's head close to Carl's and Sidney's. And then Warren on the beach that morning. He had hardly seemed surprised at finding Charlie. Perhaps he had invited her to the club to be his alibi? But no . . . that would have risked insulting Viviana, surely not his intention? Her heart revolted at this explanation, but by the time she alighted at the police station Caro was caught in a whirl of paranoia in which it was only too possible Warren was deceiving her. She realized she was still holding the tulips. She had hugged them so tightly, their pink heads were drooping.

The Super fiddled with the pens on his desk. There were now three FBI ones. It would be at least another forty-eight hours before he had a result on the murder weapon. He was going nowhere with Peabody, who had admitted nothing and given no explanation for the fingerprints. Maybe it was better to let him run . . . see where he led them. There were bigger fish to fry than Carl and Sidney.

'All right,' he said, ungivingly. 'But I'm watching you.'

Caro did not doubt it.

The Quest Natural Healing Centre was an unlikely natural venue for police officers, but when agents Benson and Hedges arrived to speak to Rumer they were as pleasant and polite as always. Caro, waiting in the lobby for her own bout of healing, saw them whisked away by Toni.

As she lay on the massage couch a few minutes later, she could not resist asking the purpose of their visit.

'Can't say, said Toni irritatingly. 'They called up after the dinner.' She ladled rosemary oil on to Caro's shoulders, 'wonderful for cleansing'.

How did she know, thought Caro, in awe again at her friend's psychic powers, that she needed cleansing.

She felt an overwhelming desire to confide in Toni, as she had in former years, but was afraid she would incur only censure. Instead she tried to relax into the massage. Perhaps, after all, she could still keep her secret.

When she got back to Four Trees, Jean had left to visit Bill, and Delia, with set lips, was cleaning the Aga. She looked out of sorts and told Caro that Craig had gone to London for a few days' research, adding that she had given him Zo's number, as StrongFellows had an excellent catalogue of New Age material.

'He'd better get there quickly,' said Caro sardonically.

Delia chipped at a stubborn stain. 'What do you think of him?' she asked, concentrating on the congealed vegetable matter.

'He seems nice,' said Caro carefully, knowing Delia was soliciting her approval.

'The kids like him,' said Delia. 'He's especially good with Harry. He took him to school before he left this morning.'

'Does he have children?' said Caro, meaning, 'Is he married?'

'One. And a grandchild. His wife is dead.'

So far, so good, thought Caro.

'It's difficult here, you know,' continued Delia, 'without Sebastian.'

Caro, terribly aware of her own need for understanding, said, 'Delia, it's your life. Whatever you do is OK by me.'

She crossed to the Aga and gave Delia a quick hug. Delia looked at her gratefully. 'Four Trees is hard work,' she said. 'Although Seb never actually did anything' – they both laughed – 'he was there for me morally. I'm not sure how long I can cope alone.'

Caro said, 'We'd all miss you terribly if you decided you couldn't.'

Delia gave the Aga top a swipe. 'This bloody thing wouldn't.'

It was lunchtime before Jade descended, yawning. She was wearing one of Deen Perry's shirts. She had not returned to Caro's room at all the previous night. Whatever Deen's flirtation with bisexuality, he was obviously not entirely of the 'other persuasion'. She avoided Caro's eye as she made coffee.

'Any news?' she said casually.

None, thought Caro, I am going to tell you. 'I went to see Bill Plummer,' she said. 'He's going to be all right, thank goodness.'

Jade and Deen had returned from the pub in time to see Bill being wheeled out to an ambulance.

Caro watched her daughter, stunning in the grubby shirt, as she pottered barefoot round the kitchen. Jade's hair was glamorously messy; her shapely legs seemed even longer under the shirt-tail, which barely concealed her small, neat bottom. Caro saw those legs wrapped around Warren, his hands on those pretty buttocks, and felt a strikingly unmaternal jealousy.

'Heard from Zo?' said Jade, over her shoulder.

'No,' said Caro, immediately feeling guilty. 'I'll call her at home later.'

'Mm,' said Jade, her mind not really on the subject.

'Oh, and Briar called for you. Wants to know when you're returning.'

Jade pulled a face, dashing Caro's hopes that it might be soon. She picked up the second cup of coffee and wafted to the door, saying vaguely, 'Oh well, see you later.'

Caro stared after the disappearing shirt-tail. Her daughter's actions were, as always, incomprehensible.

TWENTY-TWO

Blossom Cottage was awake early the next morning. Agents Benson and Hedges were off to London on undisclosed business and Jeremy was determined they wouldn't leave without a proper breakfast. He was, he realized, quite enjoying this B & B business. He loved to cook and had more or less stopped bothering, Darryl's recent appetite had been so pitiful. Jeremy popped another egg in the pan, letting its cheerful sizzle rid him of thoughts of Darryl's unacknowledged illness. It had been bad enough when Guy . . . no, he wouldn't dwell on that, the mushrooms wanted turning.

When bacon, tomatoes and toast were *au point*, Jeremy went to the hall and banged a tiny gong, a relic from his days in antiques and a nice touch, he thought. Shortly afterwards the agents descended, straightening ties and cuffs distinguished by gold FBI cufflinks. Darryl, unusually, came too, though he was still in his dressing gown.

As the agents sat at the prettily dressed table – Bruges lace cloth, another antique bargain; early roses in one of Toni's ceramics – they exclaimed over the wonderful spread.

'Gee, is that jelly home-made?'

'Yes,' said Jeremy, feeling obliged to add, since after all they were police, 'but not by me. It's one of Marsha Snelgrove's.'

Darryl went to collect the *Warfleet Chronicle* from the letter box. Its headline silenced them all.

PEABODY RELEASED WHEN LOVER, CARO, COMES FORWARD.

Yet again Glyn Madoc had achieved a scoop.

'Is he trying, d'you think, for a job on a national?' tittered Darryl into the hush.

Jeremy snatched the paper and read the paragraph. He was so concerned he barely heard Darryl and did not see the look which passed between the agents.

'Excuse me,' he said. 'I must call Caro ... in case she doesn't know. This is so distressing!'

'Warren Peabody was released from police custody yesterday, when Caro Radcliffe provided him with an alibi. Radcliffe (49) swears they were together at the time of the killing, admitting she and Peabody were lovers,' Jeremy read to Caro over the telephone.

'Oh my God,' said Caro, shivering in her nightshirt.

'Yes,' said Jeremy. 'You'd better be prepared. It'll only be hours before the nationals run it.' The town was indeed still swarming with their stringers.

'What shall I do?' whimpered Caro.

'Get a solicitor. Threaten Madoc with an action if he reveals any more.'

'But it's true,' said Caro.

'Bluff it out,' said Jeremy. 'At least to him. But you'd better tell Zo, hadn't you?'

Caro replaced the phone and stood as if rooted to the Indian carpet. Delia, also still in nightclothes, came out of the kitchen where she had just read their own paper. She took Caro by the arm. 'Come in here,' she said kindly, drawing Caro out of the hall and into the curtained living room. She pushed Caro, who was now shaking badly, into an armchair and put a large brandy in her hand. After a moment's hesitation, she poured herself one for moral support. The two women sipped in silence in the dark room. Trickles of sunlight escaped the heavy curtains and striped across last night's ashtrays and soiled glasses.

'Well,' said Delia at last, 'look on the bright side. You're only forty-nine this time.'

Caro burst into tears.

'Lordy lord,' said Delia, bringing over the brandy bottle, 'that was supposed to make you laugh. Here, have another one.'

Caro gulped the brandy, feeling it scald down her throat and settle in a tight ridge across her ribs.

'I'm sorry,' she said, 'I know how it must look . . .'

Delia waved away the apology. 'Like you said to me yesterday, you only have one life.'

Caro tried to smile. Delia's generosity was warming.

'I think you should go up to town. See Zo.'

It was true that could hardly be worse than facing Jade and the others. While Caro pondered, the phone rang again. Delia answered it.

'Oh, Delia, Glyn Madoc. Is Caro there? Just wanted a quick word.'

Delia covered the mouthpiece and mouthed, 'Glyn.'

With a sudden burst of rage, Caro snatched the receiver and snapped, 'Yes?'

'Good morning, Caro,' said Glyn, sounding not in the least contrite. 'I wondered if you'd be interested in an interview? Features page? You know, age gap, older woman, younger man sort of thing—'

'Fuck off, Glyn,' said Caro, her voice low but vicious. She slammed down the receiver as if it was burning.

Delia, watching, said, 'Bastard. Get dressed before the others are up. I'll take you to the station.'

On the train, everyone appeared to be reading the *Chronicle*. The headline stabbed Caro from all sides, as she hid behind a headscarf and dark glasses. She cowered in her seat, willing away the miles so she might get to Zo before the papers.

Jean Plummer was late, having stopped to visit the hospital.

'Bill's doing well,' she said to Delia. 'He's out of intensive. But he won't be home for a bit. Just as well, as I've got Warren!'

Jade, sitting staring at the paper, a look of stunned disbelief on her face, turned to her. 'Warren's at your house?' she questioned.

Jean gave her a look; she didn't approve of Jade. Or at least, not in relation to Warren. 'For a few days,' she said guardedly. 'He thought it best.'

Privately, she told Delia as they changed the bedlinen that Annabel had thrown him out. 'Just looking for an excuse!' she concluded with disgust. 'That girl's never had no compassion.'

Delia refrained from commenting that Annabel had had rather a lot to put up with.

Jade had instantly formed the plan of visiting Warren. She would rather have caught him, as in a wildlife programme, in his home environment, but at least at Jean's they would be undisturbed. She cursed herself for having let her trail go cold, sidetracked by her liaison with Deen Perry. How could she have been blind to what was going on between Caro and Warren?

She was furious with her mother, who was both disgusting and embarrassing, but Caro had defected. In her absence there were one or two things she had to say to Warren.

The Plummer, formerly Peabody, household had come up in the world since Jade's last visit. As she paid the taxi, she recalled the sad, pebble-dashed house of former years. Now it was gay with paint, the pebble-dash replaced with bright blue weathershield; the windows double-glazed; the garden, patioed and tubbed, a riot of brilliance.

The front curtains were drawn, and when she rang the tuneful bell there was no reaction. She rang again and banged the letter box, knowing Warren was inside. After a few moments, an upstairs window opened a crack and Warren poked his head out. 'Yes?' he said warily, then recognizing Jade, 'Oh. Just a minute.'

He opened the door, barefoot and unkempt, his long hair straggling at the collar of his hastily donned shirt. It was open and showed a gold neckchain and his smooth, brown torso.

'Can I come in?' said Jade, trying to smile as several emotions coursed unexpectedly through her. Anger, curiosity, jealousy, desire, she could identify immediately; she prided herself on being rather good at self-analysis.

Warren reluctantly stood back and allowed her into the hall. 'Thought you were a journalist,' he said unwelcomingly as he padded into the kitchen. 'They've been phoning up all morning.'

Jade followed him, noting the fitted carpet, central heating, bowls of fake flowers. The kitchen, half decorated in alcopop colours of fizzy lime and crushed orange, awaited completion of its 'cottage-style' stripped pine cupboards.

'Went back to bed,' said Warren briefly. 'I 'spose you read the paper.'

He'd reverted very quickly to his adolescent ways, thought Jade with a certain spiteful satisfaction. Warren, looking moodily handsome in the late morning light, was spooning instant coffee into a mug.

'How's Caro?' he said.

'She's gone to London,' said Jade. 'I haven't spoken to her.'

Warren made a distracted gesture with the spoon. 'She must be horrified,' he muttered.

'She and the rest of Warfleet,' said Jade, then, unable to stop herself, 'Whatever were you thinking of!'

Warren stared at her. 'What do you mean?'

'She's my mother, for Christ's sake! She's old enough to be yours!'

'So?' said Warren challengingly.

'Have you no sense of . . . of . . . propriety!'

Warren began to laugh. 'I see you are still concerned with what other people think.'

'It's not funny,' interrupted Jade, 'it's revolting!'

Warren stopped laughing. 'There's nothing revolting about love,' he said quietly.

There was a pause, then Jade said falteringly, 'Love?'

'Yes,' said Warren. 'Remember it?'

They looked at each other. A look of antagonism laced with sexual memory.

The kettle broke the moment, letting off steam for them

both. Warren picked it up and filled his mug. 'I know it's hard,' he said. 'I can't explain. It . . . it just happened.'

Jade took a deep breath, fighting to get back control. This wasn't at all how she'd planned the encounter. 'You told me,' she said in a more measured tone, 'that you were happy . . . with Annabel and your children.'

Warren dropped his head and his hair fell forward, masking his expression. 'I was,' he said, 'at least, I thought I was . . . it's all so complicated.'

Jade thought, If I'd known back at the funeral, but she shook the thought away. It was too late now. Besides, her purpose with Warren was different.

Warren said, 'Is that what you came for . . . to tell me off?' He grinned his charming lopsided grin and his eyes glinted green-gold with amusement. Jade was impressed that in the circumstances he had held on to his sense of humour. He had always been essence of cool, she remembered.

'No,' she said. 'I didn't mean to do that. I'm sorry.'

Warren bowed his head, acknowledging the apology. Then he said, 'Shall we go into the garden?'

He opened the kitchen door and led the way into the small but crammed back garden. It was grassed over, with splendid herbaceous borders just coming into bloom; there was a swing, a rockery and a bird table. The sunlight was piercing without being warm and Jade was glad of her leather coat. Warren seemed unbothered in his shirt; he was as impervious to cold as ever.

He sat on the swing and rocked gently, sipping his coffee. 'So. What did you come for?'

'I wondered,' said Jade, finding a spot in the sun on the rockery, 'what you could tell me about Charlie.'

Warren groaned. 'Well. First I didn't shoot him.'

'I never thought you did,' retorted Jade. 'Not at all in character.'

'Tell that to the police,' said Warren. 'They'll have me back given half a chance. I'm still their number one suspect.'

'What about Sidney and Carl?'

Warren shook his head. 'Hah. They're terrified of shooters. They won't find the murder weapon in that lot.'

'How can you be so sure?' said Jade. Then when he didn't answer, 'How are you involved with them?'

Warren poked at the grass with a bare big toe. 'I always have been.'

Jade had not forgotten. In the past, Warren had served a prison sentence rather than betray Carl. Was he going the same way now?

'Look, Jade, there's things . . . for your own good . . . I can't tell you. There's bigger players . . .'

The delicious threat of danger spurred Jade to demand, 'Who?'

Warren gave a half-admiring smile. 'You're incorrigible. Believe me, your life wouldn't be worth living. Nor,' he added dourly, 'would mine.'

'It has to be the Italians,' said Jade, but when Warren smiled on, saying nothing, she urged, 'It's classic Mafia . . . bullet through the head like that . . . or perhaps Masonic. Left on the shore at the high-water mark . . . no wonder the police were so keen to nail you. They wouldn't want to go after their brethren.'

Warren guffawed. 'You've been reading too many books,' he said. Jade's ability to turn every situation into high drama had been a feature of their relationship.

'It could be,' insisted Jade. 'Let's face it, a hit man only costs a couple of hundred quid.'

But Warren just shook his head, still laughing.

'OK,' sighed Jade, conceding he would not be drawn. 'What do you know about Charlie?'

Warren blew out air, considering.

'If he was so in debt,' pressed Jade, 'where was he getting the money to finance the Millennium Park?'

'Drugs?' said Warren, adding quickly, 'But that's only a guess.'

'Laundering,' stated Jade, as if it was a fact.

'Really?' said Warren, sounding amused. 'I thought that was only Swiss banks.'

Jade snorted. 'Nah, they're all at it. Property companies, films, publishing, theatre ... no one gets as far as Charlie without help from drugs money.'

Warren gave her a sceptical look. 'How d'you know all this?'

Jade tossed her head. 'Through my job. Trust me.' Warren smiled at her. She was like a child playing at sophistication. 'I'm sure,' she was saying, 'Charlie was involved with a cartel in Colombia.'

'And you think that's who had him killed?'

'Why not? A hostile takeover too far? I'd love to expose the connection.'

Warren eyed her with respect. 'Christ,' he said, 'you're determined to see us both in concrete underpants.'

Jade took out a pack of cigarettes and offered him one. Warren looked up at her through curling lashes as she bent to light it. It was a look that told of his former fascination; she was now, more than ever, a beautiful woman.

Jade flicked him a glance. 'So will you help me?' she said. 'It's in your own interests.'

Warren drew back. 'I don't see what I can do.'

'Viviana,' said Jade. 'She knows plenty.'

Warren shook his head firmly. 'It's her who shopped me, I'm sure.'

'A woman scorned?' said Jade lightly. She gave him an openly provocative smile. 'You have been a silly boy, haven't you?'

The corners of Warren's mouth twitched. She was so outrageous, it was impossible not to succumb. He said, 'I'll think about it.'

TWENTY-THREE

The restaurant, Del Mundo, Zo had chosen for lunch was fashionable and packed. Not, Caro thought, the best place for the sort of conversation they were about to have. Waiting in castle Fong's sunless atrium that morning, Caro had received a message that Zo was busy and would see her for lunch later. By now, of course, she would have read the papers.

Her heart full of dread, Caro made her way to the appointed table. Zo was already there, poring over some document. She looked unusually smart in a dark designer suit, which flattered her strong shoulders and close-cropped blond head. She looked up as Caro pulled out her chair and said, 'Hi. How're you doing?' Her brown eyes were searching, but not without warmth, and Caro felt tears rise quickly to her throat. If only this meeting were normal, how pleased she would be to be having lunch with Zo, exchanging gossip and ideas, loving looks and little touches. How had they let it all go wrong?

'Not good,' she managed to choke out as she sat, glad the other lunchers were obsessed with their own conversations.

'Sorry about this morning,' said Zo in a friendly tone. 'All our HoDs were called to a meeting with the receiver.'

Hence the suit, thought Caro.

'He's OK, actually. Quite humane.' Zo gave a small laugh. 'Like a stun gun.'

A waitress came to take their order. Caro could not imagine swallowing more than water, but Zo, she noticed, ordered two substantial courses, ending with 'and for my friend, a bottle of champagne'. That was so like her.

When the waitress had gone Zo said, 'Well, your press coverage is unbuyable. Pity no photographs.'

Caro stared at the weave of the tablecloth. 'I wish you hadn't found out like that. It's bad.'

'Is there a good way?' said Zo, apparently lightly.

Caro looked at her, amazed. Was she going to keep up this amused, distant banter?

'I don't know how to explain,' she said softly. Indeed, there was no explanation. Her collision with Warren was like a force of nature: unavoidable and potentially destructive.

'Don't then,' shrugged Zo. 'I'm sure you had your reasons.'

'It's funny,' said Caro. 'I know you've been unfaithful lots of times . . . oh, don't bother to deny it, I've always known . . . but somehow this is different.'

'Because you haven't?' Zo sounded more chastened now.

Caro nodded slowly. 'I can't understand myself . . . can't accept it.'

Zo said, 'I won't deny it's a bastard shock.'

'To me too,' said Caro.

There was a pause. The waitress came with the champagne and filled their glasses. Zo clinked Caro's glass, meeting her eyes, and said, in a not unfriendly tone, 'So what do you want to do?'

'I wish I knew,' said Caro. 'It's all impossible.'

Zo drummed her fingers on the table. '*I've* been pretty impossible,' she said. 'I realize I've . . . given you cause.'

'Don't blame yourself,' said Caro quickly, 'that's absurd.'

'No. I've neglected you. That's true. Career's been all-important.' She gave a painful laugh. 'Look where it's got me.'

'What will happen with StrongFellows?' said Caro, grasping at the diversion.

'Worried about your book? We'll salvage something. Marcus has drawn up a business plan. The receiver seems impressed with it.'

'No more David and Goliath,' said Caro wryly.

'I'll drink to that!' said Zo. 'It's an ill wind.' She looked at Caro over her glass. Her eyes held some of her old humour. 'I always knew I was a stepping stone,' she said. 'I told Jade years ago.'

'What do you mean?' said Caro. 'Don't say that.'

'It's not so bad,' said Zo, covering Caro's twitching fingers with her own square hand. 'We've had a few good times together.' She grinned her sweet gap-toothed grin, cocking her head slightly as though expecting acquiescence.

Caro pulled her hand away. How could Zo dismiss the intensity of their relationship as a few good times? Was that really all it had meant to her? Or was this Zo's way of letting go gracefully? Admitting that life, and people, moved on? If so, she was more of a grown-up than Caro. But then, despite her comparative youth, Zo had always had a way of seeming older and wiser.

Caro said, rather stiffly, 'You speak as if it's all over between us. Is that what you believe?'

Zo responded with a comical grimace. 'I hope not,' she said. 'Time will tell.'

'But aren't you angry?' said Caro. 'Don't you care?' Perversely, she now wanted some show of proprietorship from Zo; some admission of jealousy; pledge to fight.

Where was the youthful page who'd once charged to her rescue?

Zo said defensively, 'You know me. I'm not . . . possessive, territorial, like that.' It was true. At least of her private life. Caro had had the freedom to roam where she pleased, but had not, until now, taken it.

Zo's first course arrived and she began to eat while Caro crumbled bread and looked round the restaurant. To her discomfort, she saw Miriam sitting at a central table with a man who looked vaguely familiar. She must have taken a later train from Warfleet.

'Who's that man with Miriam D'Abo?' she asked Zo.

Zo flicked them a glance. 'Eddie Flynn. Ex-drug dealer. His story's all over the papers. Typical Miriam!'

So that was where Caro had seen his face; it was lined but had a raffish attraction, as did his long but well-cut greying hair. Not at all the Saturnalian look Caro would have associated with a drug dealer. Zo snorted into her champagne. 'I'm pissed off with him. He turned me down to do his book. I offered a quarter of a million.' She attacked her seared tuna, leaving Caro to digest the quarter of a million. She took another surreptitious glance at Eddie, impressed by a man who could turn down such serious money. Miriam had taken off her owlish specs and was smiling up at him ingratiatingly. Eddie returned the smile but his eyes were wandering. They rested for a moment on Caro and he appeared to wink. She turned quickly back to Zo.

'Miriam's staying at Four Trees,' she said. 'I hope she hasn't seen me.'

'Oh,' said Zo, 'speaking of Four Trees, a Craig O'Connell's been in. Looking for ley lines or something. The way he went through the files, you'd have thought he expected to find them in the building.'

'Well, Charlie *was* into feng shui,' said Caro, attempting to match Zo's spirit. 'As a matter of fact I think Delia's keen on him.' The gossip was a welcome way back to normality.

'Really?' said Zo. 'I hope she's careful. There's more to him than meets the eye.'

'In what way?' queried Caro. To her, Craig seemed exactly as he met the eye.

'Dunno,' said Zo, raising her shoulders. 'Just a feeling. He was asking a lot of questions.'

Miriam and Eddie were leaving and Caro ducked her head behind the menu, praying Miriam would not be on the same train home. Eddie stopped, however, at their table. 'Ms Acland, isn't it?' he queried, giving a graceful half-bow which set his wavy hair dancing. Zo acknowledged him with an unsmiling nod.

'No hard feelings, I hope. I was flattered by your offer.'

'But you had a better one,' said Zo shortly.

Eddie smiled, a roguish merriment lighting his craggy features. Now he looks like a gypsy, thought Caro, watching; with his soft Celtic accent a spinner of yarns, a troubadour.

'To be honest,' he was saying, 'I had wind of the ... difficulties ... ahead. I thought it better to save you embarrassment.'

Zo looked at him with more respect.

'I knew Charlie,' went on Eddie, his smile dying. 'I'd hate to see people damaged by this. If there's anything I can do ...' He took a card out of the pocket of his casual linen suit and laid it on the table. 'Give me a call.'

Miriam's face had gone gooseberry sour, as if she'd

swallowed a large pickle. 'We must go, Eddie. I'll be late.' She turned to Caro and Zo. 'I'm interviewing a Bosnian war criminal.' Then flashing Zo a malicious little smile, 'Pity you're not in a position to pick up *his* story.'

Eddie nodded goodbye, his eyes lingering for a moment on Caro. They were brown as sugar, deep with experience and, she had to admit, sexy. They seemed, with their knowing glint, to be inviting her to something. Something that would be fun. But perhaps it was just her current erratic hormones.

There was a brief hiatus after they left. Both women were, in their different ways, evaluating the encounter. The second courses arrived. Zo ate her steak steadily and Caro played with some rocket leaves.

At length Zo said, without looking up, 'Are you going back to Warfleet?'

Caro nodded. A look of disappointment crossed Zo's face. Caro said falteringly, 'I feel . . . I can't . . . abandon them.'

'Yep,' said Zo. 'I can understand that.'

'It seems,' said Caro sharply, 'that you understand everything.'

Zo looked at her, the regret still on her face. 'Oh, Caro,' she said sorrowfully, 'I wish I didn't.'

To Caro's dismay her eyes filled. She had rarely seen Zo cry, let alone in public. 'Darling,' she whispered and touched Zo's arm, 'don't. This will blow over. It's just a . . . just a madness.'

'Maybe,' said Zo, fighting her way back to a smile. 'Anyway we'll still be friends if it doesn't.' She looked at Caro anxiously for validation. It was a long time since Caro had seen her so vulnerable. Zo refilled their glasses and said, 'A toast. To us. And being friends if it doesn't.'

Caro felt unhappy admitting the possibility that they

would be only friends, but really, as she lifted her glass, she was toasting Zo. Her honesty.

They drained their glasses, then Zo, apparently recovered, looked at her watch and called for the bill. 'I was going to suggest going off to a hotel and making mad passionate love,' she joked shakily, 'but the receiver waits for no woman.'

'I've got an appointment anyway,' said Caro. After wandering aimlessly in Chelsea all morning, too depressed even to shop, she had called Noelle and fixed to see her that afternoon, assuming Zo would go back to the office.

They parted outside the restaurant. Zo said, 'Try to keep out of the headlines. It's not good for a girl's morale.' Then, with a lingering brush of Caro's lips, she was off down the street, leaving Caro standing, watching.

Noelle's office, in a ramshackle building behind Wardour Street, was the usual pickle of papers, dirty coffee cups and partially hidden wine glasses. The air was a smog of secondary smoke with some underlying rot . . . wormy manuscripts? Or decaying clients, perhaps.

Noelle seemed startled to see her: probably she had forgotten. Yet there, spread on her desk, were the papers detailing Caro's fall from grace. She quickly recovered herself, pushing back the reading glasses which had slipped to the end of her nose and offering Caro a 'medicinal libation'. Caro shook her head, still unsteady from the champagne, but Noelle brought a half-finished bottle of red wine from the floor by the side of her desk and poured herself a generous glass anyway.

She leaned back, sipping it, and regarded Caro, 'Well?' she said, sounding slightly slurred. It was three-thirty.

Caro opened her hands wide. 'It's all there,' she said,

indicating the papers. 'Except I never admitted we were having an affair.'

'But,' said Noelle, 'you are though.' Caro nodded. There was a pause, then Noelle let out a cackle of laughter. 'Good for you,' she said. 'It's about time you made some changes.'

Caro had not been expecting this. 'But,' she stammered, 'it's awful. This kind of exposure.'

'You could,' admitted Noelle, still chuckling, 'have chosen a less explosive route. Still . . .'

'What do you mean, time for a change?' asked Caro, puzzled.

'I mean,' said Noelle, polishing off her glass, 'you've been in stasis for some time.'

'Stasis?' pressed Caro, wondering how Noelle had divined her personal problems.

'With your writing!' said Noelle, banging down the glass and picking up the bottle. 'The personal is art, love. Whatever happens, use it.'

Caro instantly recoiled from the notion. 'You mean,' she said frostily, 'my affair is good copy?'

Noelle flapped a hand over the newspapers. 'See for yourself,' she chortled. 'Your first book was direct experience, your second disjointed, unsatisfactory. Now in the new one you can draw on this trauma.' She gulped down the last of the wine as if to underline the finality of her statement.

'How was your lunch?' she said, after a fraught silence had fallen.

Caro dropped her head. 'Sad. Upsetting.'

Noelle nodded. 'I'm sure. But Caro dear . . .'

Caro was surprised at the sympathy now in her agent's tone; she was used to the other Noelle, brusque to the point of brutality.

'. . . that relationship has been over for a long time.'

Ah, that was more like it. Caro fixed her with fiery eyes. 'What are you saying? That's outrageous!'

Noelle pointed a wavery finger. 'You can bluster all you like, but it was plain for everyone else to see. It was past its sell-by.'

Caro swallowed, choking on denial. Noelle was saying things she had not even dared to think. But she recognized the truth of them.

'I have to go,' she said, needing to escape more awful pronouncements.

Noelle patted her arm. 'Don't take offence. I'm telling you for your own good. Which is' – she gave another bray – 'the best you can expect from an agent.'

Somehow Caro got down the twisting stairs and out into the fresher street.

She leaned against the front door for a few moments, trying to recover her equilibrium. A beggar went by and held out his hand automatically. She gave him 20p, all she had in her pocket. 'God bless you, lady,' he mumbled. 'I can see you're lucky.'

TWENTY-FOUR

Don Martini's Pasta Palace, the flagship of the Martini empire, lay out of town a little, close to the beach and the sailing club. It was a handy haunt for the sailing crews and windsurfers, who entered rugged and reddened after downing many pints in the sailing club bar. Predictably, it had a reputation for late nights and roistering.

Of all their hostelries, it was the one at which Ugo and Fabio were most likely to be found, particularly as it was also a favoured spot for the Stourbridge CID, whose expenses ran to the over-inflated prices. The brothers made a point of being civil.

Jade and Warren agreed to meet there that evening. Jade dressed for the occasion, determined to catch the eye of at least one brother. She wore a low-cut velvet bustier over a short, tight skirt, with very high heels and very long earrings. Warren, waiting by the mock Venetian fountain in the mock marble hall, did not suppress a soft whistle; she looked absolutely stunning.

'Didn't want to let you down,' she said, tossing him a smile. 'A man who's been dumped by his wife has to keep up his profile.'

'No one,' said Warren, his eyes drawn to her uplifted breasts, 'could accuse you of being low profile.'

Ugo, who was standing, tuxedoed, at the bar, looked less than happy to see Warren. Nevertheless he came smoothly forward with his arm raised and clasped Warren's shoulders. 'Good to see you, my friend. And who is this lovely young lady?' His black eyes lingered on Jade's cleavage.

Jade introduced herself, holding out her hand. Ugo took it caressingly and, lifting it slowly to his lips, dropped a kiss on it. 'Can I offer you a drink?' he murmured, indicating the bar. 'Mario, champagne for my guests.' He led the way, seeming unwilling to relinquish Jade's hand. At the bar Jade hitched her skirt even shorter to accommodate the stool, making sure Ugo got the benefit of her Lycra-clad legs. As he turned away to collect the champagne she gave a droll wink to Warren.

'How are you, Warren?' said Ugo, handing him a glass. 'I was worried when I heard about your . . . trouble.'

'Fine,' said Warren, with a twist of a smile. 'You've no need to worry.'

Ugo tapped an incisor, which had, Jade noted, a small diamond set into it. 'Good, good,' he said softly, his eyes not leaving Warren's face. He appeared to be looking for something.

Warren did not flinch from the study, but neither did he respond, and after a moment Ugo turned his attention back to Jade. He was an attractive man, she thought, not sorry she had talked Warren into this visit; his skin was supple olive, his thick blue-black hair sharply cut, as was his tuxedo; a persuasive smile decorated his handsome features.

'This is your first visit, Miss . . . may I call you Jade? Please, take a look at our menu.' He handed her an elaborate sheet topped with the Martini brothers' logo, two stallion heads, nostrils wide, staring in opposite directions. Jade started. Hadn't she seen somewhere . . . *The Godfather* perhaps . . . that horses featured in Mafia killings?

Warren said, 'I'm not sure we're staying to eat . . .'

But Ugo held up a finger. 'I insist. I particularly recommend the fegato this evening. I tried it myself.'

Raw, most probably, thought Jade. She had the feeling that to refuse would be to offend Martini honour.

Ugo led them to a table, summoning a waiter to whom he said menacingly, 'Piero, these are my special friends. Anything they want. Immediately.'

He helped Jade into her white, wrought-iron chair, brushing his palm lightly across her shoulders. She gave an involuntary shiver, not sure if it was from fear or pleasure. Ugo glided away leaving them with the champagne and an aura of aftershave.

Warren gave Jade a dry smile. 'You're certainly getting the treatment.'

'He oozes Tuscan charm,' she giggled.

'Mmm,' responded Warren. 'Via an ice-cream parlour in Thanet.'

Jade looked around the large room, clearly modelled on the super-restaurants of London. The decor was a little rococo for her taste, depending on stucco angels and heavy gold-leafed mirrors, but she had to admit the effect was stylish and no doubt impressive to the burghers of Warfleet. It was still early and not many tables were full. There was no one she recognized. 'Who comes here?' she asked.

'Golfers, sailors. Stourbridge constabulary.'

'Really?' said Jade, looking more intently at the tables.

'Later. They come to drink. And,' he added, almost to himself, 'to exchange information.'

Jade was instantly alert. 'What sort of information?'

'Whatever,' said Warren, smiling at her irritatingly. 'Choose your dinner.'

'I'm not having the fegato,' said Jade. 'I don't know who it belongs to.'

When they had finished their first course, excellent Parma ham and melon, Jade went to the ladies, labelled 'Powder room'. This was appropriate as its peachy furnishings smelt of things powdery. She looked in the flattering mirror, re-applied lipstick and wriggled further into her corset. Pleased with her image, she returned to the restaurant to find Ugo at their table. As she approached, he turned his diamond-enhanced smile on her. 'Everything is good.' It was a statement rather than a question, but she nodded enthusiastically. It would take a brave person to complain in here, she suspected. He touched her arm, managing to graze a breast, and slid away to glad-hand someone at another table.

'What was he saying?' Jade demanded, automatically lowering her voice. The whole place was suffused with an atmosphere of intrigue.

Warren said reluctantly, 'There's a meeting at the Hall tonight. To discuss the future of the estate. Ugo says Viviana wants me to go to it.'

'Playing into our hands,' whispered Jade delightedly.

'I said no!' Warren had alarm in his voice.

'Don't be absurd,' said Jade, pouring more champagne. 'Of course we're going.'

Caro took a late train back to Warfleet. She had dithered over staying in town, but in the end something had stopped her. A fear of cowardice? A sense of responsibility? She had invested so much of herself in Warfleet, both literally and metaphorically; a fact her ex-therapist, Ingrid, had often invited her to address.

'Have you considered, Caro, what a lot of yourself you feel obliged to give away? Perhaps you want other people to take care of it.'

She made it sound like litter Caro had carelessly dropped. But whatever the baggage, the town was still in many ways her touchstone. She had meant what she'd said when she'd told Zo she couldn't abandon it. Besides, although she loved Zo – she was in no doubt about that – there was something else, some unknown part of herself, to which these extraordinary events were a key. Despite everything, as she alighted from the train into the sharp April night she felt, largely, relief.

There were no taxis so she walked from the station, savouring the cool night air on her hot head. She wondered where Warren was and what he was doing. Her body yearned for his touch, but now, of course, that would be impossible.

The quickest route took her through back lanes nudging the Tolleymarsh estate and down through the copse which joined it to Four Trees. The narrow lane was free of traffic and she began to enjoy the walk, stopping to sniff the heady, night-scented hawthorn and listen to the assorted squeaks and rustlings from the hedgerow.

She entered the estate via a stile and took the path dipping through the trees which bordered the long drive to the Hall. There was the calming, resinous smell of pine; the moon had emerged from behind banked clouds and white light filtered down, turning the birch bark luminescent.

Distantly Caro could hear the sound of a car and as she

meandered, lulled by nature, headlights appeared, sweeping through the trees before glancing off to follow the bend in the drive. Caro stopped in her tracks. In the moonlight she could see clearly that the vehicle was Warren's jeep. She could make out the top of his silvery head and next to him, fully lit by the brilliant beam, the laughing face of her daughter.

There were few lights on at the Hall; it loomed hugely out of the blacker surrounding darkness, like a stranded liner or the House of Horrors in a Gothic fantasy. Warren took them in through a back way, one obviously familiar to him, noted Jade, and down dimly lit stairs hung with amateurish paintings vaguely erotic in content. 'Henry did these when he was younger,' Warren said. Jade stifled a giggle. It was hard to imagine enfeebled Henry as a lusty Don Juan. No wonder they were consigned to the basement.

A web of passages, not at all like the sumptuous rooms upstairs, ended in a door upon which Warren, holding his ear close to it, knocked. After a moment it was opened by Viviana. She flung her arms round Warren's neck and drew him into an embrace which left Jade in little doubt about their relationship. Greek tragedies flashed through her head. There was little of the stepmother in Viviana's attitude.

'You bastard,' Viviana was breathing, as she covered Warren's face with kisses, 'you drove me to eet—' She stopped abruptly as she saw Jade. She dropped her arms and her face assumed a shuttered expression.

'Hi, Viviana,' said Jade, as though the situation was normal.

Viviana was barely polite. 'Thees ees a beezness meeting,' she said sulkily.

Looking around, Jade could see the large, subterranean room was set up for a party. There were long low sofas in boudoir pink, discreet lighting, relaxed music, little tables with dishes of nuts and olives. In the corner lit with Day-Glo fairy lights was a bar with several beautiful young women lounging at it. The whole impression was of a club. Or brothel. With Viviana, in a revealing Versace, as the expensive madam.

Viviana let them pass, then followed them to the bar. There was a waiter mixing drinks, and as they waited to be served one of the women ran her hand up Warren's thigh.

'Not him,' snapped Viviana, slapping the girl's hand. The girl gave a careless shrug and turned back to her companion.

Jade was entranced. This was better than her wildest dreams. She tried to attract Warren's attention but he sat with his head down, looking extremely embarrassed. She wondered if he had been at these 'meetings' before. She would question him later. As they sipped their cocktails Viviana's mobile phone rang. She moved away to speak into it, then disappeared through the entrance door.

Jade nudged Warren. 'What's going on?'

'You'll see,' he returned gloomily. Then with a burst of anger, 'I shouldn't have brought you.'

Jade stopped herself saying that wild horses . . . even Mafia ones . . . could not have kept her away, as Viviana re-entered with Ugo and Fabio. Though they were not twins, there was a strong family resemblance. Fabio too was handsome; a little older and taller than his brother, with a careful streak of silver in his black hair. Behind them came a posse of men in badly cut suits and garish gold jewellery.

'Stourbridge drug squad,' muttered Warren.

Ugo did not seem surprised to see Jade. Viviana had had

time to tell him there was a slight hitch in their plans, she supposed. He crossed towards them, bringing Fabio in his tow, and introduced him. Fabio bowed low over Jade's hand. Like his brother, he seemed taken with her costume.

The policemen were introduced by first name only, Len, Colin, Nigel, Chris. A couple of them gave Warren suspicious looks, but were quickly deflected by drinks and female attention. Viviana turned up the music. The barman continued to mix the mind-numbing cocktails; watching Viviana toss one down her throat, Jade was reminded again of stepmothers: wicked ones with poisoned chalices. None the less, when Ugo handed her a third foaming glass, she drank it without a tremor.

Someone had dimmed the lights and people began dancing on a small square of parquet. The young women, who were all skimpily dressed, pulled the policemen away from the bar, lolling against them provocatively. Ugo invited Jade to dance. He held her close, moving his hips insinuatingly in a sort of bossa nova rhythm easy to follow. She was quite drunk now and let him run his hand down her back and rest it on her buttock. As he steered her, fluid as oil, she checked on Warren, who still sat moodily at the bar. The next time she looked Viviana was draped over him, whispering in his ear.

Fabio came over with another drink and without interrupting the beat took her from Ugo and continued dancing. They were a seamless double act, she had to admit. Fabio's movements were more insistent. He pressed against her as she swung with him; she could feel his cock hardening.

Several drinks and dances later she noticed Warren and Viviana had left the room. She looked around, sobering slightly. The room was whirling, but she stood still until it came to rest, and noticed a small ante-room off the main one. While Ugo and Fabio were refreshing drinks for the drug squad she swayed towards it. From the doorway she saw three girls and two policemen, Nigel and Colin, splayed on couches. They were all partially undressed. One girl had her breast in Colin's mouth and another her hand in his flies. Nigel watched as the third girl chipped up a large pile of white powder on the table. 'Pure Colombian,' she said, noticing Jade. 'Want some?'

Jade knelt at the table. She loved coke and it wasn't often she was offered something this good. The girl, Karin, divided it into serious lines then rolled up a ten-pound note, offering the first snort to Nigel. Everyone took a turn, then sat back, sparkling. The girls redoubled their efforts with Colin, one bending to take his cock in her mouth, the other stripping off her top and straddling him. Karin turned to Nigel, who was pawing eagerly at her miniskirt. She took his hand and placed it between her legs, pressing his face into her protruding bosom.

As Jade stared, fascinated, she felt hands encircling her own breasts from behind and smelt Ugo's now familiar aftershave. His lips were on her neck and he bit it gently as his hands massaged the flesh above her bustier. She was confused but excited and leaned back a little so that he could slide a hand down her cleavage. His fingers cupped one breast, while his other hand searched under her skirt and edged beneath her G-string. From the corner of her eye she saw Fabio, at the doorway, watching. On the couch before them, both policemen had their trousers down and were being vigorously manipulated. The girls swapped positions frequently, pausing to tongue-kiss and suck at each other.

Jade wriggled as Ugo's fingers found their target. As he rubbed and squeezed, she collapsed against him and let him take her hand and pull it back to feel his stiffness. He blew into her ear and whispered Italian endearments, 'Bella . . . dolcessa . . . mia bambola,' then forced her head around so he could sink his tongue into her mouth.

Just as her last reserve crumbled and she began to kiss him in return, she felt another pair of hands grip her shoulders. In her dizzy state she assumed it was Fabio. The brothers, it seemed, shared everything. Then she was jerked to her feet out of Ugo's grasp, and found herself staring into Warren's furious face. 'Come on,' he said roughly, 'we're going.'

Jade tripped and stumbled as Warren hustled her out of the room. At the door they passed Viviana, looking livid; behind them, as Warren marched her away, she could hear Ugo and Fabio laughing.

TWENTY-FIVE

When Jade awoke next morning it was to a towering hangover. Jean Plummer's face as she handed her a cup of tea registered every kind of objection: to Jade, asleep fully dressed, if that's what she called fully, on her sofa; to the state of her make-up; to the suspicious smell of alcohol; to her presence in the house at all.

'I suppose you still take one sugar?' she said, her face corrugated with disapproval. 'It's eight-thirty. I'm off to the hospital. You should be going home, young lady.' Jean had no intention of leaving Jade alone with Warren, if she could help it.

Jade focused blearily on her surroundings as the shameful events of the previous night hiccuped back into her pounding head. She buried her face in Jean's hard, floral cushions and groaned softly.

I should think so, Jean thought but did not say. Really, she did not know what to make of the Radcliffes, both of whom were now implicated in Warren's downfall. She had been fiercely devoted to Caro when she had first gone to housekeep at Four Trees and fond of Jade when she was little. She still felt loyalty to them as 'family', but Warren was her son, her first-born, and as such untouchable.

She left Jade to her discomfort and went to chivvy the

younger children into readiness for school. She would drop them on her way to see Bill. Through the half-open living room door, Jade heard shouts and scuffles in the kitchen, Jean issuing orders, then the front door slamming on the chatter and footsteps on the path outside. When the flying particles had settled, she dragged herself into an upright position and stumbled to the gilt-edged mirror hanging over the eternal flame gas fire. It reflected a sight every bit as wretched as her inner turmoil. She couldn't remember how she'd got to Jean's, or indeed anything beyond being hustled out of the party by Warren. That image had stayed, embarrassingly, along with the touch of Ugo's hands. She was still trying to piece the rest of the evening together when Warren entered the room. Compared to her own state, she registered sourly, he looked devastating in jeans and a camouflage vest.

'Oh. You're awake,' he said sternly.

'Barely,' muttered Jade, avoiding his eyes. 'Got any real coffee?'

Warren raised his eyebrows in mock despair. 'What the fuck are you like?' he said, sounding almost awed.

'You can talk!' said Jade, stung into inelegant retort. She hardly needed Warren to lecture her.

'Really,' said Warren sarcastically. 'I didn't get drunk, snort God knows how much coke and nearly involve myself in an orgy.'

'You took me,' said Jade petulantly.

'I wouldn't have done if I'd known it was going to be that kind of an evening.' There was a hint of an apology now in Warren's tone.

'What were you expecting then?' Jade seized the advantage. 'A boardroom meeting? You seemed quite at home there.'

Warren shrugged without agreeing.

'Stop staring,' commanded Jade, attempting to straighten her costume, absurd in the cruel morning light. 'Lend me a shirt or something.'

Warren went out and came back a moment later with a faded sweatshirt. Jade snuggled into it, oddly comforted by the unforgotten smell of Warren's skin and hair on the garment. 'Oh, let's not argue,' she said with a placatory little smile. 'I agree I behaved badly.'

'You don't know what a lucky escape you had,' said Warren, less judgementally. 'I suppose you realize that was all being videoed?'

'Videoed!' exclaimed Jade.

'Yeah . . . and you were nearly the star. Imagine trying to make your "truthful" documentary of Charlie when Viviana's got you on tape with your knickers down.'

Jade swallowed hard, imagining. 'But why?'

'Use your head,' scoffed Warren, 'what's left of it. The Italians want stuff on the drug squad. Quid pro quo, as you might say.'

'I don't get it,' said Jade, rubbing her eyes. In her befuddled state her Latin had deserted her. 'Quid what?'

Warren sat opposite her and after a moment said, in a more considered manner, 'I'm going to tell you a couple of things. In *strict* confidence.'

Jade was instantly alert, hangover forgotten. 'I'm listening,' she said, leaning forward.

Warren weighed her up, as though doubting his own judgement, then with a sigh began. 'It all started a long time ago, before Viviana . . . or Charlie. Or,' he added, almost as an afterthought, 'Annabel.'

Jade drew up her legs and nestled down in her chair as though preparing for a fairy story.

The morning was not going well at Four Trees. Jean Plummer arrived in a sullen temper and threw things about in the kitchen. Delia seemed out of sorts. Caro worried that their moods related to her and tried to make awkward appeasement. 'I'll make my own bed, Jean. Anyone for toast?' She was put into her own spin by the *Warfleet Chronicle*, which Jean launched, missile-like, at the table. On page 13 was an article about older women with younger men, headed WOULD YOU LET YOUR SON MARRY ONE? and accompanied by a picture of herself, squinting into the sun, neckless. It was a photo, she eventually realized, taken by Seb on a Spanish beach years ago. How Glyn had acquired it was a mystery. This, coming on top of a troubled night full of wild assumptions about Jade and Warren and an early morning phone call from her mother ('I shall have to move,' Cynthia had wept, 'I simply can't bear the humiliation'), was enough to make Caro heartily regret her return to Warfleet. When Jean had huffed off to hoover, Caro put her head down on the table and let one self-pitying tear squeeze out of her eye and drop to scald the photo.

The listening Jade was sunk deep in resistant scatter cushions, her eyes huge and her thumb in her mouth. 'God,' she said as Warren concluded his tale. 'Now I really need some coffee.'

Warren rose and sloped to the door. He turned before he went out and gave Jade an anxious look. 'I hope I've done the right thing, telling you. Last night I realized you were in real danger.'

'Thanks,' said Jade, subdued. 'I appreciate it.' She followed him into the kitchen and stood staring vacantly out of the window on to the lawn until the acid spring green hurt her eyes. The smell of coffee brewing turned her round. 'I still don't see,' she said, 'how Viviana fits in.'

'Viviana,' said Warren. 'She's a wild card.' His voice had a sort of affection in it, as though, in spite of everything, he liked her.

'Was she a prostitute?' said Jade bluntly.

Warren waved a hand. 'If you were born in a Bogotá slum, you'd use everything. She's naive in many ways. No idea what she's walking into.' He fixed Jade with amused eyes. 'Quite like you, really.'

'Bet she gave you a hard time when she took you off last night.' Jade chose to return his jibe with interest.

'She had another go at persuading me to play along. Offered management, money, lawyers, protection.' He dropped his head. 'Mostly she wanted to know about Caro.'

'She's obsessed with you,' said Jade. 'I saw it straight away.' The coffee had restored her vigour. 'They're like wasps to a honey pot.'

'You're the wasp,' said Warren sharply. 'If I wasn't a modest man, I'd say you sounded jealous.'

'Touché,' Jade had the grace to concede. 'Actually, now I'd rather have you as a brother.' She smiled impudently until Warren was forced to relent. 'So where do we go from here?'

'Nowhere.' Warren was firm. 'My best advice to you is to go back to town and forget the whole business.'

Jade put her head on one side sceptically. If Warren seriously thought she would consider doing that, he didn't know her as well as he thought he did.

*

She took a taxi back to Four Trees, having for once been circumspect and refused a lift in Warren's jeep. On arrival, she saw her mother wandering in the orchard. Though the morning was raw, Caro was wearing no jacket; her hair was uncombed, her feet unshod, and she appeared to be shredding the *Warfleet Chronicle*. Despite a returning sense of outrage, Jade felt a moment of anxiety for her. Caro looked gaunt and dazed; on the edge of calamity. She didn't notice Jade's approach and, when Jade put a hand on her shoulder, started like a frightened animal. Some relief crossed her face when she saw it was her daughter. 'Oh, it's you,' she said, managing a cracked smile.

'What were you expecting?' said Jade. 'Arrest?'

Caro laughed; a hoarse, unconvincing sound. 'You'd think I should from people's attitude.'

'It's not exactly pretty,' said Jade ungivingly.

She was uncomfortably divided between anger at her mother and pity for her plight. She was affronted on Zo's behalf and annoyed that she herself had misjudged the situation. This conflict did not help the sick ache which had settled like a hat on her forehead. When Caro said awkwardly, 'Jade, we need to talk,' her immediate instinct was to refuse, yet she heard herself agreeing.

'I'll get changed,' she said. She was still wearing Warren's sweatshirt, at which she saw Caro cast a questioning look. Over her short skirt, high heels and laddered stockings it made a bizarre costume. 'What about the Quest?' she suggested. 'Maybe Toni can give us a massage.'

Caro at once nodded agreement. Apprehensive though she was about Toni's response, the Quest could not be worse than Four Trees.

They were both silent on the short journey. Delia had said

she didn't need the car. 'Where am I going to go? Safeways?' Her tight face, as she handed over the keys, worried Caro. She knew her friend to be upset, but her own problems were more pressing. Jade drove, assuming her mother incapable. She only took a couple of wrong turnings.

Toni was busy when they arrived, so they went first to the newly installed steam room. This was Toni's *pièce de résistance*, paid for in part by the windfall and in part by the improved business events in the town had brought them. It was splendid with marble slabs, Norwegian wood floors, power showers and aromatic steam, though Jade insisted she could detect a tinge of Chinese dumpling.

When Toni was not occupied in the massage room, she would scrub clients down with a spray hose and loofah. They awaited this treatment with some trepidation.

As it was still early, the steam room was empty. Caro and Jade entered, discreetly saronged in large white towels, and took up opposite benches. Neither knew how to begin. Jade, besides, was acutely embarrassed at her mother's semi-nudity; it provoked unwelcome reminders of her sexuality.

They sat without speaking for several moments. Then, as though the words were wrenched from her, Caro blurted, 'What were you doing with Warren last night?'

Jade was taken by surprise. She'd been expecting an apology, an explanation at least, not this confrontation.

'Nothing,' she stammered. 'I mean . . . we had dinner.' Then, regaining her ground, 'How do you know I was with him?'

'I saw you in the jeep, in the woods. I was walking back from the station.'

Jade considered the implications of this, then said carefully, 'We were invited to a party. At the Hall. It was by chance. Really.'

Caro's face said she was doubtful. But she said nothing.

'Look, Ma,' Jade began in a more conciliatory tone, 'there's nothing between Warren and me, if that's what you're thinking. He was helping with my research. That's all.'

Caro nodded, her expression painfully exposed. 'I know,' she said, 'I have no right to ask. I have no claim on Warren. I've been a fool. I *know* all that. Believe me.'

Jade was struck with sudden compassion for her mother. It was, for her, an original feeling. She said in a low voice, 'Don't, Ma.'

'Don't what?' said Caro, seeming drained by her confession.

'Punish yourself any more. You once told me love comes in many packages.'

'Love?' said Caro. Her daughter's sympathy was confusing.

'Warren loves you.'

Now Caro focused properly on Jade. 'Does he?' she asked almost timidly.

'He told me so,' said Jade.

A look of great joy spread slowly over Caro's face. It reached her eyes last and she began to cry silently, releasing the tears she had suppressed since her exposure.

'Oh, Ma,' said Jade, exasperated. She hated it that her mother had the power, still, to move her. Dropping her towel she ran to Caro, clumsily catching her round the shoulders and pressing her head to her small pointed breasts. 'Come on. You'll live. It's just another experience.'

'Not to me,' Caro choked out. 'I feel I've destroyed so many people.'

'Ego,' said Jade bracingly. 'You flatter yourself. They'll recover.'

After a moment Caro began to laugh.

'What now?' said Jade, alert for hysteria.

'I was just thinking how odd it would look if a stranger came in now.'

'Another scandal!' giggled Jade. 'Saucy pranks in the sauna.'

With the laughter Caro's crisis receded.

Outside in the restroom Toni had thoughtfully provided a corner for smokers. Caro took a drag from Jade's cigarette and said, in a tone approaching normal, 'So how's your research going?'

'We-ell,' Jade proceeded cautiously, aware her mother was really querying Warren's involvement, 'I still haven't found out who killed Charlie, but I've eliminated a few suspects.'

'Yes?' said Caro quickly.

'If it's Warren you're worried about, I'm sure he's in the clear as far as any conspiracy goes.'

Caro breathed out and took another quick lug of the cigarette.

'It's drug related, I'm sure. The Italians are still in the frame, but then so is Viviana, or StrongFellows, or Talk TV. The trouble is, Charlie had more pies than he had fingers.'

'Yes,' agreed Caro. 'But you're convinced about Warren?'

'Absolutely,' said Jade, nodding emphatically. 'But I don't think it's fair to say any more.' Warren had sworn her to secrecy. 'You should ask him yourself.'

'If I get the chance,' said Caro dully.

'Why not?' said Jade cheerily. 'Let's face it, you've got nothing to lose now, Ma!'

It was true, of course, but only her daughter's matter-of-fact acceptance made it seem possible. Caro had often regretted Jade's over-sophistication; now it was both wise and welcome.

'How did Zo take it?' Jade did not resist asking.

'With amazing grace,' sighed Caro, 'as usual.'

Jade turned serious. 'She does love you a lot, you know. She'd do anything for you.'

'I explained it was just menopausal madness.' Caro gave an apologetic smile. 'It wasn't a lie; it's what I believe, ultimately.'

'Well, maybe,' said Jade with reservation, 'but I wouldn't undermine it.'

Toni bustled in, rolling up her sleeves. 'Right. Who's first?' She snatched the cigarette from Caro. 'It had better be you by the look of it.'

Toni gave Caro a hard massage and an even harder lecture. She posed uncomfortable questions about loyalty. Adultery. Deceit. Caro's only replies were grunts and whimpers. Toni finished with an admission that she was hurt that Caro hadn't confided in her.

'I wanted to,' said Caro lamely, 'I just couldn't bear the thought of your reaction.'

Toni gave a sharp slap to her buttock, as though to admonish her for such feebleness.

Caro spent the afternoon alone in a cinema in Stourbridge. The film reeled by with love and war and plane crashes, but Caro was oblivious of it. She was grateful only for the dark. There was much for her to think over.

TWENTY-SIX

Nothing happened for a couple of days. A pall hung over the residents of Four Trees. Each was wondering why they were still there. But the hypnotic drama held them all in suspended animation.

The food had deteriorated markedly. Delia was listless and, as the weather turned warm again, made do with cold offerings. The residents, who looked forward, sometimes with desperation, to the supper bell, became disgruntled.

Jean Plummer maintained her sulk, speaking directly to neither Caro nor Jade, but dropping many hints about their behaviour. This led to a nasty row between Jade and Deen Perry, which broke out one night at the supper table. They barely stopped short of tossing Delia's salad over each other. After that, Jade removed herself to Neil's vacated room, indicating the brief affair was over.

Miriam returned from London full of arch references to her time with Eddie Flynn. 'He's quite a supporter of the arts, you know,' she insisted by way of justification. 'Apparently that's how he knew Charlie.'

Jade privately thought there might be other reasons for the acquaintanceship and resolved to grill Miriam as soon as opportunity offered. She had no intention of giving up on her planned exposure.

Caro slept a great deal. In her conscious moments she attributed this to shock. Her unconscious ones were luridly coloured with death, loss, destruction. She was relieved when Jeremy rang one morning and asked her to supper. He sounded very depressed, but wouldn't say much on the phone except that the FBI agents were still away in London and he had no one to cook for.

Caro made an effort for the evening, knowing the couple's love of style. For days she had neglected herself, but now she bathed and waxed her legs, blow-dried her hair, making a mental note to get her roots fixed, and dressed in a summery linen suit. April was progressing mildly towards May and the days were getting pleasantly long; as she left Four Trees to walk into town, the early evening light was hopeful with blackbirds.

Blossom Cottage was candlelit. Jeremy, too, had made an effort. The table was laid in the window bay. For two only, Caro noticed.

'Darryl's in bed,' said Jeremy, offering her a gin and tonic. 'Not feeling well.' The insouciance with which he usually made such remarks was missing.

'So, my dear, how are you bearing up?' he said when they were seated in the lounge with drinks and peanuts.

'I've been sleeping,' said Caro.

'Good. Good,' nodded Jeremy. 'Best remedy. I tell Darryl . . .' Before Caro could enquire into Darryl's health, he hurried on with, 'The whole town seems bemused. The police are at a standstill.'

'Have you heard from the agents?' asked Caro.

'Not a word.'

It flicked through Caro's mind that Delia hadn't, as far as she knew, had a call from Craig either.

'Yes. Everyone's running round in circles,' Jeremy went on. 'The stress is getting to them.'

Caro settled comfortably into the velvet armchair, preparing herself for gossip.

'There've been ructions at the Admiral Nelson,' said Jeremy, warming to what he most enjoyed. 'You know of course that the landlady's an alcoholic?'

Caro didn't, but she nodded encouragingly.

'Well, with the extra trade she's had to take on lots more staff, and she's been having an affair with one of them . . . a Stourbridge man, I believe . . . anyway, he's a boozer too, and the other night they had a frightful row . . . something to do with him insulting a journalist, one wouldn't think one *could* really . . . and she threw him out. In retaliation he pitched all her window boxes through the windows. Can you imagine! Glass everywhere, punters covered with soil and geraniums.' Jeremy began to chuckle, appreciating his own anecdote. 'The police were called. He's run off. And now she's refusing to press charges.'

Caro couldn't help laughing. Jeremy's stories were so deliciously subversive.

'Oh, and there's been a terrible falling-out in the Warfleet Players.' This, at least, was normal. 'Marsha insists on a gay mystery play and Teddy wants to do a topless *Twelfth Night*. He feels, at last, they've got a cosmopolitan audience.'

'I'm not sure *any* audience would be ready for that,' remarked Caro.

'Me neither,' twinkled Jeremy. 'Laurel's appalled. She says they'll be savaged by the critics. She's got her reputation to consider. What with fund-raising . . . they're in deficit as usual . . . and running the B & B, she's had to go on Prozac.'

'Seems to be epidemic,' said Caro, glad Jeremy had steered clear of the scandal she was creating.

'The town council's having a communal collapse. They say it's inappropriate to hold the regatta under the circumstances, whereas the local traders see it as an opportunity to expand. They want to invite the Queen Mother.'

'Would she survive it?' said Caro, suffused with giggles.

'This could,' agreed Jeremy, 'be the finishing of her. Oh, and do you remember Gary?' Caro looked puzzled. 'Our resident shoplifter.'

'Oh yes,' said Caro. Until recently he had provided Sergeant Plummer with most of his business.

'Had to leave town. Can't half-inch a tea bag with all the new security cameras.'

Caro wiped her eyes; wedded as she was to the town, it was cathartic to laugh at its absurdities.

'Let's have supper,' said Jeremy, 'before my boeuf en croûte is ruined.'

Dinner was superb and they drank a bottle of excellent burgundy with it. Caro felt a mellow warmth travel up her body and with it a desire for a more frank conversation. For all his camp humour, Jeremy was a dear and trusted friend and in difficult times a good adviser.

'I've been wondering what to do,' she said. 'I seem to have caused so much damage.'

'A catalyst,' shrugged Jeremy. 'This town was an accident waiting to happen.'

'What do you mean?' said Caro.

'Poor, abandoned, ignored by the world. But take the lid off and it's full of seething passions; a perfect example of Little England.'

'Greed, crime, sudden death,' Caro murmured thoughtfully.

'Talking of death,' Jeremy lowered his voice, 'I'm terribly worried . . . about Darryl.' Caro nodded, at once understanding that Jeremy was sharing an unwonted confidence. The amusement had left his face and his hands, as he poured the last of the wine, were trembling. 'He won't admit, you see, that he's ill.' Jeremy's voice broke suddenly and he put the bottle down and covered his face with his napkin.

'Oh, Jeremy,' said Caro, reaching for his pudgy hand, 'I'm so sorry.'

Jeremy wagged his head from side to side and took a deep breath. He let the creased napkin fall and Caro saw his eyes were full of tears. 'It's a terrible strain,' he said in a choked voice. 'Pretending.'

'Mmm,' said Caro. 'I know.'

'I can't talk about it to anyone, you see. Toni's always been . . . I don't know, she's never *approved* of Darryl. She was wonderful when Guy died, of course, but she warned me then we should both get tested.'

'And you didn't?'

Jeremy's jowls quivered. 'Couldn't bear to. Didn't want to know. Now the worst has happened.'

'But,' said Caro, 'there's all sorts of new treatment. It's crazy not to go to hospital.'

Jeremy sighed. 'I know. But as I say, Darryl's in denial. Gets furious if I question his state.' His face crumpled like his napkin and tears spilled down his plump cheeks. 'I'm so afraid of being alone. And lonely.'

Caro pushed back her chair. Going round to his side of the table, she took him in her arms. He hung on to her, sobbing quietly, until at last he had exhausted himself. 'Oh dear,' he said, pushing her away slightly, 'what an exhibition. As if you didn't have enough on your plate.'

Caro offered him the napkin to dry his face.

'What else are friends for?' she said. 'You've always put up with my problems.'

'I've made a lovely pudding,' said Jeremy, covering his discomfiture with activity. He went into the kitchen and came back with a tureen of crème brûlée, saying as he put it on the table, 'This used to be Darry's favourite.'

Four Trees was empty that evening. The camera crew, having finished filming, had departed leaving a space as vacuous as their presence. Jade and Miriam had gone for a drink in the Admiral Nelson. Harold was making his weekly visit to his mother in Stourbridge. Deen, who'd hardly spoken since the row with Jade, had slammed out about his own business. The children were in bed, for once asleep, and since Delia was at home, Anthea had begged leave to go clubbing.

At a loose end, Delia wandered from room to room. She was unused to idleness, and after the recent whirl it left her feeling particularly empty. How long was it since she'd read a book, she thought, picking up one discarded by a guest. It used to be her whole life, yet she hardly seemed to miss it. Perhaps it was enough to be surrounded by artistic endeavours.

The thought of reading gave her a headache. She dropped the book on page 2 and went to find some painkillers. The bathroom cabinet had an array of stuff Anthea used for the children and, tucked away at the back, some pills Seb had been prescribed for his last illness. The writing on the packet was blurred, but Delia knew them to be effective. She popped a couple into her mouth, thinking that the cupboard needed a good clear-out, and put the rest absent-mindedly in her pocket.

Back downstairs she turned on the television, but it was some unfunny comedy show. The other channels had glum news or the blaring laughter of quiz shows. A flat misery settled on her. This was when she most missed Sebastian. She *could* do the ironing. It was usually Jean's job, but, still put out, she had been minimal in her services that week. Reluctantly Delia went into the kitchen. The door was open on to the warm night and a faint smell of early jasmine drifted in. I'll have a drink, she thought. Lord knows I deserve one. Delia was not an aficionado of alcohol, though Sebastian had always kept a generous cellar. She went down and searched out a bottle, the dustiness of which proclaimed its decency, and poured herself a defiant tumbler. Then she put on the radio . . . a Russian drama was running its stilted course . . . and hoiked out the ironing board.

Connex South Central had axed many of the late trains to Warfleet. No demand, they said. Craig O'Connell caught the last one by the skin of his teeth and stood at the sash window of his compartment for some time, recovering from his race down the platform. He passed the rest of the journey calmly enough, mulling over his progress in the capital and reading the evening paper. He had followed events in Warfleet closely, and scanned the paper swiftly for further developments. A small paragraph on page 5 told him the police were still awaiting a ballistic report. In the absence of any hard news, the case had lost some of its profile.

Darkness had fallen by the time the train drew into Warfleet and the station was deserted. Craig, carrying his small holdall, strode out towards Four Trees. He took the most obvious route through the town, slowing for a moment outside the Admiral Nelson. The revolving door spat fluorescence and Britpop on to the pavement and Craig decided against it. The high street was lively with wandering groups, the cafés loud and jostly. Craig quickened his pace, eager for restful Four Tress.

Only Delia's car was parked in the drive. The front door was bolted. Detecting a glow towards the back of the house, Craig skirted the shrubbery and opened the side gate which led to the kitchen. The back door stood open, letting in a buzz of moths attracted to the lamp on the table. Its light fell on an empty wine bottle and a scattering of pills. An ironing board stood in the middle of the floor and there was a distinct smell of scorching. It took Craig a moment to realize that the room was not empty. In the dim light he stumbled across a pair of feet, and saw, spread between the table and the Aga, Delia's unconscious body.

'I wasn't trying anything,' protested Delia feebly. 'It was just a mistake.'

'Drink,' ordered Craig, putting a mug of coffee to her lips. Delia was sitting on the edge of the bath, a towel held to her chin. There was a bloody gash on her forehead. She did as she was bid, but immediately slid to her knees again and thrust her head down the lavatory. Craig held her while she retched until, at last, only dry heaves shook her body.

He left her slumped against the bath and went to search out a blanket. 'Big chest. Landing,' she called weakly as she heard him opening and shutting doors. He returned with the duvet from his own bed, which he wrapped quickly round her.

'Can you stand?' he said, and she nodded. He helped her

up and circled her with his arm, leaning her into his shoulder so he could support her weight; then together they moved shakily down the passage. Craig steered her into her own room, in which he had been sleeping. She protested as he eased her carefully on to the bed.

'No. This is your room. I'm all right, really.'

'Hush,' he said firmly. He took off her shoes and, unwinding the duvet, began to undo her clothing. Delia lay, unable to remonstrate further, and let him slip off her skirt and jumper. His movements were assured and she had no sense of immodesty. It was as though he were a priest, or a doctor. Craig pulled back the sheets and lifted her effortlessly between them. Then he drew up the duvet and, because she was still trembling, slid under it beside her.

When Delia came down to the kitchen, rather late, the next morning, there was a large plaster on her forehead. The residents had by now all dribbled in and were sitting, nonplussed, at the table as Craig cooked a hearty Texan breakfast. He had already told them that Delia was indisposed, having fallen the previous evening and hit her head on the Aga. 'A little concussion and a tear. No stitches required,' he said cheerfully as he tossed pancakes with the aplomb of a professional. Privately he told Caro, the first down, that drink and drugs were involved. 'Silly girl,' he said, shaking his head reproachfully at Caro, who immediately felt guilty of neglect. 'She took some painkillers with which you absolutely should not drink, then polished off an entire bottle. It was lucky the iron didn't set fire to the place. I arrived in the nick of time.'

Again, thought Caro. If this man planned to be hero he certainly had immaculate timing.

Delia sat and drank coffee, her pale face with its pink plastic strip and purple bruising a matter of concern for the residents. They, not she, were allowed accidents, turns, vapours. This was a faith-shattering reversal; the Aga Goddess felled by her own totem. Delia said very little, allowing Craig to fill her plate and pour maple syrup over her pancake. Occasionally she rewarded his solicitude with a shy smile. Caro, watching covertly, knew they had slept together. The looks and touches implied a new understanding. She was filled with envy. They at least could conduct their affair without fear of calumny.

TWENTY-SEVEN

Dear Warren,

This is a hard letter to write. Partly because I don't know what I'm really saying. Jean has mentioned that Bill is coming out of hospital and she feels you must leave Cherry Tree Walk. Do you know where you are going? I don't ask idly; I feel . . . responsible. If there is anything I can do to help, please let me know.

Your friend (I hope) Caro.

The letter sat on Caro's desk for a full twenty-four hours. It was Jade, finally, who persuaded her to send it. 'Go for it, Ma. Could be your last chance.' Caro was unsure whether she meant last chance with Warren, or last chance in life. But Jade's attitude to the relationship had certainly undergone a revolution.

She posted the letter, thinking Jean would be affronted if she delivered it in person, and for a further twenty-four hours was on tenterhooks, wishing she hadn't sent it. His phone call, asking her to have lunch at the oyster bar, set her heart thudding, but provoked instant withdrawal. 'Oh . . . I don't know,' she fluttered. 'It's very public.'

'Fuck 'em,' said Warren briefly. As if to give weight to his attitude, Caro was cut dead by Laurel Hopcraft, who was shopping in the newly sprung-up street market.

The oyster bar was packed. Prices she noticed had doubled. Most of the clientele were strangers, but any apprehension she felt was dispelled by the sight of Warren. He sat on a high stool at the bar, looking moodily beautiful. His hair, still wet from the shower, was neatly ponytailed; he wore a crisp cotton shirt over clean blue jeans and turned a champagne flute in his long fingers. Caro slid on to the stool beside him, pleased she had put on a flattering silk suit and make-up. For a moment they looked at each other, neither of them speaking. Warren broke first, his face crinkling into a mischievous grin.

'Well?' he said. 'Any knives out on the way here?'

Caro said, 'Laurel Hopcraft. She was bartering over a hand of bananas and when she saw me she practically swallowed them.' They laughed, each appraising the state of the other; finding it to be less extreme than in their nightmares.

'Drink?' offered Warren, indicating the champagne.

'Why not?' said Caro, almost blithely. He poured a glass and toasted her with his eyes, today the colour of the sea outside and reflecting the sparkle of sunshine. 'Doesn't it seem for ever since we were last in here?' said Caro. It was over a week since they had made love and she wanted him terribly.

Warren nodded. 'Amazing how much you can cram into a month.' He held her in a long look, which cut out the world around them.

'So,' Caro passed her tongue over her dry lips, 'what are your plans?'

Warren said, 'I'm going to get a flat in Stourbridge for a while.'

'Have you got any money?' Caro realized she had no idea of his financial arrangements.

'A bit,' shrugged Warren. 'Nobody's stopped my salary.'

Annabel was still hoping then that he'd go back. Or perhaps Viviana held the purse strings.

Warren said slowly, measuring each word,'Why don't you come with me?'

'Where?' said Caro stupidly.

'To Stourbridge, of course.'

'You mean . . . live with . . .' Caro's breath deserted her before she could finish the sentence.

'We're both consenting adults,' said Warren. His voice was light but his eyes were still fixed on her intently. His arm was just inches away from Caro's; the scent that came from his skin made her feel light-headed. She sipped at the glass of champagne, giving herself time to think. But she knew there was only one answer.

They found a room in a big, plain house not far from the city centre. It wasn't romantic but it was functional. The other inhabitants, judging by the occasional swirl of spliff and pound of techno, were students. Warren paid a month's rent in advance; optimistic, thought Caro.

The moment they surveyed the L-shaped room with its haphazard furniture, their eyes were drawn to the bed. Until then they had barely touched. Each slight brush with each other . . . in the jeep, at the letting agency, on the stairs . . . had been the occasion of exquisite anticipation. Now, Warren took Caro's hand and led her gently towards the bowed double. He sat her on the edge of it and knelt at her feet, burying his face in her lap. She put her hands to his head, drawing off the band on his hair and let her fingers luxuriate in his freed locks. They were held in a silent ecstasy, feeling the quickened beat of each other's body. Warren began to kiss Caro's thighs through the thin silk of her skirt. The heat of his lips penetrated to her skin and she pulled his head closer, wanting him to burn her. He ruched up the shivery silk and let his tongue travel the flesh, pulling aside her pants so he could slide in his fingers. Now she moaned out loud, grateful for the anonymous music from the other rooms. 'No. No,' she begged. 'Not fingers. I want you, all of you, inside me.' Warren reached for his belt and with one hand released the buckle. Then he stood so Caro could see his full magnificence and slowly let himself down upon her. She sighed under his weight and they were still for a moment. Then her hands urged him on, seeking and guiding until she had every bit of him deep inside her body.

Agents Benson and Hedges stood on each side of the desk in Detective Superintendent Cooper's office. Though the day was warm, they were formally garbed, having returned that morning from London. Detective Superintendent Cooper felt disadvantaged in his shirtsleeves.

'Well, Bob,' said Frank agreeably. 'That's how it is.'

Laurie nodded to reinforce the impression that although their views were mildly expressed, they were uncompromising.

Bob Cooper stood, in an attempt to wrest back some status, and said testily, 'But where's the evidence? We can't just arrest a man on the say-so of some psychic.'

'Well now, Bob, it's a little more than that,' said Frank, steel entering his tone. Laurie nodded again, more forcefully.

'You haven't any proof at all, let alone a weapon.'

'We feel he's close to cracking. That's our information.'

The detective superintendent placed his hands on the desk and leaned forward. This was, to say the least, an awkward situation. Ballistics hadn't got a result; none of the guns matched the bullet. They held Carl and Sidney for illegal possession of weapons but not, it seemed, for murder, and the pair had point-blank refused to implicate others, terror fleeing across their faces at the mere suggestion. His force had turned up no other real leads, despite assiduous cross-referencing (twice he'd had to reprimand Armitage for playing Formula One video games on the compulsive computers).

He already had one over-hasty arrest behind him and now these two ... *interlopers* ... sauntered in and demanded he make another. On the other hand, press disquiet was mounting, his superiors had been on the blower ... something must be seen to be done, or he would be a laughing stock.

'Where is the suspect?' he demanded, changing his tack.

Frank put a slip of paper on the desk. 'This is the address. We advise instant action.'

Laurie, as if to stress the necessity for speed, said, 'He does have powerful connections.'

TWENTY-EIGHT

When Caro looked back on the days and nights she spent with Warren, she saw it as an idyll, a honeymoon, removed from any reality.

They ventured out rarely, blinking in the light. In a few days it had turned into summer. They pottered in the nearby market, buying lovers' delicacies. Smoked salmon, they decided, was the food of love and they picnicked on it with candles and wine. They bought touching gifts for each other, favourite tapes and CDs. They chose cheap Indian throws and cushions for their garret then, overcome with the need to make love, hurried back to it. The ugly room had become paradise; every crack in the walls, every patch in the carpet, made magical by their passion.

It couldn't last, of course, but none the less Caro's heart almost stopped when she went out for supplies one sunny afternoon and saw agents Benson and Hedges loitering in the market. They smiled and nodded hello to her, but she saw only serpents' heads beneath their golf caps. Mechanical with shock, she hurried back to warn Warren. There was a note saying he had gone to see his children. She threw down the shopping (how pathetic the pasta and salad seemed now) and paced the worn carpet in agony. She had forgotten the children. Forgotten Annabel, the pregnancy, the agents, the crime. Everything, in fact, but their life in this room.

In his absence all her doubts about Warren came hurtling back. Why had she not done as Jade suggested and insisted on the truth ... was it because she feared it? She hurried to the window to check if the house was being watched. The sun-dappled street was empty.

By the time Warren returned, bearing flowers, that evening, she was huddled in the middle of the floor, convinced he was a murderer and, worse still, that he'd left her.

'Caro, my love,' he said, squatting beside her. She turned to him, exhausted, unable to speak, and thrust her head into his shoulder. He rocked her, making soothing sounds, explaining. Annabel had called on his mobile; the children, she said, were missing him. He had taken them swimming and to buy some shoes. It all sounded so normal.

'I saw the FBI agents outside today,' Caro managed to croak. 'You've got to tell me everything.'

Warren pulled away and looked at her searchingly. 'You still believe I had a hand in it.' His hurt expression tore at her heart, but she could not stop now.

'No ... I don't know. It's something to do with your old involvement with Carl.'

Warren dropped his arms and stood up. He crossed to the table and opened the bottle of wine Caro had bought to grace their intimate supper.

'You're right,' he said, as he poured two glasses. 'I suppose I wanted to ... save you. I know how much you love Warfleet.'

'I'd rather know the truth,' insisted Caro, 'than keep my innocence.'

Warren took the wine glasses to the sofa and offered one to Caro. She crawled across and sat at his feet, sipping.

'The truth is the Italians have been drug-running ever since they came to Warfleet.'

Caro started at his bluntness and Warren patted her head sympathetically.

'I know, I know, but you've got to understand. Half of Warfleet's been off its face for ever.'

This was hardly extraordinary, Caro knew, in a depressed seaside town, but still . . .

'What about Carl?'

'He used to score from them. Then he got into dealing. One thing led to another and soon it became big business.'

'And you?'

'I bought from them . . . who didn't?'

'But the dealing?' pressed Caro, her thoughts flying back to their first conversation. How long ago that beach walk seemed.

'I've always resisted. But, as you say, Carl and Sidney are my mates from way back . . . it's difficult.'

Caro nodded. It was as she had thought. Blood-brother loyalties.

'Besides,' continued Warren, 'I don't agree with the law on dope. And I've never been one to toe the line with authority' – he gave a rueful grin – 'as you well know . . .'

He caressed Caro's hand, as though asking for her forgiveness.

'I soon realized the boys were using the club as an outlet. I turned a blind eye till I found the guns.'

'The guns were at the club?' exclaimed Caro.

'Crates of them. In the cellar. They'd used it before, once

or twice, but this shipment seemed odd. The boxes were so much bigger and heavier. I got suspicious. A bit of dealing's one thing but I wasn't having the club used as a dumping ground. I opened one of the boxes.'

Caro pictured the scene, the frightening discovery in the dark, dank cellar.

'Carl and Sidney were horrified. They'd been told it was tobacco.'

'They'd been used,' said Caro. 'You all were.'

Warren nodded. 'Fucking right. I went ballistic – no pun intended – I called them everything from a pig to a cow for being so bloody stupid.'

'What did you do?'

'Shifted the whole lot to Sid's hut. I wasn't having them on the premises.'

Hence the fingerprints, thought Caro.

'I told them, that was that. Finito.'

'God,' breathed Caro. Her heart was racing as though she herself had been present.

'My punishment was a tip-off to the drug squad.'

'By the Martinis?'

Warren nodded. 'That's how the club got busted. The Range Rover mob are in their pocket. Have been since day one.'

Caro's eyes widened.

'Don't look so shocked.' Warren almost laughed. 'It's normal practice. The Martinis have stuff on them, they have stuff on the Martinis. They bust me as a favour . . . looks good for them too. Collar the small fry now and then, less suspicious.'

Caro took a gulp of wine, struggling to grasp this arcane, underworld balance.

'The message was clear: play ball or face ruin. The Martinis knew the estate was in difficulties – I'd had to borrow money from them to open the club – and they had big plans for the future.'

'That's what you meant when you said they had their toe in the door.' Then, leaping ahead, 'They must have got an awful shock when Viviana brought in Charlie.'

'They were fucking furious.' Now Warren was chuckling. 'They thought I'd put her up to it.'

'Did you?' said Caro, thinking pillow talk.

'As if. I was as pissed off as them.'

'Did the Martinis have Charlie killed?' Caro could still not dismiss the memory of Warren's posse huddled in the Admiral Nelson.

'They certainly stood to benefit. With Charlie gone Viviana's dream crashed. She wanted me to negotiate the Italians in . . . by then she'd worked out what they were up to.'

'Why didn't she do it herself, then?'

'Doesn't like them. Wanted to keep out of it.'

'Wanted to keep you in it, you mean.'

Warren shrugged. 'I refused anyway. In fact I said if she went ahead, I'd expose their entire activities.' He paused. 'Whatever you think . . . I do draw lines. I wouldn't want to see Warfleet as a centre for arms dealing.'

The idea seemed absurd. Yet Caro could now see there was every possibility.

'That was brave,' she said, honouring Warren's stand.

He waved aside the compliment. 'Largely bluff. I traded on the hope she wouldn't want me dead.'

While she might still have you in bed, thought Caro.

'She nearly blew the whole thing when she shopped me to

my stepdad. Poor old Bill.' Warren shook his head wonderingly, 'But that's Viviana.'

Caro mirrored his action. She could barely comprehend the wickedness of it all. Despite herself, she was shocked.

'The Italians are definitely taking over. Viviana's done the deal. Annabel told me.' His face was woeful.

'Oh, Warren, I'm so sorry.' Caro put an arm round his knees and hugged them tightly.

'I must seem very weak to you,' he said in a small voice.

'No.' Caro looked up at him. 'A little ... gullible, perhaps.' It was only too clear how it had happened. 'Overloyal to the wrong people.'

'Arseholes.' Warren looked close to tears. 'Like Jade used to point out, I'm just not clever.'

'Don't say that.' Caro was fierce, thinking of their confidences over the past few days; Warren's face inspired as he'd talked of his ambitions for Tolleymarsh and the town. He was loving. Giving. Perhaps too much so. She was guiltily aware that she too had benefited. 'Is it too late to go to the police?'

Warren turned his head away. 'I won't put people I love in danger.' He paused. 'Believe me, the Martinis'll stop at nothing. Anyway, don't forget, I'm still a prime suspect.'

The bland smiles of the agents rose before Caro. Perhaps, even now, they were outside, waiting, watching. She scrambled on to the sofa and gathered Warren into her arms. 'Oh, Warren, what shall we do?'

His answer was to kiss her.

Afterwards they lay side by side and shared a cigarette. The smoke hung peacefully on the sepia candlelight, but everything had changed. The real world had crashed in, ending for ever their idyll.

TWENTY-NINE

Things returned to some semblance of normality at Four Trees. Jean rallied; fortunately she knew nothing of Warren and Caro's love nest. Only Delia and Jade were party to that information. The residents were persuaded to do their own washing and even take turns with the shopping, and Craig, an excellent cook, put himself in charge of the kitchen.

Of course it wasn't normal that Delia kept to her room except when persuaded by Craig to a lounger in the sun-warmed conservatory or summoned for one of his dinners. Nor was it normal for the guests to see a man presiding over the Aga, though his enthusiastic experiments partially won them over. When he was absent Delia spent time with her children; they, at least, benefited from the change in their mother's habits.

Jade, however, was deeply frustrated. Partly it was Deen's continuing presence – couldn't he see it was vulgar to remain? – and partly the lack of progress in her investigations. After all Warren had told her, she was more certain than ever of the Martinis' and Viviana's guilt. But there seemed no more leads to follow.

In her enforced idleness she kicked about her childhood garden, discontented with what her life had become. A rare, introspective depression descended. Briar called several times demanding her return, and even Jed had left a message. She didn't respond. She had no intention of returning to London with the mystery unsolved. She longed to contact Warren, but felt, with unusual consideration, that he and her mother deserved their privacy.

Her conversation with Miriam, though entertaining, yielded only that Eddie Flynn knew Charlie as a player in the arts. Since finishing his sentence and writing his book about the drug trade, Eddie had been very busy on the arty-party circuit.

Miriam turned interestingly pink when talking about him. 'He's a terrible flirt,' she said, 'charm the birds off the trees.' The girly tone she adopted sounded more like a budgerigar. 'Knocks about with girls half his age.'

Jade got the impression Miriam regretted having let Eddie breach her usual professional defences.

'Of course he's got loads of money,' said Miriam, sounding envious; an arts presenter's salary wasn't what it used to be. 'He's using it philanthropically, he says, backing the arts and so on. Feels a need to atone, apparently.'

Jade pulled a disbelieving face and tossed off her gin and tonic. 'Atone for what? Helping people get high? Doesn't exactly make him the devil.' Miriam's expression turned disapprovingly prim and Jade could not resist adding, 'Oh, come on, Miriam. The TV industry would collapse without coke. Bet you know people on it.'

Miriam clammed up after that, either resenting the implication or aware she had given herself away over Eddie. Jade was left hungry for hard facts. Eddie's connection to Charlie, she was certain, pre-dated their emergence as benefactors.

At least Jean Plummer seemed to have forgiven her. Revelling in a crisis, Jean was back on course at Four Trees and as full of prattle as ever. 'Bill's a lot better, but he's got to take it easy. I tell him now's the time to retire, but he won't hear of it. Feels it would be a disgrace because of Warren.'

'Bit unfair on Warren,' said Jade, struggling with a pillow case; she was helping Jean 'do' the bedrooms, for Jade an arcane experience, 'to make him guilty by association. It's Carl and Sidney who work for the Italians.'

Jean clicked her teeth. 'Those bloody Martinis. You'll never believe what they've gone and done now. Only applied for lottery money!'

'For the Millennium Park?' said Jade. The news that a deal had been struck had circled the town within instants.

'They've got Scott Harvey-Dickson on their side. He's in that what d'you call it Ministry?'

'Culture?' said Jade.

Jean nodded. 'That's it. He's been involved with the brothers for years.'

'How?' said Jade, distant bells beginning to chime. Dust arose from the mattress Jean was pounding as though it was Scott Harvey-Dickson's head. 'Backed their takeovers ... helped with planning permission ... got them licences through the Masonic ... they'd never be where they are today without him. Of course he used to be a Tory.' Jean delivered this last remark as though it explained everything.

This was curious news to Jade. She had never considered a link between the local MP and the Martinis. 'Does he have shares in their business?' she asked, wondering if he had declared them on the members' register.

'Wouldn't be surprised.' Jean tittered. 'He eats at Pasta Palace often enough.' She went to the airing cupboard to find duvet covers. 'I've got to hurry this morning,' she said, 'I've promised to rehearse for the May Day pageant.'

'May Day?' said Jade, who had forgotten the season of revelry was almost upon them.

'They've lost the back end of the hobby horse,' said Jean. 'I promised I'd take over.'

'Oh . . . the pageant,' said Jade, rumours coming back to her.

'It's going to be big this year,' said Jean. 'The committee got an unexpected contribution. Course Laurel Hopcraft nabbed most of it for the Warfleet Players, but there's the parade, and bladder football – Teddy Forbes wants to do a tour bus of the murder site, but some of the committee think that's a bit tasteless – morris men, and in the evening dancing round the maypole.' She checked her watch. 'Oh lor', I said I'd be at the Seafarers by eleven.' The Seafarers' Centre, a large Gothic hall downtown, had once been a mission; there the Warfleet Players were rehearsing their rites of spring offering.

'I'll finish up,' said Jade stoically. She wanted time to adjust to the new information.

Jean chucked a pile of linen on the bed. 'That's Deen's and Delia's, you'll have to go to the other cupboard for yours. I've got that behind with the ironing.' She scurried to the bathroom to put on some lipstick. Even the back end of the hobby horse had its pride.

Jade left Deen's pile of linen outside his door. Serve him right if he had to wrestle with his own duvet. Delia's room was empty. She had taken Alex for a stroll along the seafront. Jade stripped the bed, observing the tell-tale stains and a man's sock beneath it. Craig and Delia had been reasonably discreet about their relationship, though it was clear to the residents what was happening, but perhaps it was just as well that Jean had been saved from more disturbing discoveries.

The emergency linen cupboard was at the far end of the

hall, beyond the bedrooms. It was little used as it housed only the non-matching sheets and random pillow cases Delia's thrifty nature could not bear to discard. Jade threw open the doors and breathed in the scent of slightly musty linen overlaid with Delia's home-dried lavender. She foraged through the pile, breaking out in a fine sweat in the mild morning air. This was normally the sort of job she paid other people to do; tottering beneath the pile of tea towels which flung itself on her head, she wondered how they managed. She had to reach into the dark recesses for a duvet cover, and as she pulled one clear something fell clanking to the bottom of the cupboard. Clicking her teeth, Jade bent to pick it up. On the boards, between accumulated flannels and hot-water bottles, something gleamed dully. Jade drew back her hand before she touched it; nestling in a pile of innocent linen fluff was the snub, metallic shape of a .38 revolver.

A short time later, Jade made an unannounced visit to Tolleymarsh Hall. She was glad, now, that Warren wasn't around, for he would certainly have stopped her. Nothing but wild instinct drove her. She was certain she had in her possession the murder weapon and equally certain that she could blackmail Viviana with it. The thought of solving the crime filled her with ambitious glee. She could almost taste the triumph. Besides, she loved to live dangerously.

The Hall was quiet and peaceful in the morning sun; like a child's jigsaw puzzle or biscuit tin lid, the picture of English heritage, with the newly leafed trees and lilac blossom. Jade didn't approach the front door, however, but, bent double, skirted through the lilac bushes to the entrance at the back she had taken with Warren. She had to stifle some nervous laughter, particularly when her heel got stuck in some newly piled compost; the whole exercise was so cloak and dagger, she felt like the Scarlet Pimpernel.

She found the door easily enough and to her surprise it wasn't locked. She crept in and flattened herself to the wall; this scene she had witnessed many times on the screen. There was no sound, except a distant radio playing *Woman's Hour*, perhaps in the kitchen. Emboldened, she moved out into the passage. This time she took the stairs going up instead of down and wound her way, as soundlessly as possible, to the first floor. The stairs finished at a small door which opened on to a corridor, panelled and shiny with polish, off which was a set of larger, more ornate doors. These, Jade was certain, were the bedrooms.

Keeping to the walls, she crept along the passage, past the wide main staircase with its spiral view down into the hall. Every tiny sound made her freeze, but the fear of discovery was also exciting. She listened outside every door and by the third one had become blasé enough to actually dare to open it. She peered through the slim chink into what she immediately realized was Viviana's bedroom. It was partly the colour scheme, gold and white, and partly the waves of overpowering perfume. The bed was Empress-sized and, with its flowing silks and encrustations of pearls, reminded her of an elephant's howdah. Though for a lady of Viviana's leisure it was still early, Viviana was not in it; only the shih-tzu snoozed, snuffling, among the lace pillows. Moments later, as Jade stood, rooted with fascination, she heard Viviana's voice. She entered the room from what must be the en suite bathroom – the tiny strip Jade could see was also white and gold – talking on her mobile telephone. Jade heard her say, '*Madre Dio!* Get off my backside! Of course I am careful!'

She made several more peremptory grunts, then snapped off the caller.

Jade edged the door open a fraction more, as Viviana moved out of view. Now she could see her standing in the bay which looked down over acres of manicured lawn. The breeze that entered through the open window lifted her frothy negligée and wound it delicately through her legs, giving a slithery, cling-filmed effect. The outline beneath wasn't bad, conceded Jade, if aided a little here and there by surgery. As if to prove this theory, Viviana plunged her hands into her topknot of preposterous curls and flung the whole piece to the dressing table, where the blond tresses unravelled like malevolent entrails. Without the foaming hair, Viviana's head seemed stranded and vulnerable.

This, Jade decided, was the moment to pounce. She pushed open the door with her foot and swung round it in a movement reminiscent of episodes of *NYPD Blue*, holding the gun in a two-handed grip and pointing it at Viviana. The perfection of her action was slightly marred by Viviana's obliviousness of it. Jade had to cough to get her attention.

'Mees Radcleeffe,' she hissed, when she finally turned and focused on Jade, 'do you theenk you are een a movie?'

Jade was, in fact, now completely embroiled in a Hollywood fantasy, but she brazened it out, saying in a tough tone, 'I've come for the truth. Don't move, Viviana.'

Viviana took her at her word, her only move being to pucker her face into a pout. 'Thees ees reedeeculous.'

Jade, who was aware that Jean Plummer's rubber gloves, snatched up in haste, did not exactly enhance her credibility, dropped her hands slightly.

Viviana sat down on a flouncy tuffet of stool. She looked

suddenly much older, small and defenceless. Her shoulders hunched forward and shook slightly. Jade felt almost sorry for her, but went on remorselessly, 'I know all about you and the Martini brothers, so unless you want me to go to the police you'd better tell me the real Charlie story.'

The fight seemed to have gone out of Viviana. She gazed vacantly at the white shag-pile beneath her high-heeled mules and said in a heavy voice, 'What do I care?'

'Don't mess with me,' said Jade, through theatrically clenched teeth. 'This gun is loaded. And I happen to know it's the murder weapon.' This was a lie, but Jade felt it was justified as it seemed entirely likely.

Viviana showed a flicker of interest. 'How do you have eet?'

'Never you mind. Let's just say if you don't talk, I'll turn it in as evidence.'

Viviana shrugged, seeming unmoved by the threat, but said in a drearily resigned tone, 'Where shall I beegeen?'

'How about with the laundering of money?' said Jade. She let the gun drop to her side; her arms were beginning to ache in the unnaturally stretched position.

Viviana pulled her flimsy negligée closer, as if early memories were chilling. 'Hong Kong. In the back of hees father's store. Leeterally washeeng yen notes . . . eef they were clean, they commanded a higher exchange rate.'

The picture of Charlie stooped over a soapy bucket tickled Jade, and she gave an involuntary snort. Viviana seemed not to notice and went on, 'He first went to Colombia when he was quite young, trouble shooteeng for JP, the beeg multee-national. He already had a yen fortune; he was a wheez keed. He got eenvolved, I don't know how, with the main cartel.'

'Drugs?' said Jade.

Viviana raised her eyebrows, thin without their pencil embellishment, as if to enquire if there was a cartel of any other kind. 'Eemport-export. Charlee's share went eento offshore accounts, friendly banks ... the Vatican ees good ... and was used to back hees beezneesses.'

'So, the money went into his enterprises and came out clean.' StrongFellows, Talk TV, and all the rest, she thought, were just so many buckets of soapy water. 'And you thought you'd get him to do the Tolleymarsh dirty washing?'

'Why not?' Viviana gave a small shrug. 'I could not stop Charlee, even eef I wanted. Why not put the money to a good cause? Eet ees better for people to have jobs. Enough to eat. No? I thought I could help.' Viviana went on, looking surprisingly humble, 'Een Colombia eet ees normal for drug barons to help the poor. They build schools, roads, houses. Breeng prospereetee. Warfleet ees poor. I thought we could do the same.'

She really does see herself, thought Jade, as some sort of Evita. 'The end justifies the means?' she snorted.

'Eet was not all my idea,' Viviana continued, as though wanting to shift the blame. 'Eet was Scott Harvey-Dickson's.'

'What?' said Jade. This was an unexpected twist.

'Of course,' said Viviana, gaining confidence. 'Charlee had geeven much money to the New Labour partee. Hee was about to be made a peer, you know.'

Jade did not know. This opened a whole new aspect of the intrigue.

'Scott wanted to get work, trade, for hees consteetuencee. He knew I was a friend of Charlee ... he suggested we get heem to eenvest here. *He* suggested the millennium project.'

'Very New Labour,' said Jade disparagingly.

'Theez theengs are eemportant. They should be marked,' said Viviana, with an almost evangelical fervour.

Yes, Jade supposed, with the background she and Charlie had had, you would need a lasting monument. Perhaps Viviana imagined a statue of herself in the ersatz millennium square, to which people would come to worship. Well, however the plan had backfired, the town was certainly enjoying a novel prosperity.

'But then the Italians got jealous and killed him?'

Viviana looked doubtful. 'Maybe. He went to the Pasta Palace that night—'

'He went to the Pasta Palace?'

'After we had deenner here. He told me he had a meeteeng weeth Scott and the Martinis. You know they said hees last meal was spaghettee?' She smiled indulgently. 'Charlee was very greedee.'

Jade, breathing fast with excitement, said, 'So the last person he saw was Scott?'

'I do not know eef he was the last—'

'Maybe they all conspired to kill him?'

'Why would they?' said Viviana. 'They wanted to join een. The meeteeng was to put themselves forward as partners.'

Perhaps, thought Jade, Charlie had resisted; a turf war would have offered a motive. 'You could just have got the Martinis in the first place,' she said.

'They deed not have the profile,' said Viviana, drawing herself up haughtily. 'Nor,' she added with a hint of contempt, 'the monee. They theenk they can walk een Charlee's shoes. They are not beeg enough.'

Clearly there was no love lost there, thought Jade. Viviana obviously resented her need for the common Italians.

'But you didn't,' she pursued, 'tell the police about this meeting?'

'No,' said Viviana. 'Scott asked me not to.'

Of course, thought Jade, if Scott knew the truth about the brothers' nefarious 'business', he would want to keep the authorities as far away as possible from any dealings he had with the Martinis. Viviana, in the grip of powerful men, presumably did as she was bid when her own financial future was at stake. And perhaps she was telling the truth. Jade suspected she was told things only on a 'need-to-know' basis.

Viviana cast a sly look at her. 'Eef you want to know who killed Charlee, I theenk eet was a drug dealer. You have heard of Eddee Flynn?'

'Eddie Flynn?' Jade's heart began to beat faster. Her intuition was right, then. 'What makes you think that?'

Viviana played with the frill on her peignoir. 'They have an old feud from Colombia. Eddee worked for the same cartel. Charlee became suspeecious of heem . . . I don't know why . . . and alerted the authorities. Eddee was arrested. He served ten years. You would want revenge, no?'

Judging by her behaviour over Warren, thought Jade, it was certainly high on Viviana's agenda. Perhaps, though, this was a red herring, thrown in by Viviana to deflect her. There was still no explanation of how the gun came to be between the sheets at Four Trees. Until that moment, engrossed in the unwinding of the tale, Jade had forgotten the gun. It dangled from her fingers, pointing harmlessly at the carpet. She quickly raised it again while she considered her next move. There was the sound of a creaking board outside.

'That will be Henree,' said Viviana, her face assuming an expression of distaste. 'He always comes een at thees time.'

Jade looked swiftly around for somewhere to hide. She didn't want to be responsible for delivering the *coup de grâce* on the ailing Henry.

Viviana pointed to a door by the bathroom, and as distinct footsteps became audible Jade made a dive for it. She found herself in a dressing room stuffed with clothes and shoes, and just had time to pull the door closed before the footsteps entered the bedroom. She pushed silently through the forest of coats and frocks and squatted at the back, assaulted by beads and tulle and the suffocating smell of Viviana's chosen perfume, Poison.

She could hear the man's voice, and then Viviana's. But the clothes deadened the sound and she could not make out what they were saying. It was hard to breathe, and she hoped desperately they were not about to engage in conjugal passion. She held the gun upright, pointed at the door, just in case of discovery.

After a few moments a silence fell. Jade tensed. The gun in her hand was shaking, the pink rubber glove trembling like blancmange, and she shifted her position to support it better. At that moment the cupboard door was flung back and through the dangling designer hems Jade could see a man's shoes and trousers. It was surely not Henry. He would never be wearing trainers and jogging bottoms.

An eternity seemed to pass as Jade's whole body went into silent seizure. Then a man's face appeared through the fabric on a level with her own. Jade recognized it, although she had never seen such ruthless flintiness on its normally benign features. The man held out his hand for the gun. 'I'll take that now, Miss Radcliffe.'

Mesmerized, Jade relinquished the weapon into the large hand of Craig O'Connell.

THIRTY

'An arrest has been made by the Stourbridge constabulary in a massive undercover operation. The suspect wanted for questioning in the Charlie Fong murder case was last night returned to Warfleet.'

So said the bold black of the *Warfleet Chronicle* to the sleepy-eyed dwellers over their morning coffee. The town was quickly on red alert with conflicting theories, paper boys, delivery vans, cars and school buses carrying the news and views to the furthest branches of its nervous system.

Those involved in the May Day rehearsals at the Seafarers' Centre could hardly bear to drop speculation and begin rehearsal.

'Warren Peabody,' said Teddy Forbes, struggling into heels as high as stilts for his Hades. 'They should never have let him out of custody.'

Jean Plummer had yet to arrive and her lateness caused comment. Marsha Snelgrove, playing Persephone, Goddess of Spring, was on her second bun. She shook her head, spitting currants over the table. 'I heard it was someone from London.'

Sonny Delgardo, mending last year's Source costume, a waterfall of unsubtly blended aquas, opined that she couldn't see anyone in Warfleet having the imagination.

'Speak for yourself, dear,' snapped Teddy. His costume, now paraded in front of the mirror, certainly showed no lack of it.

May, on her knees, was pinning Ashley into the jester's many-coloured motley. 'Jeremy says the FBI definitely found the suspect,' said Ashley, wriggling in his playing card diamonds.

May coughed. 'Keep still, Ashley,' she said crossly. 'You nearly made me swallow a pin.'

'Sorry,' said Ashley. 'It's scratchy.'

Teddy pulled on a feathered bonnet. 'Rumer would know, of course. She gave them the vital clues.'

'Did she?' said Peggy Bacon, who'd come in with a case load of footwear.

'Oh, yes' supported Marsha, reaching for a chocolate biscuit. 'They got on to the trail after she did them a tarot reading.'

A hush fell as Rumer herself entered. She was taking the part of Demeter, Queen of the Earth, and processed through the hall as if already in character. The Players looked at her expectantly but, cloaked in an air of regal mystery, Rumer was saying nothing.

Laurel Hopcraft came out of the loo, dragging on the last of her Gauloise. 'Ah, Rumer,' she croaked. 'Now we can begin. Places, everybody.' Laurel took her role as director very seriously; the pageant was only days away and the show must go on regardless.

Detective Superintendent Cooper stared at the prisoner on the other side of the table in the interview room. DI Malton stood at a respectful distance. A tape recorder on the table was running. Neil Kenton was huddled in the steel-framed chair, clinging to its sides as if he were drowning. Tears had blotched his face and soaked into his shirt collar. He could hardly speak for the convulsions in his throat, let alone make a statement. He had put up no resistance to arrest; on the contrary, he had seemed relieved. Yet no murder weapon had been found on his premises, a trendy mews conversion in Notting Hill Gate, and they had yet to get a confession. Any minute now Neil's lawyer would arrive and they could kiss goodbye to a result. Detective Superintendent Cooper had no intention of letting that happen. 'Now then, Neil,' he said, laying a brotherly arm on Neil's shuddering shoulders, 'let's try again, shall we? You got as far as, Charlie Fong was the backer of your musical . . .'

Caro and Warren received the news of an arrest with cautious optimism. Some kind of hoax, worried Warren. Meant to draw out the real culprit? There was always the possibility the *Warfleet Chronicle* had got its facts wrong. Glyn Madoc relied far too much on bar-room hearsay; it wouldn't be the first time he'd led with an unsubstantiated story.

The lovers were still in bed, every moment doubly precious now, revelling in the spring sunlight which cast motey beams across the bed, warming their bodies after love-making. Warren stirred to prepare breakfast and brought croissants and coffee to the bed on a tray. He buttered a piece of the warm pastry for Caro, but as she began to nibble they were startled by a knock on the door. Caro pulled Warren's towelling dressing gown around herself while Warren crossed quickly to the door, adjusting the striped lungi Caro had bought for him in the market. 'Who is it?'

A woman's voice gave a muffled reply, and Warren opened the door to let in a solemn-faced Jade.

'Darling,' exclaimed Caro, at once embarrassed and relieved. It was the first time she had seen her daughter since she had left Four Trees.

Jade came quickly to the bed and gave Caro a hug. It betokened unusual news, since Jade only did this *in extremis*.

'Sit down. Have a croissant,' said Caro, immediately falling to mothering.

Jade shook her head. 'Coffee.'

Warren poured, remembering, Caro marked, that Jade took it black and without sugar, and the three sat on the bed in a kind of awkward complicity. Caro could not suppress the amused thought that a photograph of them would have shown the ultimate post-modern family. But Jade was clearly not in the mood for levity. She said, 'You've seen the news?' The *Warfleet Chronicle* lay on the Indian coverlet. 'The man they arrested is Neil Kenton.'

Caro and Warren exchanged startled glances. He was the last person they would have expected.

'How do you know?' said Warren.

'Your mum told me.' Jade permitted herself a small smile. 'When she came in this morning. Apparently PC Armitage came to visit Bill yesterday.'

Warren gave a grimace. 'Mum's a terror.'

Jade picked up and put down a corner of croissant. 'I think they've got the wrong man,' she said abruptly.

'Jade, what have you been up to?' said Warren warily. He and Caro drew together almost imperceptibly, surveying Jade as though she were a troublesome adolescent.

'Well . . .' said Jade.

After Craig had taken the gun and helped Jade out of her ignominious corner, he shepherded her, one broad arm firmly round her back, through the bedroom and out into the passage. Viviana stood as though turned into a pillar of salt. Only her eyes followed their exit. Craig returned to the room and said something to her in a low voice. Jade did not hear an answer. Then he collected Jade, who was leaning on a carved banister feeling rather sick, and led the way calmly down the main staircase as though nothing untoward had happened.

The marble hall was empty, though there was the sound of a distant Hoover. The main doors were open to the sunny morning, now heading towards noon, and in the drive, looking inappropriately normal, was Delia's shiny little Clio. Craig politely assisted Jade into it, his good humour apparently recovered, and as he pulled away across the forecourt switched on the radio. It was tuned to Classic FM and the sound of Delius's pastoral *A Cuckoo in Spring* filled the car.

They cruised down the drive without speaking. When they stopped at the main road Craig said pleasantly, 'I'd like that tape also.'

Jade reached into her pocket and took out the small tape recorder. It was still running. She extracted the tape and handed it to Craig, who nodded an acknowledgement before slipping it into his anorak. He was dressed, thought Jade, as though for a stroll in the country. Nothing more was said until they arrived at Four Trees.

Craig opened the car door for her and offered her a gentlemanly hand. When they stood face to face, he said, without smiling, 'Miss Radcliffe, don't you go meddling in things you don't understand. You could get yourself hurt that way.' He paused, as if waiting for the message to be absorbed, then dipping his head courteously said, 'You have a nice day now.'

Jade stood rooted as he walked into the house; she had no idea why she was so compliant, except that his authority was frightening. And absolute.

Many options occurred to her during the rest of the day; police, the press, Jed, Zo, the FBI agents. She contacted none of them. It was scary to be in the house with someone whose involvement in the crime was obvious, who might even be the murderer, and yet do nothing about it. She felt like Trilby under the power of Svengali.

At supper time, as she watched Craig carving a splendid roast, joshing with the guests, who had now completely accepted him, acting with chivalry and affection towards Delia, Jade was struck with doubts about their encounter's having occurred at all. She felt in the grip of a surreal nightmare, like the doomed wife in *Gaslight*. She checked several times before attempting to sleep that the bolt on her door was working.

When she read the paper the next morning and heard Jean's expansion of its contents, her one thought was that she must tell *someone*. The only possibility was Warren.

When Jade finished her account, Warren and Caro said nothing. Caro was struck again by her daughter's obsessive attraction to danger. Was it some fatal mistake in her upbringing? Warren was regretting the loss of the gun, which might have cleared him categorically. A cloud passed over the sun and the room turned grey and misty. Caro shivered and got up to put on some clothes. While she was in the bathroom, Jade said, 'Have you told her the rest?'

Warren nodded. 'Yes. She knows everything.'

Jade nodded, wondering, but not liking to ask, what effect it had had on their relationship. It must be strange for a woman of Caro's generation to be plunged into this world. She had no idea about her mother's attitude to drugs, though she knew Zo was a frequent user. When Warren volunteered nothing more, she said, 'I've got an idea. Have you still got access to your office?'

THIRTY-ONE

Later that day agents Benson and Hedges presented Detective Superintendent Cooper with exhibit A. The murder weapon. The Super drew in his breath and gave them a nasty look.

'May I enquire where you got this?' he said with barely concealed rancour.

'Laurie said carefully, 'A colleague.'

'A colleague,' repeated the Super, with heavy irony. 'Really?'

'We firmly believe this is the weapon used in the killing,' said Frank; Laurie added, 'Bob, we only want the best result for everybody.' Both agents nodded, as if to underline their best intentions.

Bob Cooper leaned back in his chair and pointed his choleric face at the ceiling. There was a savage resentment in his breast, but his choices were limited. He had extracted a statement of sorts from Neil Kenton, who maintained that he had accompanied Scott Harvey-Dickson to the Pasta Palace the night of the murder, at Scott's instigation. Afterwards he had walked with Charlie to the beach, alone, wanting a private conversation. There, unfortunately, his memory about the incident went blank. He was saved from searching it further by the timely arrival of his lawyer. In the meantime, the assistant constable had been on the blower again, moaning about the cost, the bitch, and now here was a convenient tie-in.

The detective superintendent took in a lungful of air and, fighting to control his tone, said, 'Look, lads, why don't you give me a bit more to go on?'

Frank said, 'We interviewed Mr Harvey-Dickson in Westminster. He gave us information leading to Neil Kenton, which was corroborated by our . . . other sources.'

'I think,' said the Super, holding up a hand, 'we'll get Harvey-Dickson to make a statement.'

'Rumer sent them to Scott,' said Toni. She and Caro were sipping camomile tea at the Quest, Caro questing in more than one sense. 'Remember that day they came for a consultation? She told them Charlie had been in for a tarot reading. He wanted confirmation on the Millennium Park, never closed a deal without psychic advice. Very sensible.'

Caro held her peace on that, though in this instance it appeared the advice had been far from sensible.

'In the reading, Rumer kept turning up the same cards. The Page of Swords . . . that could be a gun, you see; and the Fool . . . that's theatrical. There was the Empress . . . well, that's obviously Viviana . . . and another figure, the Juggler, which often means a politician. She also warned Charlie about the Lovers . . . that's the Italians, I'm sure those two are incestuous . . . and behind them all a shadowy figure who always indicates conspiracy, the Prince of Darkness. The last card was the Hanging Man. And we all know what that means!'

'Well,' said Caro. 'If Charlie really believed in all that, he was potty to do the deal.'

'You shouldn't fly in the face of the cards,' agreed Toni,

shaking her head gravely, 'that's hubris. After Rumer had told them all that, she did another reading and turned up the same cards again! Which is practically undocumented, except by Aleister Crowley. Well, it didn't take long to put two and two together; everyone knows Scott's in bed with the Italians. And off they went to Westminster.'

'Did Rumer tell them Neil Kenton had shot him?'

'She'd never be that categoric. She always says readings are like weather reports: they show the possibilities.'

By now it was late afternoon and le tout Warfleet knew the possibilities; Toni clearly felt it was breaking no confidence to talk about them.

'What about the wider picture?' said Caro. 'Does Rumer suspect some kind of conspiracy?' She hadn't mentioned Jade's account, dismissing it on reflection as her daughter's usual romance with the dramatic. The idea of kindly Craig as a killer was surely preposterous?

'The cards never lie,' intoned Toni, Cassandra-like. 'It certainly looks like it.'

Warren and Jade were in Warren's office at Tolleymarsh, searching the Net for conspiracies. The office had a melancholy air, despite the sunny day. The under-manager had been 'let go', and though the safari park was due to open on 1 May everything was on hold during the financial crisis. The wall of superhighway equipment, Warren's pride, had previously been useful mostly for estate matters. Now, the two sat in swivelling leather chairs, hypnotized by the large screen in front of them.

When the pages on Charlie revealed only a long list of business interests, they turned to the pages on 'Money laundering'. There was an extensive catalogue, some of which set out step-by-step detail of how to do it.

'We could start!' snorted Jade, having regained her sense of humour.

'Yeah, I need a new job,' said Warren ironically.

Jade clicked to 'CIA involvement'.

'Easy,' Warren's tone was sceptical.

'Black Ops,' said Jade briefly. She clicked and clicked again, swiftly assimilating a detailed account of how the CIA had laundered Colombian drug money for use in the notorious 'Black Ops'; particularly the provision of arms to the Nicaraguan Contras. It was all done, according to the information, through the Bank of Panama, the main launderer being a well-known and respected businessman.

Warren sat back. 'You've lost me. I only use this to find out the price of animal feed.'

There was a knock on the door, but before either of them could respond it was pushed open and Annabel entered. Warren stood up quickly, but Jade, still glued to the uncoiling data, barely noticed.

'I must talk to you, Warren,' said Annabel loudly.

Jade half turned as Warren hurried across and took Annabel's arm.

'What's she doing here?' Annabel snatched her arm away and took several steps towards Jade. Her arm was raised as though she might strike her.

'Just using the computer.' Warren, gruff with embarrassment, caught his wife's shoulder.

'How many more of your bitches have I got to tolerate!' Annabel's voice was rising with every word. It was clear she was out of control.

'Annabel . . . calm down. Let's go outside.' Warren, now the colour of his terracotta walls, urged Annabel back towards the doorway. Jade stared, round-eyed with astonishment. 'We'll go to the house.'

Annabel subsided, suddenly aware, it seemed, of the undignified figure she cut. She brushed Warren aside and, flinging up her head, stalked through the door. Warren, with a wild glance at Jade, followed, shutting the door behind them.

Jade sat looking at the heavy stripped pine for some moments. It reverberated from the slam, but nothing further happened. She thought of going after them to explain . . . but what would she say? Warren's problems were of his own making and besides, resolution beckoned.

She spun back to the computer and resumed the chase, scrolling backwards and forwards, clicking and tapping. Soon an exhilaration possessed her. Dissatisfaction, depression, boredom forgotten, she whistled through the Net. 'Yes,' she muttered under her breath, and once or twice, 'Jesus!'

Charlie, JP, narco-guerrillas, Craig. Eddie, Craig, the cartel, Charlie. Craig, the CIA, Charlie, Eddie.

The whirligig revolved endlessly as bit by bit she untangled the web of connections. This was what she was good at. Jade the huntress.

After an hour she sat back, shaking from the tension of total concentration. She lit a cigarette and puffed the smoke upwards, her eyes fixed unseeing on the ceiling. The feeling of euphoria subsided and was replaced by apprehension. What on earth was she to do with all this information? With a sudden sense of responsibility, she knew she couldn't burden Caro and Warren. For the things she had uncovered, she was sure, had put her life in danger.

THIRTY-TWO

Scott Harvey-Dickson did not take kindly to being commanded back to his constituency. 'Really,' he protested, 'it's most inconvenient. I'm swamped with work at Westminster.' None the less he appeared at the police station in the late afternoon. Detective Superintendent Cooper undertook to examine him personally; after various things the FBI agents had told him, he felt it better not to involve a third party.

Scott, attired in his trademark Prince of Wales check with dandy-collared shirt and canary-yellow tie, sat with his legs neatly crossed and an air of contemptuous irritation.

'As I told agents Benson and Hedges . . . charming fellows . . . I had dinner with Neil Kenton and Charlie Fong at the delightful Pasta Palace on the evening of Mr Fong's death.'

'And what was the purpose of that meeting, sir?'

'It was to discuss the possibility of the Martini brothers going into partnership with Charlie.'

'On the millennium project?'

'Yes,' said Scott, looking a little evasive. He shifted in his chair, and ran a hand over his immaculate auburn toupee.

'I understand the brothers weren't best pleased at Mr Fong's intervention in Warfleet?'

Scott cleared his throat. 'They were not . . . entranced, certainly.' He added quickly, 'But they were eager to do a handsome deal. It was a perfectly legitimate business proposition.'

'I don't doubt it, sir. I don't doubt it. And they asked you to broker it?'

'I took it upon myself to persuade Mr Fong to stay a little longer and hear them,' conceded Scott. A rim of perspiration had broken out on his top lip.

'Because you have other interests with the Martinis—'

'It's a matter of record,' intervened Scott hastily.

'I wasn't suggesting otherwise, Mr Harvey-Dickson. Also, of course, you had backed Mr Fong's new enterprise.'

'Correct.' The MP dropped his eyes from the Super's face to the scattering of papers on his desk.

'Yes, thought Cooper, and I'll be bound the Italians weren't best pleased with *you* either. 'I gather you had to bring a certain amount of pressure to bear on Mr Fong?'

'Pressure?' Scott Harvey-Dickson's orange eyebrows shot up.

'Mr Fong isn't noted for embracing partnerships. Indeed his entire empire is a testament to single-mindedness.'

'Er . . . that's true, but in this instance—'

'In this instance, you had certain information with which to, shall we say, *persuade* him.'

'What are you implying, Superintendent?' A dull red rash had begun to travel up the MP's neck.

'You had a document compiled by the DTI on Mr Fong's financial difficulties. It cited unaccounted-for funds and tax evasion and stated he was under FBI investigation.'

Scott visibly started and clutched one arm of his chair.

'You . . . suggested . . . if you leaked this document to the press, it would put paid to Mr Fong's chances of a peerage.' The Super permitted himself a foxy smile. Not for the first time had his Masonic connection come in handy. He'd had a drink at the lodge that lunch time with Glyn Madoc.

'That's an outrageous suggestion,' Harvey-Dickson was blustering. 'If any such document existed, it would have gone straight to the Cabinet.'

The Super broadened his smile. 'Well, perhaps it did, sir. I can't imagine they'd want it made common knowledge. After all, Mr Fong was a financial saviour during the election. He deserved the honour they were about to bestow.'

Scott Harvey-Dickson gaped like a netted goldfish.

'So you put it to Charlie, at that dinner, that your mates in the DTI would suppress the document, get him his barony, as long as he played ball with the Martinis.'

Scott Harvey-Dickson sank back in his chair, showing every sign he considered the game to be up.

The Super chuckled gently. This was more like it. His morale felt quite restored. 'Now, sir, the question I want to ask you is, what was Neil Kenton doing at this dinner?'

Scott passed a swollen tongue over pale green lips. 'He's an old acquaintance,' he gasped.

'On this occasion, not "forgot",' jested the Super, thoroughly enjoying himself. 'Wasn't he more of a confidant? Weren't you very close to a member of his company?'

Rumours of Scott's homosexuality had reached even his backwater constituency. Scott said nothing, but his eyes registered terror.

'Well, be that as it may. You knew Mr Kenton was down here because your ... "friend" ... in the company had recommended Four Trees and you knew Mr Kenton was angry because Charlie Fong had backed out of his show, causing it to close. So you took him along to add a little extra ballast?'

Scott managed a jerky nod.

'Now, would that ballast be anything to do with drug-running?' Scott Harvey-Dickson swayed sideways in his seat; it looked as though he was about to faint. 'Would you like a glass of water, sir?' The Super pressed a button on his intercom and after a moment PC Armitage appeared. 'Some water, Armitage,' the Super barked.

'Yes, guv,' said PC Armitage, his fresh face goggle-eyed with curiosity.

'There you go, Mr Dickson,' he said, returning immediately with a glass.

'*Harvey*-Dickson,' said the MP in a petulant whisper. He had used the moment to reassemble himself somewhat.

'You see, *we* think,' said the Super, when the door had closed on the reluctant Armitage, 'that Charlie was involved with drugs money and that Kenton knew this and that the Italians were smuggling drugs and possibly guns, and that you knew this, and that the Italians wanted in for much more than the theme park. They were after a piece of Charlie's global action and the meeting that night was to blackmail Charlie into agreeing.'

There was a short silence, then Scott Harvey-Dickson gathered himself into a parliamentary reaction. 'That is a disgraceful and totally unfounded allegation and I demand that you withdraw it immediately!'

'Well then, sir, if there was nothing untoward about this meeting, can I ask why you didn't come forward about it when you heard only hours later that Charlie Fong had been murdered?'

'As I explained to agents Benson and Hedges, I was out of the country – in Montserrat, actually; we're funding a film and theatre complex there – for several days, and when I got back it simply slipped my mind.'

Really, thought the Super, he was quite an impressive liar. One could see him in the Chamber. 'Slipped your mind ... that you were possibly one of the last people to see Fong alive?'

'Well, I knew *I* hadn't murdered him.' The MP was almost camp in his refutation. 'And I had no reason to believe that any of my associates had either.'

'Until the agents called on you.'

'I did tell them then all I recalled, which was that the last I saw of Charlie was him setting off for a walk with Neil Kenton.'

Yes, thought the Super, you dropped Kenton right in it. 'So, to summarize,' he said, putting his elbows on the desk and his fingertips together, 'you know nothing about any illegal activity on anyone's part. The evening was amicable and ended with Mr Kenton and Mr Fong leaving for a sociable walk together.'

'Just so,' said Scott Harvey-Dickson.

'Was a deal struck over the Millennium Park?'

Scott Harvey-Dickson hesitated fractionally. 'Mr Fong said he'd think about it.'

'Think about it,' the Super drolly repeated. 'Well, he didn't get long to do that, did he?'

'Unfortunately not,' said Harvey-Dickson, now completely in charge of himself. 'He's a great loss to us all.' He checked his watch. 'If there's nothing more, Superintendent, I'd like to get back. I've got a function tonight for the Ministry of Culture.'

'Certainly, sir. We'll be in touch. Oh ... and do let us know next time you're leaving the country.'

Harvey-Dickson flounced out in a cloud of disdain. The Super smiled to himself. The MP would be straight on the blower to the Martinis. Good job they'd already been picked up by the boys from Stourbridge.

THIRTY-THREE

May Day roused Warfleet with blinding beams. The town was in an early bustle; the celebrations were due to begin at noon, but there was much to be done in preparation. Bunting fluttered madly across the narrow streets. Fairy lights had been rigged for later. The procession was to begin in the square, the floats wending their way to the clifftop, where the maypole had been erected. There, the Warfleet Players would perform their pageant, before organized games and the morris men competition. The day would end with the Marcia Banks School of Dance demonstrating maypole dancing.

In Stourbridge, too, the morning light had driven Caro, Warren and Jade early from sleep. Not that they had had more than fitful bursts. Jade had returned to the Stourbridge flat the night before to find her mother pacing. 'You've been ages,' she snapped. 'Where's Warren?'

'Er . . . he went to the dower house to see,' she paused, 'to see the children.'

Caro's face tightened. 'Oh.'

'The office is only a few hundred yards . . .' Jade found herself reasoning.

Caro flung herself on the sagging sofa. 'I know. I know.'

Jade brought a bottle of Chardonnay out of her bag and

opened it. 'You need a drink. Honestly, Ma, you've got to give him *some* space.'

Caro took the proffered glass and drank deeply. 'What did you find out?' she said.

'Oh, nothing much,' said Jade, as airily as she could manage, 'me being a drama queen. It's probably Kenton. God knows he murdered his shows.' Her amateur acting talents were finally being realized, she thought. Perhaps she would make a video of herself telling the brave, investigative truth to camera. She would be dead before it was shown, of course, but posthumous fame was better than nothing. 'Ma,' she said, her voice wavering slightly, 'is it OK if I stay the night? I'm too knackered to go back to Warfleet.'

'Of course, darling,' said Caro, still distracted. 'This sofa's rather awful, but you're welcome.'

Warren came in late. There was a large scratch on his cheek which both the women pretended not to notice.

Warren had promised to take the children to the May Day festivities and he set off early to collect them, agreeing to meet Caro and Jade at the Delphinium Tearooms later. Jade had woken that morning wondering where to run. The May Day celebrations seemed good enough; there was safety in numbers. She borrowed clothes from Caro, and the two women took a minicab to Warfleet, Jade dismissing the bus as 'boring'.

The day, though brilliant, was blustery. The streets were crowded with merrymakers, those not in costume defying the wind in shirtsleeves. The shops and taverns were all doing excellent business. Fast-food stalls had sprouted all round the square and the air carried the intoxicatingly greasy promise of hot dogs and doughnuts. The Delphinium was packed; Jade and Caro squeezed into a corner and ordered coffee. Caro, nervous of the impending encounter with Warren's children, her first as his lover, could eat nothing and Jade despised breakfast.

Toni entered, dressed in extravagantly patterned saffron. Spotting them, she waved and came over. 'No sign of Jeremy?' she asked, draping her robes around the table.

Caro shook her head.

'Not surprised.' Toni looked grim. 'Darryl's very poorly. They've charged Neil Kenton, you know. Murder.'

Jade gave Caro a nudge, which made her spill a pool of froth from her coffee.

'And they've got the Italians in custody. Carl finally cracked and spilled the beans. Apparently . . .'

Caro and Jade feigned surprise as Toni, voice only slightly lowered, conveyed the now familiar tale of the dark undertow of Warfleet.

'Who'd think it? Here of all places. Of course, they're foreigners. I suppose Carl put them in the frame, so he'd get a lighter sentence.'

'If he lives,' said Jade darkly.

Toni ordered a scone. The telling of the news had given her an appetite. 'It's one thing having a sensational murder. But this corruption has been going on for years!'

'Centuries,' murmured Caro, mopping her coffee.

Toni tucked into her scone and Jade lit a cigarette. She offered one to Caro, who reluctantly refused, aware of Toni's watchful presence.

Warren appeared in the doorway holding Jasper by the hand and Dickon in the crook of his arm. Caro's heart lost several beats as she saw them. Their three blond heads were perfectly angelic; a medieval painting, with New Man replacing the Madonna.

He looked harassed as he negotiated the children through the crowd. Jade pulled up another chair and waved to attract a waitress. Warren put Dickon on to Caro's lap and lifted the chattering Jasper on to his own. Toni stiffened visibly. Caro swept the room with her eyes to see who else had noticed, but le tout Warfleet were about their own excited business this morning and most of May's festively garbed clients were strangers.

Warren had heard about the arrests. 'The police came for Viviana this morning. Everything's in a hell of a state at Tolleymarsh.'

'Oh my God,' said Caro.

'Yes,' said Warren curtly. 'Annabel's gone up to the Hall to pacify Henry. He's close to collapse. She's terrified this'll kill him.'

'They'll have a hard time pinning anything on Viviana,' said Jade, thinking with regret of her confiscated tape. If her calculations were correct, there was no way that would surface.

A brass band fanfared outside the café windows and the children clamoured to be allowed out to see it. The Marcia Banks School of Dance was parading by, pirouetting and twirling red pom-poms to a medley of Andrew Lloyd-Webber. The procession had begun, and even Toni, who was agog to hear more of Viviana, joined the crowd pushing towards the doorway. Warren carried Jasper and Caro Dickon as they were propelled along the pavement, Jade and Toni following.

The floats were splendid, every trader represented. Jim and

Peggy Bacon had done High Street Heels as a giant boot. Peggy, wearing gingham and a ginger wig, was the old woman who lived in it with a troop of Brownies as her children. Transco's truck had an eternal flame. 'Wish I could get one out of my cooker,' said Toni, laughing. The Warfleet Players were frozen in a Spring Tableau on a truck bedecked with paper flowers and AstroTurf. Marsha and Teddy had arrived at a compromise; some of the women were dressed as men and the men dressed as women were topless. The Martinis' float, prepared before their arrest and flying the flag in their absence, was a giant cake in the shape of a gondola. 'With any luck,' said Warren into Caro's ear, 'that's the closest they'll get to Venice.' Behind the floats jingled teams of morris men, clacking sticks and heels as they limbered up for the competition. The hobby horse wove in and out, plunging and neighing. Jade recognized Jean Plummer's sparrow legs, thrust into furry hoof slippers.

There were many familiar faces, particularly outside the Admiral Nelson where they were already flushed, and many strange ones; Warfleet's May Day was famous and people had bussed in from all over the county. Toni, shouting something, was borne away by the crush. By the time the procession had snaked up the hill, Jade had got separated from the others.

The cliffs were Disney-bright in the sunshine, the white chalk fluorescent and the grass a dazzling green. Below, the sea was a perfect foam-capped blue, the waves in regular cartoon-like animation.

The carnival masses milled about, eating, drinking, laughing and shouting, as the Warfleet Players began their pageant, flooding the area with unnatural pink and orange. It was a retelling of Demeter's triumph over the dark forces of Hades.

The legend had a bizzarely camp spin, with male fairies, court to Teddy, King of a rococo Hell, prancing about in Day-Glo organdie, but the audience, entranced with the pageantry, seemed not to notice.

It was extraordinary, Jade thought disaffectedly, as she reached the summit, how into heraldic ritual the British were. It was almost their only way of expressing emotion, having taken the place of religion, politics, morals. No wonder so many had favoured Charlie's millennium project. Ethereal taped music circled from loudspeakers above their heads, creating a trance-like atmosphere. Soon Jade too, despite herself, was held in some pantomime enchantment.

In the stillness, broken now only by muffled whispers and the artificial piping on stage, Jade hunted on tiptoe for her friends. Among the crowd of spellbound people gazing towards the stage she saw only one face she recognized; it was Craig O'Connell's and he was looking directly at her. Panic raced through her. She froze and then, as though pursued by the demons on stage, turned and ran.

She hurtled through a rowdy gypsy family catcalling and whistling at the gay japes, dodging beefy men, colliding with a strapping woman, evading a barking dog. On the other side she snatched a glance over her shoulder – she could no longer see Craig – and dived into the morris men, practising team strategy. She criss-crossed through hopping legs and handkerchief-whirling arms, panting now, and dashed beyond, narrowly avoiding having her head cracked. She could hear distant sounds from the fairground. Screams and laughter; disco music. Her plan, if plan such frenzy could be called, was to lose Craig in the mêlée, then double back and find Caro and Warren.

To her dismay the crowd began to thin, but mindless now

she ran on and on. At last there was nothing but the clifftop path and the dizzying edge. A dagger-sharp pain sliced into her side and completely winded her. The stitch forced her to stop, bent her double. She heaved in several breaths, then straightened, holding her ribs, and turned to face the crowd. Every head was riveted to the stage, but a few yards away, approaching at a steady pace with one hand raised, was Craig O'Connell.

'No,' whispered Jade (in the movie he would use crowd confusion to push her over the edge). 'No!' She took a step back and the crumbly cliff edge gave way beneath her foot. She swayed, clutched at air, then twisted, almost in slow motion, towards the technicolour sea. Suspended in time she hovered, gazing down at the churning waves upon which were superimposed scenes from her childhood; then, as though suddenly released, she hurtled swiftly towards them.

Her fall was interrupted by a sudden painful jerk. Someone had her by the ankle, then the thigh. Strong arms gripped her waist, pulled her back and deposited her, swooning, on the spiky crushed grass. Her eyes were still open and she saw, far distant, the dense blue sky; counted puffy clouds hurrying across it. The sea, she remembered, had looked picture-book blue and inviting.

After a time which went on for ever she struggled on to her elbows. Craig O'Connell was sitting cross-legged in front of her. His hands rested on his knees, and despite his bulk he looked completely at ease in the position. On his broad face was an expression almost mischievously puckish.

'Well, Miss Radcliffe,' he drawled, 'I arrived in the nick of time.'

To Jade, in her out-of-body state, it seemed he must be the devil. Or at least one of his messengers.

THIRTY-FOUR

'You can kill me,' said Jade, 'but it won't do you any good. I e-mailed the whole story to Jed Rosenbaum.'

Craig raised an amused eyebrow. 'Yes. Good move. I must admit technology has made my job harder.'

'You know?' exclaimed Jade. She had recovered a little after a swig from Craig's brandy flask. He had even obligingly lit her a cigarette, producing her own brand, though he himself did not smoke.

'Indeed,' he smiled. 'We have people at Talk TV.'

The cigarette slipped in Jade's fingers. Really, their network was astonishing.

'We don't need to worry about Jed.' Craig laughed heartily. 'I don't think he'll be acting on the information.'

'He's not . . .' Jade's voice dropped to a squeaky whisper and she could not complete the sentence.

'Dead? Heavens no. He'll live to make another buck.' Craig roared again. 'No. We have certain facts on him we can use any time.'

'The money scandal,' pounced Jade. 'He *was* involved. I *knew* it.'

'Very observant,' said Craig, nodding approval. 'You seem to have put most of it together.'

'So I was right,' even now Jade found the trail irresistible, 'about Charlie and drugs and Eddie.' Craig merely raised his eyebrows. 'And you?' finished Jade, falteringly.

'Whoa.' Craig raised one of his great paws, 'I didn't shoot Charlie. Contrary to what you appear to believe,' Craig chuckled, 'we don't often kill our operatives.'

'Charlie *was* working for you?' Even in danger Jade was triumphant. 'CIA, right? That's what you are, isn't it?'

Still smiling, Craig inclined his head.

'And it was Eddie Flynn who killed Charlie.'

'You're wrong there. Eddie's one of us.'

'Eddie! But . . . he went to prison, and . . .'

'Well, we couldn't stop that . . . would have blown his cover.'

'You mean,' said Jade, 'he was already one of yours back in Colombia?'

'Indeed,' said Craig. 'One of our finest.' He shook his head. 'We were sorry to lose him, but it goes with the territory.'

'It doesn't make sense. If Charlie was working for you too, why did he have Eddie busted?'

'Ah,' said Craig, 'you went a little off-centre with that.'

Jade dragged irritatedly on the cigarette.

'You rightly surmised that when Charlie started working for JP he encountered the paramilitary squads . . . the so-called "narco-geurrillas". JP uses them to intimidate, coerce and if necessary liquidate anyone who gets in the way of their progress.' Craig delivered all this as a matter of fact, no moral analysis necessary. 'Through them Charlie connected with a cartel and started his own dealings.'

'Laundering?' checked Jade.

'Indeed . . . through JP. Now Eddie was already in the field for us – the US has interests in JP – and he was watching

Charlie. Actually we were considering getting him on board—'

'Black Ops!' put in Jade. 'The middlemen made staggering profits. Over two mill in one transaction.'

'Well,' twinkled Craig, 'I see you can do the math.'

'Except getting two and two to make four, apparently!'

'Don't be pissed. You were nearly there. Eddie's cover was running drugs for the cartel. Charlie got suspicious of him and told them he was a CIA spy. The cartel "arranged" to have him busted.'

'Why not just killed?' Jade thought of a deserted road in Los Llanos, a band of narco-guerrillas . . .

'He was lucky,' said Craig. 'It wouldn't have been the first time. But the cartel was keen on a deal with us. It wouldn't have been . . . polite to take out one of our agents.'

'How come Charlie started working for you?'

'We recruited him to replace Eddie.'

'Knowing all he'd done?' Jade was appalled. 'He was a criminal!'

Craig dropped the smile. 'He was a businessman . . . and a damned good one. Don't be naive, Jade. I'm sure you realize a number of our operatives are drawn from the criminal classes.'

Jade stubbed her cigarette butt into a pile of dried rabbit droppings. Cynical as she was, the truth was even more Byzantine than she'd estimated.

'He's been very useful to us . . . until recently.'

'The FBI investigation?'

'Charlie didn't know when enough was enough. Great men and hubris.' Craig shook his head, sighing. 'Eddie alerted us to the problem.'

'He still works for you, then?' Jade could not resist, but Craig just smiled annoyingly.

'Charlie was about to become an embarrassment. I was on my way down here to check it out when—'

'Not from Agincourt?' interrupted Jade again, remembering Craig's original story.

Craig gave a shout of laughter. 'From Sark. Charlie used small companies registered there for many of his transactions. But' – he looked out across the indigo depths of the Channel – 'I did go there via Agincourt. It's best to stick as closely as possible to the truth.'

'You're not really a professor?' Jade was still sceptical.

'Indeed I am. And I'm researching a paper. It was ...' Craig paused, looking serious, 'my love of history ... fascination with its lies, I guess ... that got me involved in the first place.'

'Your day job?' said Jade satirically.

'You need it,' said Craig. 'Believe me.'

'Were you going to check out the Italians too?'

'Hah!' hooted Craig. 'Characters! What we call independents. We had an idea what they were up to, but Neil Kenton—'

'He's not an agent, is he?' said Jade, prepared now to believe even Jean Plummer might be.

'Nope. Strictly left field. I must say, it took us by surprise.'

There was a pause, while both assembled their thoughts. Jade was as shaken by all Craig had confirmed as by her dice with death. According to Craig, this had been unnecessary. His hand had been raised in warning about the cliff edge, not in threat to push her over it. But why was he letting her know all this? It was very puzzling; hardly proper, if he wasn't going to kill her.

'Why are you telling me?' she blurted.

Craig leaned back a little and scrutinized her, his face straight. 'I have a proposition to put to you.'

Jade sat upright, a slow suspicion burning in her.

'I think you're looking for a change in your life . . . you're bored, right?'

Jade held her breath.

'You like excitement. You're a good sleuth . . .'

'Are you *recruiting* me?' breathed Jade, her eyes widening with visions of undreamed-of power.

'What d'you think?'

'Yes . . . oh God . . . yes. Definitely.'

Craig surveyed the family groups dotted around, munching on hot dogs and sandwiches. 'It's no picnic, I assure you. You can forget normality.'

'Suits me,' said Jade, adding contemptuously. 'Normal people are dickheads.'

'We'll have to do something about that attitude,' said Craig admonishingly. He had become the professor again. 'You've got a lot to learn, young lady. Now. How many other people have you told?'

'No one,' said Jade quickly.

'Warren and Caro?' tested Craig.

'Nothing that matters.' She looked him in the eye. 'Honestly.'

Craig patted her with an avuncular hand. 'You know, I believe you. Under that tough crust you're pretty staunch. That's a useful quality.'

Staunch, thought Jade. She liked that. No one had ever attributed strength to her before.

'Are you ever wrong about people?'

'Rarely.' Craig's face took on the ruthless expression Jade had last seen in Viviana's closet. She shivered a little, sure those about whom he was wrong were swiftly eliminated.

'What shall I do about Warren and Caro?' she asked, thinking that, above all, she must protect them.

'Up to you,' said Craig. 'How you handle it will be the first test of your integrity.'

Integrity, thought Jade, was an interesting word to use in the circumstances. She had no doubt Craig believed in his rectitude. 'What about Viviana? Does she know who you are?'

'She may suspect. It depends how much Charlie told her. But she won't be charged. We'll take care of that. We may have other uses for her.'

'To take over where Charlie left off?' said Jade, excited by a new puzzle.

Craig gave her a quizzical look. 'Now, Jade, you don't have to know everything.'

'And Delia?'

Craig's face turned troubled and he sighed. 'You know, I really care about that lady.'

Jade could see Craig's life was not easy.

'Craig! Jade!' Delia, looking well and happy and for once dressed with care in a flowery summer print and neat jacket, was approaching with Anthea and Harry and Alex in his pushchair.

Craig leapt to his feet and went to meet them. Jade watched as he kissed Delia and took Harry's hand, his face alive with pleasure. The change in him had been instant. Practised.

Was this, then, how it would be for her? Lying, dissembling, trusting no one? Not unlike, she thought with inner irony, life in television. Well, why not? She was heading for a thirty-something, marriageless, childless life; it wasn't much to look forward to. Craig's was an offer she couldn't refuse. It really would be like living in a movie.

THIRTY-FIVE

The police charged Neil Kenton with murder when they got the result they wanted from ballistics. Neil's fingerprints were a perfect match. Thanks to the rubber gloves, Jade's had not been lifted. Confronted with this, Neil had broken down and confessed all he suddenly 'remembered'.

He and Charlie had left Pasta Palace to walk home via the beach. In the light of what had been revealed during the evening, Neil had tried to persuade Charlie to back the reopening of his show.

'Blackmail him, you mean, Mr Kenton,' put in Detective Superintendent Cooper. Then, 'Go on. Go on,' he urged, when Neil's lips began to wobble.

Charlie had refused. Said the show was terrible – 'As if he'd know the difference,' Neil added bitterly – and a row had broken out.

'Whereupon, I took out the gun and shot him.' PC Armitage, his lips moving, wrote the sentence out laboriously. The Super liked back-up, even though the tape was running.

'You had the gun with you, then? Just in case?'

'I got it weeks ago. To shoot myself.' At this point Neil broke down, weeping.

The Super ordered him a cup of tea. When he'd drunk it,

he admitted that Eddie Flynn, another of his backers, had first told him Charlie's money was dodgy.

'He told me he was going to crash. And not to get involved with him. I paid no attention. Beggars can't be choosers.' He agreed that after he'd shot Charlie, he'd arranged the body to look as much as possible like a Mafia killing. 'I read it in a book. I was thinking of doing a musical from it.' Neil muffled another sob with the Super's handkerchief. 'I had no car, I couldn't carry him. I thought, after what I'd found out about the Italians, everyone would think they had killed him.'

'And just what did you find out about the Italians, Mr Kenton?' said the Super in a honeyed voice, pushing the tape recorder closer.

By the time Neil Kenton had finished his statement he'd put the Martinis and Scott Harvey-Dickson firmly in the frame.

'I don't know much about the arms,' he insisted, 'but the dope ... through Scott they're supplying half of Westminster.'

The Super was well pleased. He could see promotion looming. Put that bitch at the top in her place. Besides, he hated New Labour.

'I hope we can expect a lesser charge after this,' snapped Neil's lawyer, as PC Armitage dotted his last i. 'We'll put our hand up to manslaughter while the balance of mind was disturbed. My client was suffering from post-traumatic stress disorder.'

May Day with Warren and his children had been an experience of equal pain and pleasure for Caro. The toddlers were delightful and brought back all her own buried maternal feelings. Warren was very good with them, treating them with a kind of tender offhandedess which allowed them to feel both grown-up and cherished. Watching him feed Dickon, rub Jasper's scraped knee, cuddle them both, pointing out balloons, clowns and funny costumes, Caro couldn't help feeling how wonderful it would be for them to have a child together. She dismissed the thought instantly; it would be not only wonderful, but miraculous.

That night he was late returning to Stourbridge, and when he came in, to find her resolutely pretending to go through her notes, he admitted that he'd had another emotional encounter with Annabel. 'She's upset, of course, about her dad and Viviana and everything, but she's refusing to have an abortion. Says at nearly four months it's too late.'

'She wants you back,' said Caro in a dead voice. She knew, with primitive female instinct, it was inevitable.

The next morning, Caro set off to visit Jeremy and Darryl, having had a distressed phone call from Jeremy the previous evening. When she arrived, it was to find Toni and Rumer already there and the little house redolent with incense, aroma oils and the hush of healing.

Jeremy, exhausted from a night of vigil, was on the sofa having his feet massaged by Toni. Rumer, with crystals, was upstairs with Darryl. Toni gave Caro a warning glance as she came in bringing Darryl's favoured brand of gin and tonic.

'The doctor's just gone,' she whispered, when Jeremy's eyes had finally closed. 'Come into the kitchen.'

Toni shut the door, then in a low voice said, 'I'm afraid there's no hope.'

'No!' said Caro. The speed of it was obscene.

'Pneumonia,' stated Toni. 'He's too ill even to be moved to hospital.'

Caro could think of nothing to say. It was all so avoidable. Why hadn't Darryl done something sooner? Why hadn't Jeremy made him?

'I know,' Toni put a hand on her arm, 'what you're thinking. Believe me, I did my best.'

Caro nodded, knowing well the bossiness of which her friend was capable.

'He just wouldn't alter his lifestyle,' continued Toni. 'I console myself that the alcohol would have carried him off anyway.'

This was certainly true, thought Caro. Darryl had been bent on self-destruction for years. 'Can I see him?' she asked.

'We'll go up together,' nodded Toni, 'while Jeremy's sleeping. Poor lamb, I hate to think what will happen to him. He'll be lost without Darryl.'

They climbed the stairs carefully and pushed open the door to the master bedroom. Darryl was lying in the great swagged bed. His eyes were closed and there was an oxygen mask over his face. He looked tiny; a mere shrivelled twig in the huge bed. Rumer sat by his side, crooning softly. She held one of his hands. In her plump red fingers it looked featherlight, just pale skin and bone.

Caro crept forward, still carrying her gifts, which now seemed completely inappropriate. As she neared the bed, Darryl opened his eyes and acknowledged her with a slight smile.

'Darling,' he gasped, making sucking noises on the oxygen, 'I need a stiff one.' He gave the old Darryl cackle and Caro laughed too, though her throat hurt and her eyes were stinging. Darryl drifted away again and Rumer raised her voice a little. It was some strange chant she was singing. 'North American Indian,' Toni mouthed to Caro, 'for the passage of the soul.'

He's not dead yet, Caro wanted to shout. Surely there was something that could be done? Where was the doctor?

'The doctor will be back soon,' said Toni, again reading her mind. 'He had to visit another patient.'

Caro's rage subsided. It was all too clear Darryl was dying. She just hoped he was at peace.

'The drugs are marvellous,' reassured Toni.

Rumer's chant ended and they sat in silence, each, in her own way, praying for Darryl. Soon his troubled spirit would be tranquil and the pressing problem would be how to deal with Jeremy.

Jade spent the morning in bed recovering from her trauma and considering her subterfuge. She dreamed up various complex plots, but in the end decided she would tell Caro and Warren simply that she had been mistaken. It was a laughable suggestion that Craig was CIA. He had not been following her to Tolleymarsh Hall, but had chanced upon the scene with Viviana in his hunt for ley lines. He'd taken the gun and tape for her own protection and, of course, handed them to the police.

Pleased with her story – it fitted nicely with Craig's instruction to stick as closely as possible to the truth – she got up to make herself some lunch. She was less sure how she would deal with the London end of things. She supposed she would go back to Talk TV; a cover job seemed essential. How much could she hide from Jed? But there again, perhaps he would be liquidated.

Deen Perry sat at the refectory table busy scribbling. They

had hardly spoken since the night of the row, maintaining an icy indifference at mealtimes, and Jade was disconcerted to encounter him with no one else present. He looked even odder than usual. His hair, now straggling to his shoulders, was knotted with small beads and green garden twine; his usual unkempt stubble had coalesced into a wispy beard. His feet were bare and filthy, and he was wearing a long shirt of brown sackcloth. The only thing missing from this apparition, thought Jade, was ashes.

He looked up as she entered and said in a voice unlike his usual high-pitched whine, 'I forgive you.'

'Thanks,' said Jade satirically. She stomped to the Aga and banged the kettle on the hob. Jean Plummer had mentioned that Deen had gone 'peculiar'. He'd been seen wandering in the woods, calling to the birds and eating berries.

'No, really,' Deen was saying, in the strange sing-song voice of a sermonizing vicar. 'I realize my anger with you was all prompted by envy.'

Jade let out a derisive snort.

'Scorn me, I don't mind. It's all been revealed to me now.'

'Ah,' said Jade. 'I might have known it was a revelation.'

'I expect to be misunderstood,' said Deen. 'I will be mocked and reviled.'

'Critics are bastards,' agreed Jade, beginning to enjoy Deen's self-abasement.

'Yes,' he said. 'They won't receive this book well. I've decided to write it in the person of Jesus.'

'Unblocked at last!' Jade had to turn back to the Aga to hide her laughter.

Deen nodded solemnly. 'I was obviously being prepared for this. Being shown I needed to change my ways.'

'Does that mean no booze or dope?' said Jade, keeping irony out of her query.

Deen looked less certain. 'Well . . .'

'I don't think Jesus was into coke,' said Jade warningly.

'No. But hallucinogens . . . in the desert . . .' Deen certainly gave every sign of having taken many.

'Of course, to research it properly, you'd have to be crucified.'

Deen shot her a malevolent look, but recovered himself quickly and said, 'I may be.'

'Yeh,' agreed Jade. 'By your editor. What's happening at StrongFellows, by the way?'

'All being sold off. Zo Acland and Marcus Croft are starting their own company,' said Deen, his voice rising an octave. 'They've asked me to go with them, but it's going to be a lesbian and gay imprint.'

'Well, there is an argument that Jesus was homosexual.'

'I have it on good authority,' said Deen crossly, 'that he wasn't.'

'Did God tell you?' said Jade, bringing her toasted cheese to the table.

Deen eyed it hungrily. Presumably researching Jesus required him to eschew food as well as narcotics.

Delia and Craig came in loaded with shopping bags. They spilled food from them on to the table. Delia, looking flushed and healthy, said, 'Craig's going to cook a farewell dinner.'

Jade looked up quickly. Craig was smiling, his face its usual kindly mask; his eyes told Jade to say nothing.

'Sabbatical's up,' he said regretfully. 'But Delia and I are going away for a few days with the kids before I have to go back to America.'

Jade glanced at Delia. She seemed happy enough; quite on her old form, bustling about the kitchen clearing plates and sidening food into cupboards.

Jade followed Craig out of the kitchen and in the passage caught his arm.

'Don't worry,' he said softly. 'We'll be in touch.'

'But shouldn't I give you an address . . . a contact number?'

Craig gave her a teasing look. 'You think we don't have it?'

Somewhat shaken, Jade returned to her lunch, catching Deen Perry in the act of cutting a hefty slice of the crusty brown loaf Delia had placed on the table.

THIRTY-SIX

The death of Darryl Willoughby was announced in the *Warfleet Chronicle*. He had 'slipped away peacefully' the day after Caro's visit. The funeral was set for the following week. 'So much to do,' said Jeremy plaintively, when Caro called to give her condolences; yet, she felt, there was a kind of relief in his voice. She offered her services if needed, and was told Toni would be in touch. As she put down the phone, tears welled in her eyes. She was crying, she knew, as much for herself as for Darryl.

Warren was out. In the void created by the arrests, his presence at Tolleymarsh was essential. Someone must take care of the day-to-day running of the estate; Warren could not abandon his beloved animals.

As Caro sat musing on her future, there was a soft knock on the door. She wasn't expecting anyone; indeed, few people knew where she was. Thinking it was another lodger wanting milk or, more likely, a cigarette, she got up and answered it. Annabel Peabody stood in the grimy hallway.

The two women stared at each other in silence, both their faces stained by recent tears. Caro took in Annabel's uncared-for hair and lack of make-up, and the slight protrusion of her tummy under her flowered cardigan. Annabel, she was sure, noticed the details of her own casual and distressed appearance.

'Can I come in?' said Annabel, in an apprehensive voice.

Caro stood back and let her pass into the room, watching her look swiftly round it. 'Do sit down,' she said, finding her voice. Annabel looked fatigued, or perhaps just careworn.

Annabel sat and folded her hands over her plump tummy, causing Caro a moment of acute envy. She seemed to pick her words delicately as she said, 'Warren ... doesn't know I'm here. I came to ask you ... what you think we should do?'

You came, thought Caro, because you must. Because you wanted to see, with your own eyes, your husband's mistress. Nevertheless, she said in as reasonable a tone as she could manage, 'What do *you* think, Annabel?'

'I know he loves you,' said Annabel, in a very small voice. 'But you see, we need him so terribly. Daddy ... Daddy's ill ... I'm not sure he'll recover. I can't manage it all by myself, especially ...' She moved her hand slightly on her stomach. Caro was filled in equal part with rage and sorrow. She would have liked to throw Annabel down the stairs, kick and punch her belly, but she was also overtaken with compassion for her. Whatever the manipulative or jealous instinct that had driven the girl here, her plight was a real one.

'You're asking me,' she managed to choke out, 'to do a far, far better thing ... ?'

'I'm begging you,' said Annabel, her mouth trembling, 'to let him come back to us.'

'What about Warren?' said Caro. 'Doesn't he have a say?'

'He won't leave you, unless you make him.' Annabel stared at her knees. 'He's found something with you he doesn't have with me. But he does love the children.'

That Caro knew to be true. And of course, in a way, he still loved Annabel.

There was a pause. Both women were very still. Then Caro said, in a voice dredged from her soul, 'I'll do my best, Annabel.'

The front-page news in the *Chronicle* was a detailed account of the charges against Neil Kenton, embellished with many broad hints about allied action against the Martinis. Sergeant Plummer, reading it in the lounge at Cherry Tree Walk, sighed and called to Jean in the kitchen, 'Someone's coughing everything to blasted Glyn Madoc.'

Jean teetered in with a tray of elevenses. It was her morning off from Four Trees. 'Now, Bill,' said Jean warningly. She disliked him getting agitated, fearing it would bring on another attack.

'It's not right, Jean,' said the sergeant, accepting a cup of unsweetened coffee and a dry biscuit. Jean was also determined to get his weight down, much to his discomfort.

'Bill,' said Jean sharply, 'you're going to retire. It's nothing to do with you.'

'I'm not retiring, Jean,' said the sergeant, for once fighting back, 'leaving unfinished business.'

Jean clicked her teeth and huffed away, saying she would be late for rehearsal. Since her triumph as half the hobby horse, she had got quite involved with the Warfleet Players.

She left Bill Plummer comfortably in front of the television with his glasses, paper and biscuits within reach. He was really well enough, now, to fend for himself, but she loved to coddle him. The sergeant dozed off and was woken by the doorbell. It was PC Armitage, bringing him the *Police Review* and a surreptitious bottle of whisky.

'The FBI left it, sarge,' he said. 'They took off this morning.'

'Suppose it's the end of the job for them,' said the sergeant, thinking he'd hide the bottle in his toolbox, where Jean wouldn't find it.

'Until the trial,' Armitage nodded. 'I'll be sorry to see them go in a way. Nice blokes.'

'Yes,' said Bill Plummer, 'you said they would be.'

'It'll be funny, you know, everything returning to normal.' PC Armitage stirred his tea, his face registering disappointment.

'It won't be easy,' agreed Bill. 'You've got used to the excitement.'

'And the overtime,' said Armitage regretfully. 'It came in handy, what with the mortgage and Cherie pregnant.' Keith Armitage had recently married his long-term sweetheart.

A sudden idea occurred to the sergeant. 'Keith,' he said, 'Glyn Madoc's got hold of an awful lot of detail about this case. Things I know he hasn't been briefed with.'

Keith Armitage shifted his eyes to his boots and scuffed at a tiny blot on the carpet.

'I s'pose it's the Masonic, sarge,' he said, implying the Super's known connection.

Sergeant Plummer gave a slow, deliberate shake of the head. 'I don't think so, Keith. Cooper's not that daft. It made the Assistant Constable furious.'

Armitage shrugged. His boyish face had turned quite hard. He looked, briefly, like one of the Stourbridge drug squad. When he looked up and caught Bill Plummer's questioning eye still on him, he cleared his throat uncomfortably and drained his mug. 'Gotta be going. I'm on duty in ten minutes. Hah! Back to missing dogs and domestics.'

Bill Plummer did not join in his awkward laughter. 'I wouldn't want,' said the sergeant, not taking his eyes off PC Armitage's reddened face, 'to think it would happen again.'

'Oh. No. I'm sure it won't, sarge.'

Sergeant Plummer saw him to the door, at the last minute restoring the bottle of whisky to him. 'I wouldn't feel right, Keith. It belongs to the station.'

When Jean came back at two with a fish and chip lunch, Bill Plummer looked more cheerful. 'I've decided you're right, love,' he said. 'I'm going to put in for my papers.'

'Oh, Bill. I am glad,' said Jean. 'What changed your mind?'

'Oh, I don't know,' mused the sergeant, stealing another chip while he basked in Jean's approval. 'I've just got to the bottom of the last bit of business.'

THIRTY-SEVEN

Warfleet was splendid with sunshine and blossom the day of Darryl's funeral. Delia had kindly offered Four Trees for the reception, despite Jean's censorious lip-pursing. 'The second funeral here this year,' she said dolefully, wagging her head like the Ghost of Christmas Past. But Delia, returned from her holiday in Brittany, restored to energy and form, swept all prophecy aside and readied the handsome house for the occasion, at which, once more, le tout Warfleet would be present.

Most of the residents had left over the past few days, which was a good excuse for spring cleaning. She set to with a will, turning out cupboards that had not seen a dustpan for years and creating a great pile in the sweet-scented orchard, to be turned into a bonfire. It was as if not just Four Trees, but Delia herself, needed the catharsis. Craig had left after depositing her and the children safely back in Warfleet. If there was any intention for their relationship to continue, Delia did not divulge it.

Jade had departed for London, having explained to anyone who would listen that Talk TV simply could not survive without her. Caro and Warren, locked in their own concerns, had barely questioned her story. Only Harold was still in residence, mournful at the loss of his playmate Craig, and reluctant to return to his overbearing mother. Indeed, the whole of the town had emptied as suddenly as it had filled, the journalists fleeing to wrap up the case in analytical or cautionary copy. Warfleet's fate hung in the balance with things still so uncertain at Tolleymarsh, but in the lull it had returned to a sense of business as usual.

The hearse was to leave from Blossom Cottage, and there the principal mourners had assembled. Jeremy, pale but stoical, in an Armani suit that buttoned rather less tightly than usual, directed Ashley in the preparation of devils on horseback.

'Just a little something,' he whispered to Caro, 'to tide people over. It's going to be a long morning.'

Caro had put on a suit she knew to be Darryl's favourite. It was soft aubergine wool, flattering with her chestnut hair and bronze jewellery; with Ashley in studded leathers, Toni in barley-sugar silk and Rumer in a cloak with full arcana, the funeral promised to be a feast of camp. Darryl would have loved it.

Neither of Darryl's parents was still alive, though a handful of his extended family was present, so Caro sat with Toni, Rumer and Jeremy in the chief mourners' car. As they wound slowly along the High Street, Caro could not help but notice the differences since Sebastian's funeral. There were new shops, new cafés, a small but busy market. The town now had a feel-good atmosphere owing to the unwonted financial influx. The publicity had brought visitors who might even last over the summer. Ironically, the villainous events had restored the town's self-confidence.

Many people, friends and strangers, nodded to the hearse respectfully, but there was something about the promising weather, the contentment on the passing faces, that made it an almost joyful occasion.

Le tout Warfleet had turned out at St Peter and Paul's, and the church was luscious with late spring flowers. The Reverend Pepper had drilled the choir with Darryl's favourite Elton John numbers, much to Churchwarden Souter's disgust, and they sang out in their unbearably poignant young boys' voices. Many of the congregation snuffled; Marsha Snelgrove had a full theatrical turn, so overwhelmed with sobs she had to be supported out by Teddy. Jeremy, remarkably, did not weep, though as the choir began the *Pie Jesu* from Fauré's Requiem he gripped Toni's arm tightly.

It was odd, thought Caro, staring up into the smiling ceramic blue of the sky above the open grave and hearing at the same time the Reverend Pepper's voice committing 'earth to earth', the twittering of larks, the buzz of a bee, and the shouts of schoolchildren in a nearby playground, how everything came full circle. She looked across at Warren, who had joined her at the church, and admired again his beauty. Beneath his shining hair, flaxen in the sunbeams, his face, turned to the grave, looked sad. But she had the feeling it was not Darryl he was mourning.

Delia had really put herself out for the reception, turning it into a wake seemly for Darryl. The food was light and summery, yet satisfying; the chosen drink, champagne, provided by a wine dealer friend of Jeremy's. Ashley had invited some musical acquaintances from a club in Stourbridge; they arrived in a stoned trance, wearing rhinestone-pink jackets, and set up their instruments in the picnic area of the orchard, where they progressed from playing the Carpenters to glam rock within the space of an hour.

In the kitchen, as Jean Plummer, in her funeral best of electric blue, shuttled trays of vol-au-vents back and forth, Jeremy approached Delia.

'I wondered,' he began, 'what *arrangements* you envisage now?'

'Arrangements?' Delia said encouragingly.

'Here ... with Craig and so on. I don't want to pry, of course.'

'Of course not,' said Delia, with dry affection. Dear Jeremy. Even at the funeral of his beloved, he could not resist seeking out gossip.

'Craig is not a feature,' she said lightly. 'And before you commiserate, let me add that he's not a problem either.'

'Good, good,' said Jeremy, smiling with relief. 'I must say, you look much better.'

'I am,' said Delia, running a hand through her French haircut. 'Craig was very good for me and that's all I'm going to say about it.' The finality of her statement implied there was a good deal more she could say, and might on another occasion.

Jeremy nodded forcefully. 'Oh, quite. I understand perfectly.' He paused. 'But we wouldn't want you getting back into that state. Run down and so on.'

'I agree,' said Delia. 'I'm going to look for some help.'

'Really?' said Jeremy, his face lighting up. 'Then can I suggest myself? I would like to help you.'

'Jeremy,' said Delia with surprise.

'You'll want to think about it, I know,' said Jeremy hastily. 'It's just that I found I enjoyed the company. I love to cook, as you know ... and with Darryl gone ...' His voice quivered, but he looked at Delia hopefully.

'Done,' said Delia, holding out her hand.

Jeremy took it tremulously. 'Are you sure?' he said, almost in a whisper.

'Quite,' said Delia. 'I couldn't imagine a better partner. I want time for myself and the kids. I'm going to be taking more holidays.'

'I'd still live at Blossom Cottage, you see,' said Jeremy, expounding the plan he had already spent some time working out. 'But I could be here all day and cook as often as you like. Of course,' he turned a disparaging eye towards the cooking area, 'we'll have to get rid of the Aga.'

The guests thronging the living room were shocked to hear Delia pealing with laughter. Unconventional as it was, the occasion was still a funeral.

The afternoon drew in; a dewiness fell and the children, playing amongst the bloom-laden trees, agitated for the bonfire to be lit. As the first thin lavender wisps sidled pungently up through the nest of branches, Caro took Warren's arm and drew him a little aside from the revelries.

'Shall we go for a walk?' she said.

They had hardly communicated for days, as Warren came in tired from long, stressful hours at Tolleymarsh and fell asleep in front of the television. Caro, with new determination, had started to think seriously about her novel.

They set off towards the seafront arm in arm, comforted by the physical contact. They had become so close, in such a short time, Caro found it hard to imagine walking alone again. The afternoon, though still warm, had turned a little misty; a fine down hung over the bursting greenery and by the sea thickened to a salty fog. They said little as they sauntered along the promenade, yet by unspoken agreement they were heading for the beach hut.

Warren guided Caro, careful in her high heels, across the beach to the little brown hut, crouched like a nesting bird on the pebbles. He pushed open the door – the lock was broken again, Caro noticed; no doubt the hut had played host to other lovers – and they entered. The familiar and now nostalgic smell greeted them. The heat of the day had seeped into the wood, making the space warm and welcoming. They sat on the benches at either side of the hut and looked at each other.

'You know what I'm going to say, don't you?' said Caro, trying to keep her voice level.

Warren bowed his head, acknowledging that their spiritual connection was as great as ever. 'Annabel told me she'd been to see you.'

They were both silent. Warren leaned against the wall. The last of the sun seeping through the slats lit the mournful hollows of his face, turned his eyes into pools of longing. Oh, thought Caro, how can I bear to part with him? 'It's for the best,' she said gently. 'I know it.'

Warren nodded almost imperceptibly. It was as though he had made up his mind to accept all she said, not to fight for her.

'Are you all right?' said Caro, wanting some response from him, any response.

Warren gave a short angry laugh. 'It's such a waste,' he said.

'Don't make it hard for me,' begged Caro. 'If I could see any other way . . .'

'I know. I know,' said Warren. He came to her side and sat, drawing her head to his shoulder. She put her hands, cold now, in his and he warmed them, rubbing almost roughly until life came back to them. They sat, hands clasped, very still; absorbing, committing to memory, this last touch of each other. Caro's heart felt like stone. She had no idea how she would live the rest of her life without him.

'What will you do?' said Warren bleakly.

Caro reached into her bag and took out the letter from Zo which had arrived the previous morning. She handed it to Warren and watched as he read it.

My dearest Caro,

You will have heard by now that Marcus Croft and I are to start a company with money from Eddie Flynn. It may seem strange with all that has happened recently, but we still feel a responsibility to publishing.

Though we are committed to gay and lesbian fiction, it's a broad church, as you have discovered. Should you want to join us, there is a desk top for you here; lots of work, low pay, and best of all, *no corporation*.

Whatever you do, I hope you will be happy and I want you to know that, without strings, I am still your greatest fan and your friend,

Zo.

Warren folded the letter carefully and returned it to her. 'We can't complain we aren't loved,' he said, with a ghost of a grin.

Caro too smiled, glad to see him beginning to surface. 'What will happen at Tolleymarsh?' she said, wanting to move on to something positive.

Warren said, 'Viviana's going back to Colombia. The police released her without charges.'

'Henry must divorce her,' said Caro. 'She can't possibly inherit.'

'Oh, yes,' said Warren. 'It's all in hand. Annabel's got the lawyers on to it.' He blew out breath. 'Now all we need is a major cash investment.'

'What about Eddie Flynn?' said Caro, with sudden inspiration. 'By all accounts he's into philanthropic works and he's certainly made a pile of money.'

'Mmm,' said Warren, 'maybe.'

'Jade,' said Caro, 'I'm sure could help. I'll talk to her when I get back to London.' Zo too, she thought. She had called her on receipt of the letter and been treated to a panegyric on Eddie. Helpful ... understanding ... supportive ... generous ... the praises had reeled on, leading Caro to suspect Zo had begun an affair with him. She was still open to the occasional heterosexual dabble.

'You're going, then?'

'Tomorrow.'

Another silence fell. Caro considered how to voice her last concern.

'Warren, you once asked me to give you advice ... remember? About Carl, and so on?'

'Don't worry,' Warren pre-empted her, 'this time I've learned my lesson.'

'Really?'

'Really.'

'You're worth so much more.'

'I wish,' said Warren.

'You are.' Caro was definite. 'You could have a good life here.'

Warren nodded. 'There's a lot I'd like to do.'

'Annabel and your children adore you.'

'I know.' Warren pressed her hand. 'It's been like time out with you.' He gave a slight smile of appeal. 'But, Caro ... don't abandon me.'

The hut was almost dark now and all they could see clearly in the shadow was each other's eyes. There was despair in them. Anguish. Yet, also, an odd hopefulness.

'I won't,' said Caro. 'I love you.'

'I love you too,' said Warren.

They sat holding each other, breathing with the rhythm of those bound together, until it was completely dark and through the open door the clear night sky twinkled diamonds down on them.

As the train jolted out of Warfleet station the next morning, Caro put aside her sleepless night and determinedly opened her A4 pad. Hugging her corner seat, she gazed out of the window as the train, gathering speed, left behind the cottages, the stretch of beach alongside the track, the distant cliffs, above which a sprinkling of wings was caught in the sunlight. The little town receded until it was just a framed picture. An innocent seaside postcard.

Caro's lips twisted into a slight smile. Pen poised, she returned to her pad and in bold letters wrote the title of her new novel. *Greed, Crime, Sudden Death*. Now, at last, she had the story.